ALSO BY NATALIE D. RICHARDS

FOR MIDDLE-GRADE READERS

15 Secrets to Survival

FOR YOUNG ADULTS

49 Miles Alone

Four Found Dead

Seven Dirty Secrets

Five Total Strangers

What You Hide

We All Fall Down

One Was Lost

My Secret to Tell

Gone Too Far

Six Months Later

SURVIVE THIS SAFARI

NATALIE D. RICHARDS

DELACORTE PRESS

Visit us on the Web! rhcbooks.com
Educators and librarians, for a variety of teaching tools,
visit us at RHTeachersLibrarians.com

Library of Congress Cataloging-in-Publication Data is available upon request.
ISBN 978-0-593-64416-4 (hardcover) — ISBN 978-0-593-64417-1 (lib. bdg.)
ISBN 978-0-593-64418-8 (ebook)

The text of this book is set in 11.5-point Berling LT Std.
Interior art used under license from Shutterstock.com
Interior art used under license from Adobe Stock
Puzzles illustrated by Michelle Canoni on pp. 154, 166, 182, 201, 214, 256, 301

Editor: Kelsey Horton
Interior Designer: Michelle Canoni
Production Editor: Colleen Fellingham
Managing Editor: Tamar Schwarz
Production Manager: Tracy Heydweiller

Printed in the United States of America
10 9 8 7 6 5 4 3 2 1
First Edition

The authorized representative in the EU for product safety and compliance is Penguin Random House Ireland, Morrison Chambers, 32 Nassau Street, Dublin D02 YH68, Ireland, https://eu-contact.penguin.ie.

For Adri
My favorite animal expert

CHAPTER 1

YOU'VE WON AN INVITATION TO THE

WILDLANDS
SAFARI ESCAPE CHALLENGE

SAT–SUN APR 12–13
AT WILDLANDS SAFARI PARK

Stay in a Wildlands Camp!
*Solve brain-bending puzzles in a race
against the Wildlands Ambassadors!*

Unlock gates to access new animal areas!
Win amazing prizes!

Are you ready for a truly WILD adventure? A Wildlands vehicle will pick you up for a ride to the safari park, where you'll camp out with three other randomly drawn testers and an escape challenge counselor! After a few warm-up puzzles, you'll start Day 2 on a gated path, solving puzzles in a race against our student team of experts, the Wildlands Ambassadors!
Each solution will unlock new animal enclosures where you'll get extra close to our wildest residents. Solve all the puzzles successfully and each team member will win a Special Zoo Experience or Camp of their choice at the Columbus Zoo. And someone may have the option to shoot for a spot on the Wildlands Ambassador team!

Lucy looks at the invitation carefully. She turns it over and over. She double-, triple-, quadruple-checks the date and then the time and then the letters on the outside of the envelope from the *L* to the *A*. There are probably a few other Lucys in the town of Zanesville, but another *Lucy Q. Spagnola*? She's pretty sure she's the only one of those in the whole state of Ohio. Which means Lucy is definitely, positively, 100 percent invited to the Wildlands Safari Escape Challenge.

Even the idea of a free special experience at the zoo makes her heart flutter like there are hummingbirds trapped in her rib cage. After all, zoos mean animals, and the only thing Lucy loves more than puzzles is animals, and she knows a ton about them too. Despite all of that, Lucy takes a deep breath to try to get those chest hummingbirds to settle down. She absolutely, positively can't get excited about this. Because it's *Wildlands*. The most terrible, depressing, humiliating day of Lucy's life happened at Wildlands, and the Ambassadors were there.

There is clearly only one reasonable thing to do with this invitation. Lucy pinches it carefully between her thumb and forefinger. Then she stomps on the pedal to open the kitchen trash and drops it inside.

"No way, Santa Fe." Alex's voice is unmistakable.

Lucy crosses her arms and looks up at her big sister. Here's what she knows for sure about Alex, starting with the fact that if Lucy were a bobcat, Alex would be a lion:

1. Alex is eight years older and seven inches taller than Lucy and, much like a lion, will always be more imposing and impressive.

2. She works two jobs, as an animal care intern at Wildlands Safari Park Rescue Sanctuary and as a tutor to kids in the fourth through sixth grades. And she does all of it while studying environmental science in college (which is how she ended up with the Wildlands job to begin with).

3. She is basically the smartest, coolest, most athletic person Lucy knows (captain of her high school volleyball team and now plays in college too!), so stuff is easier for her.

4. Her superpower is knowing what Lucy is thinking.

Alex crouches in front of Lucy. Her nose crinkles, which happens when she's smiling without smiling.

"Why would you throw the invitation away? This is

a special invitation. So special that only four kids got invited."

Only four kids? Lucy thinks about that, because four kids doesn't seem like very many invitations for a giant safari park. But it does feel a little like a camouflage statement.[1] Like Alex is saying one thing but the real truth is hiding in plain sight.

And Lucy thinks that hidden thing is this: There's only one possible way Alex could know that only four kids got invited, and that's if she's the one who did the inviting.

Lucy squints at her sister. "Were you in charge of the invitations?"

"Nope."

Lucy squints harder. "Are you absolutely, positively sure?"

Alex shakes her head. "Absolutely. All the interns were asked to identify fifth and sixth graders with a variety of interests and strengths. Leah and I both tutor middle schoolers, so we had bigger lists, but it was all down to a random drawing."

Leah was Alex's lab partner a lot in her freshman year in college, so Lucy knows she's studying environmental science too and that she also tutors *and* works at Wildlands in the same internship program. Still, there's one other part of this that's a little bit suspicious.

---

1   An ant-mimicking spider is a master at camouflage. It walks into an ants' nest waving two legs in the air like antennae to convince all the other ants that it is not a spider at all. That's the camouflage. But the truth is, that spider is definitely a spider and it's there to drag off (and eat) ant stragglers.

Lucy squints even harder. "Why did you include my name at all? You know what happened last time."

The last time she was at Wildlands is what Lucy means. And what happened is that Lucy tried out for the Wildlands Ambassadors team. This did not, for the record, result in Lucy being a Wildlands Ambassador, but it *did* result in the worst day ever.

Alex takes Lucy's hands and gives them a squeeze. "I do remember, but I think you would love this! It's not a tryout, you know. It's like an escape room, *and* a hike through Wildlands, *and* a way to learn more about animals! Plus, you'll be part of a team."

"A team that's competing against the Ambassadors." Lucy looks down at her feet. She doesn't want to think about teams, especially not the Wildlands Ambassadors team. If they had a mascot, it should be a pack of wolves, because they're a super-impressive team for several reasons:

1. They are special Wildlands volunteers who are trained to help with animal care and educational programs in the park.

2. They have supercool team uniforms, complete with jerseys that each have the Ambassador's name across the back.

3. They are also the eighth team Lucy has tried out for and failed.

5

Lucy sits at the counter as she remembers all the tryouts. There was select volleyball and travel volleyball (she got hit in the face with the ball on both) and then the middle school softball and tennis teams, where she quickly remembered she has noodle arms and bad hand-eye coordination. She tried lacrosse, but that was a disaster (she didn't exactly know lacrosse rules, and there was a weird long stick involved). After that she tried a singing group at school and then the big middle school play and both of those were a no, though she did get a callback for Villager 3, a role that ultimately went to Penelope Simms.

It's always hard to look at the list of kids on the roster and not see your name. And it's even harder to get those awful better-luck-next-time calls from coaches, but none of that was anywhere near as bad as the Wildlands tryout. Partly because she did so well at first, and partly because Lucy wanted to get on the Wildlands team more than anything.

She remembers that terrible day three months ago. She thinks of that wobbly platform and her hammering heart and the tears that kept coming no matter how hard she tried to stop them.

Lucy shakes her head to try to push all those images away. "I can't go back to Wildlands."

Alex frowns and softens her voice. "I know that was hard, but think about how much you love animals. This really would be different. Think about all the animals you'll see."

"But I'll be competing against the Ambassadors. Plus, I've already seen the park," Lucy says. What she does not say is that no matter how much she loves being near wild animals, she absolutely, positively does not want to see Wildlands (or the Ambassadors) ever again.

"But this is a whole new section! Most of these animals weren't on exhibit when you were last there. It's grown, and it's going to be amazing. *You'll* be amazing!"

Lucy feels a rush of excitement. Questions fly through her brain: What animals are there? Does this mean the Canopy Walk is finished? Did they bring in the ostriches? She would love so much to see ostriches again. And the Canopy Walk! She would be up close to giraffes and zebras, and—

Wait.

Lucy didn't think of it before, but that walkway will be up high, like a platform. And a platform at Wildlands was the cause of the worst day ever. No matter how amazing animals are, she can't go through that again. "I just can't do it, Alex."

"Don't be a turkey, Albuquerque."

Alex has been doing this rhyming thing as long as Lucy can remember. And maybe it did help Lucy learn that Santa Fe is the capital of New Mexico and Lincoln is the capital of Nebraska, but it sort of makes Lucy feel like she's back in third grade. Plus, Lucy has no idea how Alex keeps track of the state capitals now that she's added in other random, noncapital cities.

Alex sighs, pulls the invitation out of the trash can, and puts it down on the counter. Even looking at the edge of the paper makes Lucy's stomach do a slow somersault. Part of her wants to snatch it up and pack her bags. All those new animals. And one of the special zoo encounters in Columbus? It's a dream come true! But that stomach somersault is a warning. Once it starts, it will keep going until her throat feels too tight and her face feels too hot, and that's when terrible things happen.

"Okay, there's one other part," Alex says, and Lucy can tell she's been saving this one. "If you win, you might have another chance to join the Wildlands Ambassadors. It's right in the invitation."

"No way," Lucy says. Her stomach is curling into a ball now, and she can feel that ball beginning to roll. Dr. Kern said that feeling should be getting better, and it has been. Mostly. But she's not taking any chances.

She crosses her arms to tell Alex she means business about not being interested. "I am never, ever trying out for that team again. Or any team, for that matter."

"Being on a team is the best thing in the world."

Of course Alex would say that. Alex played basketball and volleyball, and she was super good at both. She's been on lots of great teams. And their mom? She is an even better athlete. She played softball in college and even coached the high school team for a few years. They have so many team trophies and team pictures and team flags in their living room that Lucy sometimes thinks they need one of those glass cases like the ones near the school office.

But Lucy doesn't have anything on the wall. Not a ribbon or a trophy or a single shirt with her name on it. Because Lucy has never, ever been part of a team. And after the miserable failure of her tryout for the Ambassadors, she's 100 percent sure there isn't a single team in the world that will take her.

Except . . .

If that whole mess on the platform hadn't happened, she just might have made the Ambassadors team. She had a perfect score on the animal knowledge test, did a good job on the indoor stall cleanout (even though there was lots of poop-shoveling involved!), and aced the map memorization segment. But then she had to climb the platform to do end-of-the-day animal counts. That's when everything was ruined, thanks to a stupid panic attack. But if she could have another chance . . .

"What do you mean by another chance?" Lucy asks quietly.

Alex smiles. "If your team wins, one of the members will have the option to join the Wildlands Ambassadors team."

Lucy feels a little electric zip of excitement running through her whole body. She suddenly looks at the invitation on their kitchen counter more closely. Because now it's not just a cool-sounding overnight camp. It's starting to look like a ticket to her biggest dream ever coming true!

CHAPTER 2

Lucy's excitement feels like it will shoot her right off her chair and into the air. But then a new thought comes in like a sledgehammer. "Wait. I thought all of the Ambassador slots were full. There are only five openings, and they were filled."[2]

Alex shrugs. "They've decided to expand the program to six volunteers."

"So who would get the spot?"

"Well, it depends on who wants it. It's a volunteer position, so if more than one person wants it, the keepers will determine who might be best suited to the role."

Lucy stands up, feeling a little bit wobbly and a little bit sick and a lot bit excited. It sounds completely amazing and maybe too good to be true. Which means . . . it probably is too good to be true.

"How will you determine who's best suited?" she asks.

"I'm not sure, but I'm guessing they'd choose the per-

---

2 The five slots are filled by five kids. Adam, Amelia, Isaac, Emma, and Olivia. Lucy knows this because she saw the email announcement. And she knows Adam and Emma, who go to her school. But that email also made Lucy think that even if she hadn't had a complete and total meltdown on the viewing platform, she still wouldn't have made the team. Her name doesn't start with a vowel, which feels like it might be a requirement.

son who worked the hardest throughout the challenge and demonstrates the right aptitude."

Alex opens the fridge and looks left and right, like Mom will pop out of a cabinet. A little silly since Mom is at work, but then Alex pulls out a brown bottle from the back of the fridge, the kind with a fancy silver cap and a fancy label and high-quality root beer filled right up to the top.

"What if you just think about it?" Alex asks, pushing the bottle across the counter. "You keep saying you wish you had a team. And now you will!"

Lucy touches the bottle and sniffs the air and thinks about taking a drink. But she doesn't actually do it. Taking a drink feels like admitting she might be changing her mind. And she isn't ready to admit that. Because while she can't think of anything she wants more than to join the Ambassadors, she can't think of anything she wants less than embarrassing herself in front of them again.

Which means if she does this challenge, she has to be absolutely, positively sure she will not panic. Lucy tries to think of every panicky thing involved.

"What if I have to climb the platforms again?"

"I don't know about that. I know there are tons of very cool puzzles you have to solve to unlock different gates. That much I'm sure of."

"What about timers? Escape rooms have timers," Lucy says.

If there is one thing Lucy hates almost as much as platforms, it's timers. The timers in games that buzz and make you jump. The timers in tests that sit up in the corner counting down, down, down while you try to figure out each problem. Math is stressful enough, but having to do math while a clock is tick-tick-ticking away? No thank you very much indeed.

But Alex is smiling extra wide now, and Lucy has a squirmy feeling in her chest. Because she knows this look means Alex is not going to take no for an answer. "I don't know all the details either. I think we'll get a packet when our team meets. Oh, did I mention that I heard you also might get to help give Mwanza and Tabora a bath at the end of the weekend?"

"Tabora?"

The name pops out of Lucy's mouth before she can stop herself. She can't help it. You wouldn't be able to help it either. Because Tabora is perfect. With her twitchy tail and her round, dark eyes and her very big ears.

"She has grown a lot," Alex says. "She's over fourteen hundred pounds now."

Tabora is one of four African elephants at Wildlands and the only one who was born at the park. Her mother, Mwanza, was transferred from a small-town zoo that was shutting down, but no one knew at the time that Mwanza was pregnant.[3] So Tabora is a very big deal and a very big baby and a very tempting reason to reconsider that invitation.

Lucy chews her lip and touches the side of the root

---

3 African elephant pregnancies last twenty-two months, which is the longest pregnancy of any animal on earth! Given how long they will be pregnant, elephant moms need lots of special care, which for one zoo in Australia means a customized pregnancy workout involving elephant yoga and tire stacking.

beer bottle. Alex stands up, looking way too excited. "So what do you think?"

Lucy thinks so many things in that moment. She thinks about Tabora and the safari Canopy Walk and the platform from the tryout. She thinks of all the ways this could go wrong, and it is a superlong list of things. But then she makes the list of things that can go right:

1. She will give a baby elephant a bath.

2. She will see all the new animal exhibits, possibly including ostriches!

3. She could win a behind-the-scenes experience at the zoo.

4. She could even maybe, possibly win a spot on the Wildlands Ambassadors.

Lucy's throat feels super squeezy, but her excitement is even bigger than that feeling. She grabs the invitation with a nod. "I'm absolutely, positively in!"

"Yes! I knew you'd say yes!" Alex says. "This is going to be amazing. How should we celebrate?"

Lucy opens her mouth to answer, but instead of words, a bell chimes. She closes her mouth and it chimes again and that's when she realizes it isn't her voice at all. It's the doorbell.

Right outside the window, Lucy sees a girl waiting at the door. Even the girl's shadow is enough to make Lucy tense, because she would know those long, straight braids anywhere. It has to be their next-door neighbor Jemma Louise Sparks.

The doorbell rings again, and Jemma's shadow shifts impatiently on the porch. Lucy's stomach curls into the teeniest little knot. Lucy wants to tell Alex this is a very bad idea. She wants to remind her sister that Jemma has tried out for six of the eight teams Lucy has tried out for, but with one major difference: Jemma makes every team, 100 percent of the time.

Alex opens the door, and as the door blocks the shadow Jemma, the real Jemma appears. There is a frown on her face and a bruise darkens her left knee and she's wearing a bright blue jersey with a number *19* on the front. When she steps inside the house, she turns just enough that Lucy can see the *S-P-A* of her last name in bright white letters across the back of the blue jersey. It makes the knot in Lucy's stomach feel like a lump of hot coal.

"Jemma!" Alex says. "Leah texted me that you were drawn in the lottery too! It's going to be awesome to have both of you on the team."

"Oh, I'm super excited about the competition!" Jemma says. "But I should clarify that I'm not joining the team. Not your team, anyway."

"Wait, I thought you said you were excited," Alex says.

"She did," Lucy says.

"And I am excited. I'm completely stoked!" Jemma pauses to flick her braids over her shoulders. "Because this gives me exactly the chance I need to prove what team I belong on."

"What team is that?" Lucy asks. Because now that Jemma is standing here with her annoying jersey and her annoying braids, Lucy has a terrible, awful feeling about what Jemma is saying.

Jemma just blinks. "The Wildlands Ambassadors, obviously."

Lucy shakes her head once, twice, and then a third time for good measure. "But you weren't in the tryouts for the Wildlands Ambassadors."

And she wasn't. Lucy is 1,000 percent sure that none of her neighbors was there, especially not the one Alex tutors every Wednesday night. So why is her stomach wadding itself into a tighter and tighter knot?

"I did the tryout on the first day."

Lucy feels like she's on the balance board at the science museum, like the world is topsy and turvy beneath her feet. But she does remember the sign-ups now, the sheet that had two dates listed. Lucy just never thought to check the names on the first date.

Jemma tosses her long, sleek braids over her shoulders and lets out a sigh, like all of this is very unnecessary and annoying.

Here is what Lucy knows about Jemma Louise Sparks, other than the fact that Alex tutors her on Wednesdays and sometimes Fridays:

1. If Jemma were an animal, she'd probably be a cheetah, because she's the fastest person Lucy has ever seen. That's why she's on so many teams (soccer, basketball, softball, and track).

2. She's also on a bunch of nonathletic school teams, like competitive chorale, which is a team that sings to win contests. And if you ask Lucy (which no one did), singing to win something feels like it's sort of missing the point of singing.

3. She thinks Lucy is a baby. Which she isn't, even if she doesn't jump off the high dive at the pool.[4]

4. She almost always wears jerseys to school and almost all of them have her name written on the back. In fact, maybe she's a little like a migrating warbler? She's always wearing some sort of uniform, but they do change depending on the season, just like warbler feathers.

"Anyway . . ." Jemma draws out the word. "That's why I'm here early. I'm going to do this dumb challenge so I can get on the Wildlands Ambassadors like all of my other friends."

Alex gives Lucy a little worried glance before responding. "Jemma, I thought that after the tryouts you said you were going to be too busy with soccer anyway."

Lucy tenses when Jemma narrows her eyes. She looks very, very determined. "Well, I changed my mind. And

---

4   Jemma has no problem jumping off the high dive. In fact, last summer, Lucy (who loves their neighborhood pool, high dive or not) noticed Jemma on that diving platform a gazillion times. It seemed like she spent more time in line or climbing up the platform ladder than she actually did in the water.

now I want to know exactly what I need to do to be the best. Because I am going to win that spot. End of discussion."

But at that moment, Lucy hears a car door outside and knows it's not the end of the discussion. A few seconds later, the front door swings open and Lucy's mom steps in, carrying six million things. Lucy's mom is always carrying six million things, and today, Lucy can see her travel coffee mug from this morning, her giant laptop bag, her lunch sack, and her floppy pink purse. She drops all of these things on the little table behind the door and breaks into a huge grin.

"Hi, girls! Hi, Jemma!" Then Mom turns to Lucy with a sound that's almost like a squeal. "Lucy, Alex texted me about the invitation! This is so exciting! Tell me everything!"

Everyone starts talking all at once.

"I'm going too!" Jemma says.

"Mom, I'm glad you're here. I'm going to need you to sign a permission slip, because we're going to drive the team in one of the Wildlands trucks if it's okay with everyone," Alex says.

"The Wildlands safari trucks?" Lucy asks, feeling her heart skip a beat. The Wildlands safari trucks are *awesome*. They're like monster trucks, and they're usually reserved for the extra-expensive tours because they are super high off the ground, with big cushy seats and cupholders and a special sunroof that opens all the way up so you can stop the truck and let everybody stand up and look around.

Alex grins, and even Jemma looks shocked and delighted. "Wait," she says. "Are you talking about the big off-road things with the logos and super-cool sunroofs?"

"Yep!" Alex says. "But we can only do it if all the parents agree to me driving everyone."

Mom moves closer to Lucy, putting one arm around her shoulders. "Well, who can say no to that? I'll sign for Lucy."

And just like that, the whole thing is really happening. Lucy is going to the Wildlands Safari Escape Challenge in a totally cool off-road safari truck, and if she works really hard, she might just have a chance at winning a spot on the Wildlands Ambassadors.

Of course, she's not the only one who wants that spot. Lucy's eyes land on Jemma, who is still chattering happily with Alex while she pulls out her notebook. Lucy has never, ever beaten Jemma at anything in her life, but this time has to be different. This might be her last chance at the Ambassadors, and Lucy knows she can't afford to lose.

CHAPTER 3

Two weeks later, Lucy is zipping up her backpack in her room when she hears a car pulling into the driveway. Lucy rushes to her bedroom window to peek through the blinds. And sure enough, there it is, the big black Hummer EV with the Wildlands logo wrapped down each side of the truck. It has huge tires and a giant rack on the back for expedition gear, and even from this angle, Lucy can see the glint of the enormous sunroof. Her heart does a double thump of excitement as she steps back from the window to grab her things.

Just then, she hears the truck doors open and the faint sound of high-pitched laughter on her driveway. Even from here, she can see Jemma's soccer socks as she slides out of the giant truck. There are two boys standing in the driveway beside her, and Lucy doesn't know either of them. They must be from the other middle school, and they aren't kids that Alex tutors.

Jemma probably doesn't know them either, but Lucy can hear them chatting and laughing like they've been friends forever. Have they been friends forever? Lucy feels like it's a little hard to breathe. The only thing worse than being in a new group of people is being the new person in a group that already knows each other.

Lucy pushes the thought away and turns to grab her things. She pulls her jacket off the hook beside her door and finds a surprise note stuck to the wall.

Good luck, Lucy!

I'm rooting for you!

Love,
Mom

If Lucy's mom were an animal, Lucy thinks she'd be a crow:

1. She has straight black hair, as shiny as crow feathers, and she is extra good at solving problems, just like crows.

2. She is small like a crow too, only two inches taller than Lucy, which means she's four inches shorter than Alex, but she doesn't like to have it pointed out.

3. She is a note ninja, leaving little Post-it Notes and surprise cards all over the place.[5]

---

5 Crows do not write (at least, we don't think they do), but Lucy has read multiple documented cases of wild crows leaving regular gifts like pennies and twist ties for humans who feed them.

Outside, footsteps thump up the porch stairs. Lucy feels a rush of excitement. And maybe worry. And maybe nervousness? Maybe she's ex-wor-vous?

Before she can decide what she is, Alex is opening the front door, and she knows it's Alex because she can spot the other kids playing tag in the driveway. Lucy doesn't want to be ex-wor-vous in front of her sister or her teammates, so she decides to ignore the fluttering in her chest and instead focus on the unbelievably cool truck she gets to ride in, which she can now see has spotlights mounted to the roof!

Lucy's bedroom door is open, but Alex knocks on the frame.

"Looking sassy, Tallahassee," she says. "Are you ready to go?"

Is she ready? She isn't sure. She is sure her voice will come out in an ex-wor-vous squeak if she tries to answer, so she nods a whole, whole lot to prove that she is ready and excited and all those other things.

But she's not 100 percent sure that's the truth. Her throat feels tight and her face feels hot, and both of those things feel a lot like not being ready. Lucy takes a deep breath, just like Dr. Kern taught her, and she feels somewhat better. It's never 100 percent better, but Mom always says some percentage is better than nothing, and she's right. But every once in a while 100 percent would be nice.

"What if I have one of those . . . things I sometimes have?" Lucy asks. She knows the real term for those things is *panic attacks*, but she avoids that phrase when she can.

It makes her feel a little weird and a lot embarrassed, even though Dr. Kern and Mom and Alex all tell her there's nothing to be embarrassed about. But isn't that what grown-ups have to say to embarrassed twelve-year-olds? If they didn't, would anyone ever be able to finish middle school?

"Well, you have lots of strategies now, right?"

Alex seems so sure, but secretly, Lucy thinks it might be easier to feel good about strategies if you aren't the person having the panic attacks.

The first attack she had happened in fourth grade. Her grandpa, who lives on a farm north of Zanesville, had decided to teach Lucy to drive a golf cart over holiday break. They were in the middle of a huge field, which seemed totally safe, and for a while it was. It was also super fun, like driving a go-kart without a track. But then the golf cart hit a hole in the field. Even with seat belts, the cart jerked forward and her grandpa hurt his shoulder, and while he was calling out in pain, Lucy started to feel like her throat wouldn't work right. Like she couldn't breathe. And then like her heart was going to go faster and faster until it exploded.

It was a terrible day, but Lucy thought it was only the golf cart. But when she got back to school, the same thing happened to her when she had to take a really hard math test and was running out of time. And the most recent time she had a panic attack? Lucy has been trying not to think about that since she agreed to do this escape challenge two weeks ago.

"The last time I was at Wildlands, it was horrible."

"That doesn't mean this time will be like that," Alex says. "I think you're going to be amazing."

Before she knows it, they are stepping outside, where all of the other kids are climbing back into the big black truck. Lucy heads for the open passenger door. It's so high, she has to grab a handrail to swing herself up into the seat. And the seat! It's shiny and leather and extra, extra pillowy with armrests and cupholders and little control knobs that do . . . well, they must do something, but Lucy has no idea what.

Lucy buckles her seat belt and looks to her right, where a tall Black boy with long fingers and warm eyes sits in the other captain's chair. In the back, a small, pale boy with a ton of freckles is wiggling around in his seat like he can't quite get comfortable. Lucy looks past that boy's messy, sandy hair to Jemma, who is squinting and scowling.

So these three people are the rest of Lucy's team. Two strangers and a girl who is determined to win the open spot on the Wildlands Ambassadors. Actually, for all Lucy knows, they probably all want to win the spot. Who wouldn't? Alex gets into the truck, and Lucy's face feels very hot. When Alex starts the engine, Lucy's stomach does one somersault, and then another. Is she really ready to go back to Wildlands?

"We've got to run, Madison," Alex says.

The kid with long-fingered hands looks up toward the front seat with a frown. "Wait, I thought you said her name was Lucy."

"Sorry, Trey, I did say that," Alex says.

"But you said Madison just now," Trey says.

"Madison is the capital of Wisconsin, and I sometimes do a whole rhyming thing with famous cities."

"With the capital of Wisconsin?" Trey looks extra confused now. He also still looks very long, from his arms to his legs to his fingers. Even his eyelashes are long!

"No, with all kinds of capitals," Jemma says, rolling her eyes. "Duh."

"Do you ever say other states?" the short boy asks. "Or maybe countries? Ooh, there are a lot of countries."

"I use lots of states, but no other countries. Maybe I should look into that, Harrison!"

"That would be hard," Jemma says. "I think there are almost two hundred countries."[6]

"Good way to learn them," Alex says. "We should introduce ourselves. You all know me now. Trey, do you want to start? Maybe we can say our names and one thing about ourselves. So, I'm Alex, and I sometimes do state capital rhymes. I'm also leading the blue team, and that's all of you!"

Alex turns to Trey, who clears his throat. "I'm Trey, and I have a garden with twenty-four different vegetables and plants this year."

"Wow," Harrison says, leaning forward until his head pops through the space between the front passenger seats

---

6   There are 195 recognized countries, and lots of them have at least one national animal. The national animal of the United States is the bald eagle, but it was almost the wild turkey. If you ask Lucy (and technically no one could have asked Lucy because she wasn't yet born when this national animal business was happening), picking the turkey would have been pretty awkward on Thanksgiving.

where Lucy and Trey are sitting. Lucy notices that his hair is truly sticking up in every imaginable direction. "That's a ton of planting! Oh, I'm Harrison and I don't really plant anything, which is fine since I don't really eat vegetables, unless you count ketchup and my mom definitely does not count ketchup, even though I looked up a recipe and it's totally mostly tomatoes. I even offered to eat bowls of ketchup instead of salad, but she didn't go for it. Anyway, I'm here for the kangaroos."

The truck is suddenly very quiet, and Lucy keeps watching Harrison, who talked and talked for such a long time that she's only about 63 percent sure he's done talking now. But he's not talking now, having instead slumped back into his seat. He starts to push one of the retractable cupholders open and then closed. Open and closed. Open and closed. Should Lucy say something now? Will he stop with all the opening and closing if she does?

"Ohhh-kay," Jemma says, before Lucy can make up her mind. "Well, I'm Jemma Louise Sparks and I'm here to earn my spot on the Wildlands Ambassadors, where I should have been all along."

"I know you would like a spot on the Ambassadors, but let's remember there's more to this than winning or maybe getting on the Ambassadors. No one has seen this part of the park!" Alex says. "And you're the first-ever kids to do this escape challenge. You're like test pilots!"

Harrison lunges forward. "Do we get to fly something?"

"That would be cool," Trey agrees.

"No flying, but you're checking things out. Making

sure the puzzles work. Making sure you can get through all of the gates and stuff," Alex says.

"Okay, then what are the rules?" Jemma asks. "How do we win?"

"You will win when you make it through all the puzzles, unlocking each of the gates to lead us to the campfire location with the Ambassadors. And I suppose the rules are pretty simple. Work together to solve the puzzles. Be kind and respectful to each other and the animals. And stay on the designated trails, of course."

"That's easy stuff," Harrison says. "And you said something about a big overlook walkway?"

"Yep! You'll be the first guests to ever set foot on the Canopy Walk. Oh! And the meerkats! That's an area *only* available to special tours, and that means you!"

"And we get to give Tabora a bath, right?" Lucy asks.

"That's right," Alex says. "We have a baby elephant at Wildlands, and after the escape challenge, you guys get to give her a bath."

"Okay, that's kind of cool," Jemma says. "But I'm still here to get on the Ambassadors. End of discussion."

Lucy grits her teeth and squints so hard at the rearview mirror that she's a little bit surprised it doesn't crack. How is she going to compete with this? What if everyone wants the same spot?

"Oh, yeah, that does sound pretty cool," Harrison says. "I'm interested in that too, but no matter what happens, we *have* to win. I have a record to keep up. I love escape rooms and I've done five of them and won every single one. And this is kind of like an escape room, but even better! It's like lots of little escape rooms connected together so we have to keep solving and solving them, right? Plus, there are kangaroos, which is always good and is even better in this case, because if we win, we each get one of those special zoo experiences! I want to do the Morning with the Kangaroo Keepers, where I will get to help feed and monitor the kangaroos for ninety entire minutes. That experience is even better than a bunch of escape rooms and seeing kangaroos because it's hanging out with kangaroos. Maybe I'll get to be an Ambassador *and* hang out with kangaroos!"

Lucy's throat squeezes at the idea.

"We'll see about that," Jemma says, sounding a lot like Lucy's mom when she says *we'll see* about getting a giant ice cream sundae on a school night.

"You really do love kangaroos, Harrison," Trey says softly.

"I do."

If you ask Lucy, and no one ever does even though she's studied every review on every special experience offered at the Columbus Zoo, the best experience has to be the Elephant Bath. Which she gets to do tomorrow! Lucy reminds herself that she should really focus on the elephant bath situation and not the what-if-she-can't-win-the-spot-on-the-Ambassadors situation.

Harrison pokes forward then, looking right at Lucy. "What about you, Lucy?"

What about her? Lucy's heart drops. What does he mean? Is she supposed to give her name first? Wouldn't that be weird, since he just said it? Bluh, why does this seem so easy for everyone else?

"Yes, you should introduce yourself," Alex says from the front.

Lucy opens her mouth, but she still feels panicky and unsure. How should she start? Will her voice come out at all, or will it just be a mouselike squeak? And why *is* she here, again? Because at the moment she can't think of a single reason.

"Are you okay?" Harrison asks, and Lucy realizes she's 94 percent sure there's something sticky on his chin, but despite all that, he seems very nice.

"Oh wait, are you shy?" Harrison asks. "My sister is shy. It's weird, you know. We look alike and sound alike, but I'm not even a smidge shy. I'll talk to anyone, if you can believe that."

Lucy can, in fact, believe this. While she's only known Harrison for about five minutes, she's pretty sure if he were an animal he would be a bottlenose dolphin, because:

1. Harrison talks a lot and he does it without many breaks between words, which is a lot like the constant buzzing and chirping that dolphins produce. Frankly, Lucy isn't quite sure when Harrison (or a dolphin) has time to take a breath.

2. He moves almost as much as he talks, shifting and wiggling and bouncing constantly. This is also very dolphin-like, because dolphins are always in motion.

3. He loves kangaroos. A lot. So he might prefer it if she compared him to a kangaroo, but kangaroos are often quiet and lazy and those traits just don't seem much like Harrison to her, which explains the dolphin choice.

"We'll just pretend we're meeting for real," Harrison says. "My name is Harrison and I'm here for the kangaroos and winning and hopefully s'mores. Leah promised there'd be s'mores."

"Leah did, that's true," Alex says.

"Nice to meet you," Lucy says, and her voice comes out just as squeaky as she feared.

Harrison reaches out a hand. Lucy is a little bit afraid that Harrison's hand might be sticky, but it seems okay when she shakes it. Of course Harrison doesn't stop shaking it at once or twice. He shakes and shakes until Lucy feels like her whole arm is jiggling up and down and up and down.

"It's really nice to meet you. I heard you know a lot about animals and it's kind of a funny story because Alex wasn't even telling me, she was telling my tutor Leah while Leah was helping me in math. I need math tutoring because my numbers are all mixed up all the time, which I think is an ADHD thing, really, on account of numbers being the most boring thing in the world—anyway, when she starting talking about this, I asked if Wildlands has pins for the different animals and which ones they have, because I was thinking maybe I should collect pins or something, but Alex and Leah thought I meant pens like the ones you write with, but I meant those ones you can stick on your backpack. Like you can get them at Disney World and stuff?"

Harrison shakes Lucy's hand the whole time he's talking, which is a long time but not as long as it should be to say that many things. Harrison talks at least twice as fast as Lucy.

"Sorry if I'm talking a lot. I sometimes talk a lot. So tell us about yourself."

Lucy means to say *I'm just here because I like puzzles*, because suddenly she doesn't want to tell the truth, because she doesn't want anyone to know she wants to be on the Wildlands Ambassadors. Not with Jemma here, so determined to win, and Harrison interested too.

"Do you want to be on the Wildlands Ambassadors?" Harrison asks.

Part of her is afraid to admit it, but another part of her can't help but be excited. Because she has another chance! And if there isn't some sort of platform challenge, this time really might be different. Lucy takes a deep breath and nods. "More than anything in the world."

"Oh," Harrison says. Lucy notices the way his eyes flick over to Jemma, who is sitting right beside him. Then Harrison does something he hasn't done since Lucy has met him. He goes completely silent.

"Well," Jemma says, and she uses the same kind of tone Lucy's mom uses when she's pretty annoyed with Alex or her. "Lucy, just so you know, since there's only one spot, I'm—"

"Before you finish that thought, Jemma, we have something else to get started on."

"What's that?" Trey asks.

Alex grins and pulls a sealed envelope out of her bag. "It's time for you to start your first puzzle."

CHAPTER 4

Alex pulls the envelope open and slides a single sheet of paper out. Lucy notices her sister's eyes go wide and then Alex pulls the paper closer to her face like she doesn't want anyone else to see.

"What does it say?" Jemma asks.

"Is it a secret?" Harrison asks. "I don't know if we can solve it if it's a secret."

"Shouldn't we know the rules?" Lucy asks.

Alex holds up one finger and continues to read. Then she folds the piece of paper in half and slides it back inside the envelope.

"Aren't we going to read the puzzle?" Trey asks.

"Nope!" Alex starts the engine, which is extra low and rumbly. Suddenly a faint light appears in each cupholder and at the edges of the armrests. Lucy even spots it along the footboards beside the doors. And then small screens drop down in front of Lucy's and Trey's seats. Lucy can hear the same soft whirring behind her, so there must be screens in front of Harrison and Jemma too. It's like being in a movie theater on wheels! A tactical movie theater!

"Dudes, this is amazing," Harrison says.

"True," Trey says, and he and Lucy exchange a huge grin. Is everything in the escape challenge going to be this completely awesome?

"So, this is cool," Jemma says, "but where's the puzzle? It's not on the screens."

Jemma's right. The only thing on the screens is a Wildlands logo, which is slowly spinning left and right on an otherwise dark screen.

Lucy frowns. Where is the puzzle they're supposed to be solving? Lucy looks at Trey, who seems to be just as confused. He clears his throat as Alex starts backing out of the driveway.

"Is it an invisible puzzle?" he asks.

Alex shakes her head, her blue ponytail shifting back and forth. "It's a verbal puzzle. I have the instructions, and you have to listen carefully to solve the puzzle. You may want to take notes!"

READER NOTE!

TIME TO GET OUT YOUR PENCIL AND PAPER!

"Wait, the escape challenge is only verbal puzzles?" Harrison asks.

"I don't think so. I think each puzzle will be a little bit

different. But I can tell you that this is a verbal puzzle and I'm the only one who is allowed to see the rules. Now, are you ready?"

Lucy can't see Jemma or Harrison, but given the way she feels and the way Trey looks, she's pretty sure they're more confused than ready. Harrison is snapping and unsnapping that compartment in the back again, and even that snapping goes more slowly, like he's just not sure what Alex is getting at.

"Okay, what's the goal? Like, how do we win?" Jemma asks.

"You win by finding out which habitat is our starting point in Wildlands. You'll be solving clues I say out loud in order to figure it out. There are five distinct habitats in the park. Does anyone know what they are?"

Lucy does know the habitats, and since no one else is answering, she starts. "There is a desert, a savanna, a wetlands, a forest, and . . ." She trails off and her cheeks feel very hot all at once, because she can't remember the last one. Why doesn't she remember it?

"The last one is the aquarium, but we call that a marine habitat," Alex says. "It's used for coral reef restoration[7] work."

"Please tell me this puzzle involves swimming in the

---

7   Coral reef restoration is important and difficult work. First, growing coral takes a long time. Second, many of the fish that live in coral reefs are escape artists. Once, at an aquarium in Chicago, a particular eel leapt out of a holding tank and landed in a sink, slithering down into the drain. A maintenance worker had to quickly disassemble the sink to save the eel from certain doom.

aquarium," Jemma says. "Because I'm captain of our swim team and I'm really fast at the backstroke."

"Sorry, but no swimming," Alex says. "Okay, here's the first clue. *Our destination is cool but not awesome.*"

The whole truck goes silent and still. Even Harrison stops snapping his snap. Alex chuckles in the front, and then she says it again.

"That's the start of the puzzle, everyone. *Our destination is cool but not awesome.* Here, Lucy, you can take notes if you have your pen."

Lucy always has a pen—she actually collected them for a while—so she tugs out her favorite (a green one) and starts to jot down the sentence Alex said. She double-, triple-, quadruple-checks it, and then she feels her face scrunch into a frown. Because this isn't a puzzle, it's a sentence, a pretty boring one that isn't even technically a question.

"How is this a riddle?" Jemma asks, and for the first time since they've been in the truck, and maybe the first time ever, Lucy completely understands where Jemma is coming from.

"It isn't a question," Lucy says.

"Hmm . . . ," Alex says in a way that's a little like a question and a lot like an annoying big-sister thing to do.

"Wait, was there a song playing on the radio or anything when she said that? Or was there a sign outside the safari truck? Or is there some symbol hidden in the logo on the screen? Oh! Is the movement spelling something out?" Harrison asks. He has started the snapping and unsnapping again, and it's going faster and faster. Lucy checks the screens above and watches the logo bounce up and down and left and down again. It doesn't look like it's spelling anything or drawing anything.

"It looks pretty random," Lucy says.

"Just keep watching," Harrison says. "This could be some sort of trap! Like maybe there's a trick or hidden pictures or something like those shape puzzles that they did in indoor recess that were sometimes triangles?"

"Tangrams," Trey says.

Lucy has no idea how Trey figured that out, but maybe it's because they go to the same school?

"Bluh. Tangrams? That's so dumb," Jemma says. "Can't we *do* something?"

"You can help each other work out the puzzle," Alex says.

"No, I mean like a ninja course or a corn maze?" Jemma asks. "I need to win this thing and to win, I need to race or something!"

Lucy squints at the back of Alex's headrest, which feels a lot safer than turning around to squint at Jemma, which is what she really wants to do. Because isn't helping guests figure things out a big part of being a Wildlands Ambassador? If there's one thing that Lucy hates more than the possibility of losing another tryout to Jemma, it's the idea of losing that tryout for a team Jemma doesn't even seem to want!

"Oh, races are great," Harrison says. "Mazes are even better. We have a corn maze at that pumpkin patch out on the edge of town, remember? But I like the haunted forest there. Wait, do you remember last year when they

36

had that giant ostrich that got out and started running around?[8] Were any of you there when it happened?"

"Emu," Lucy says, "but no."

Harrison stops snapping, and Lucy's throat squeezes. Everyone is looking at her. Even Trey, who's been pretty still in his seat, turns toward her.

"Wait, I saw that ostrich too," Jemma says from behind her. "I was there and it was super annoying because they shut down the basketball shooting until they caught him."

If you ask Lucy, and she's beginning to wonder if she should just start asking herself these questions out loud, shouldn't a person who wants to be a Wildlands Ambassador be more concerned about an escaped animal than a dumb basketball toss?

"It was an emu," Alex says, instead of asking the really important question. "Ostriches require more space. But now we do have a big enough enclosure, so you'll get to see them!"

"Well, I liked that emu story," Harrison says. "He figured out how to pick the lock on his cage and kept sneaking out.[9] And he waited until the farmers weren't around to escape so that he wouldn't get caught. He even got into the gift shop and stole a box of candy."

---

8   The escapee, named Edgar, actually ran straight into the corn maze and was found happily munching, not on field corn like you might expect, but on a granola bar dropped by a human guest when Edgar appeared and scared him half to death.

9   Emus, which are the third-largest bird, after ostriches and cassowaries, have a tendency to escape. One famous pair of emus, Biggie and Kimmie, broke out of a fenced area for a wild run in North Carolina involving several police officers and some pretty funny video footage.

"That's cool. But shouldn't we talk about the puzzle?" Trey asks.

Right! The puzzle! Lucy stares at each of the words, but absolutely no answers or clues or ideas pop into her mind.

Alex pulls up to a red light and clears her throat. "Okay, let's try another clue. *Our destination is cool but not awesome.* Oh, and *Our destination has blossoms but not flowers.*"

Lucy writes down the words quickly but looks up slowly. Because if there are two clues in the world that feel less helpful and less like a puzzle than these, Lucy would really like someone to point them out.

"Wait, aren't blossoms and flowers the same thing?" Jemma asks.

"Technically yes," Trey says. "But to be fair, a blossom usually refers to a flower on a tree, especially fruit trees. But flowers are part of the reproductive system of flowering plants."

Lucy is suddenly very confused about why Trey would need to be tutored at all. He sounds like one of the super-smart kids at school. The ones who always have their hands up in class and always finish tests way before anyone else. But at least he's nice. Because if he's the superstar of the team, that would be way easier than Jemma.

Unless of course he wants the spot on the Wildlands Ambassadors too. Lucy squints at Trey, who is frowning and seems to be deep in thought. She wishes she could figure him out, but so far she thinks if Trey were an animal, he'd maybe be an elephant, because:

1. He's very tall but seems to be surprisingly quiet, and elephants are known for being surprisingly quiet.

2. He has a really good memory about plant things and maybe all sorts of things, and everyone knows about elephants and their memories.

3. He might be a very tricky person to beat if he wants to win a spot on the Ambassadors. Or he might be easy to beat. Or she might not have to worry about it because he might not want that spot at all. Really, there's no way to know for sure, because other than being tall and smart about plants, Trey might surprise everyone, just like an elephant.

"Okay, so I'm confused," Harrison says. "And I'm confused a lot, but I think this feels extra confusing, even though I'm usually pretty good with vocabulary stuff. Blossoms and flowers are almost the same, and cool and awesome are kind of the same. I guess we could rule out the aquarium, since our destination has flowers, and I don't think there are flowers underwater." [10]

"Um, no," Jemma says. Then Lucy hears her shifting in the seat behind her. "I mean, I don't think so."

"Me either," Lucy agrees, but she looks at Trey, who is obviously the plant expert so far.

Trey tilts his head back and forth like he's weighing the

---

10 While there might not be flowers in the sea in the traditional sense, Lucy does think that several anemones look like flowers.

idea in his brain. "It depends a bit on what you consider a flower, but generally no. So maybe something else?"

"Maybe the desert or savanna?" Jemma asks.

"There are apple trees in the savanna area," Trey says. "And apple trees definitely have blossoms. But there are cherry trees in the forest too. Plus, there are flowers in the desert."

"You're absolutely right, Trey!" Alex says. She sounds a little bit amused, and it's starting to make Lucy a little bit frustrated.

"I'm not sure I understand," Lucy says, feeling about 98 percent annoyed with this nonpuzzle puzzle. "We have gotten to the actual puzzle, right?"

Alex chuckles. "We have. Oh, and *Our destination is yellow but never gold.*"

Lucy writes down this sentence too, and this time she maybe presses too hard with the pen because this riddle is starting to make her cranky. Yellow and gold aren't 100 percent the same, but they are awfully close to the same. Cool and awesome? Also the same. And even though Trey knows some smart-kid stuff about flowers and blossoms, for almost everyone else Lucy knows, those words are also synonyms.

So what on earth is this puzzle getting at?

"It can't be the desert," Jemma says, sounding both bored and annoyed. Bor-nnoyed. "Deserts are dry and dead."

"Deserts are full of life and have plenty of flowers and blossoms," Trey says.

Lucy has seen plenty of documentaries about desert

40

wildlife, and Trey is right. But she still doesn't remember anything particularly gold in the indoor desert exhibit area at Wildlands. Mostly everything is brown or orange.

"I bet there is goldenrod all over the savanna right now," Trey says softly. "Which is yellow and a flower, but there are yellow trout lilies in the forest too."

"Right again!" Alex laughs again, sounding absolutely delighted.

"Okay, but isn't gold like metal and shiny?" Harrison asks. "Maybe it's a magical forest! Magical forests always seem to have gold things. Like mystical golden apples and stuff. And unicorns. Wait. I think unicorns are usually silver."

"Agreed," Trey says, and then arches one eyebrow at Lucy. "But I don't think Wildlands has magical forests, does it?"

"I don't think so," Lucy agrees with a grin.

"Then where on earth are we going?" Jemma says. "If it's the forest, then maybe we'll have a tree-climbing contest."

"Hmm, would you like another clue?" Alex asks.

"Yes!" All of the kids speak in unison.

Lucy spots the Wildlands Safari Sanctuary turnoff sign on the road just before Alex turns onto the private drive leading to Wildlands. A giant iron gate arches over the road with WILDLANDS spelled out in curving metal letters right over the road. A slim sign hanging below the park name shows a message in bold red letters: PARK CLOSED THIS WEEKEND FOR PRIVATE EVENT.

A single guard shack sits at the entrance, with a friendly

grandpa type sitting on a stool. He has crinkly blue eyes and a kind smile, which makes Lucy feel a little better about being back at the park.

"Hello there, Alex! Do you have our adventurers here?"

"I sure do! Mr. Swendel, this is Harrison, Trey, Jemma, and my little sister, Lucy."

"Nice to meet you all," Mr. Swendel says. "The Ambassadors are already gathered in the south side of the park, but don't worry, they won't get started until you guys are ready."

Lucy feels her whole body go cold. *The Ambassadors are here. I mean, of course they are.* Alex said they would be, but Lucy didn't really think about it until right this minute. What if they remember her from the tryout? What if they laugh at her or—oh no, even worse—what if they are extra, extra nice to her because they think she's a baby and someone they have to be extra careful with?

"Of course, you guys won't have their help," Mr. Swendel says with a wink. "They'll be on the opposite side of the park, solving the same puzzles, but not going through the gates like you guys!"

"Leah is with the Ambassadors," Alex says. "We'll all be together for the big campfire at the end, though, so it will be lots of fun."

"Oh, and the keepers gave me a sneak peek at your path yesterday," Mr. Swendel says. "You can't imagine how close you'll be to some of the animals! And the camp is really neat."

Lucy feels like her whole body is lighting up. Trey is

sitting up extra straight beside her too, so she's not the only one who's getting excited. She wishes she could make this go faster, but Mr. Swendel doesn't seem to be a speedy person. In fact, though she doesn't know him at all, if he were an animal, she's sure he would be a sheep, because:

1. He's got lots of bushy white hair not unlike a sheep's wool.

2. He has dark, gentle eyes.

3. While she can't speak for the rest of his diet, she can see a whole bag of apples inside the guard shack, and she happens to know that sheep love to have apples as treats.

"Are the animal care teams still here?" Alex asks him.

"They just finished up, but Josie told me they'll be back at sunrise and for the picnic."

"Oh, that's right," Alex says. "Well, hopefully Phoebe didn't forget about us bathing the elephants."

"Well, I've got good news and bad news on that front," Mr. Swendel says. "Phoebe has Tessa and Ruby in the off-exhibit barn. Tessa hurt her foot,[11] so she's trying to keep them a little less active while she has time to heal, and I don't know about baths."

---

11 Elephant feet carry a whole lot of weight, so they require lots of special care; keepers need to check the skin and file the nails. And since picking up an elephant foot is about as easy as picking up a small pickup truck, trainers at zoos teach elephants special foot tricks so that they'll voluntarily present their feet for inspection and care.

"Oh, I'm sorry to hear that," Alex says. She looks back into the truck at everyone. "Tessa and Ruby are sisters. And Phoebe is our head elephant keeper."

"But don't you worry. The four of you will get extra time with Mwanza and baby Tabora no matter what. If not a bath, then you'll help with enrichment play."

Enrichment play? Lucy has to hold in a little squeal. The last time she was here, she lost a tryout because of a panic attack at the top of a viewing tower. But this time she could bathe or have a playdate with Tabora, the cutest, smallest elephant in the world? [12]

"So!" Mr. Swendel claps his hands. "You guys know the rules, right?"

"No," Lucy and Trey say at the same time.

"We went over them on the way, so we'll get started as soon as we get to camp," Alex says. And then Lucy can see her sister's face pinch with worry. "Mr. S, I have to ask. Has anyone in security heard anything more from you know who?"

"From Happy Time Farms?" Mr. Swendel shakes his head. "Thankfully that good-for-nothing hasn't shown his face in two full weeks. Josie thinks we should be in the clear."

Lucy does not miss the way her sister's shoulders slump with relief. What's going on? Lucy is 96 percent sure Alex

---

12 This is technically untrue, because Tabora is a baby African elephant, and the smallest elephants are Borneo pygmy elephants, which are just a little bit taller than a camper van. An adult African elephant, on the other hand, is almost the same height as two camper vans stacked on top of each other.

was worried when she asked about *you-know-who,* so whoever it is, it's a good thing he's gone.

"That's so good to hear," Alex says. Then she turns to look over her shoulder at Lucy and the other kids. "Josie oversees the keeper team."

"Our walkie-talkies have been on the fritz for the last couple of hours, so if you need me and can't reach me, just drive on up," Mr. Swendel says. "Oh, and Archie is out on a run."

"Again?"

"He's always up to something," Mr. S says with a chuckle.

Mr. Swendel waves as Alex pulls out a special ID card, which she holds up to a sensor with a red light on a pole. The sensor beeps and the light turns green. The giant, heavy gate begins to grind and groan. The gate lifts up, up, up, and Lucy's stomach drops down, down, down. All she can think about is standing on top of that tower. What if that happens again?

Alex drives them inside and Lucy takes a deep breath, trying not to think about towers or security incidents or whoever Archie is and why he's always up to something. But the thoughts are still there, hanging out like spooky shadows at the corners of her mind.

CHAPTER 5

"Who's Mr. Happy Time Farms?" Jemma asks.

"Oh, he was just a temporary employee who was a little sneaky about trying to get into unauthorized animal areas," Alex says. "But like Mr. Swendel said, he's long gone. And good riddance!"

A second or two after they're through the gate, Lucy turns back to see it closing behind them. Her neck feels hot and her stomach flops over the way it always does when she's worried or nervous. Or both. Which could be ex-wor-vous-ness, but no matter what she calls it, it still feels awful.

She doesn't know these other kids, and while the truck bumps its way down the path, she tries to figure out what she knows about her team so far:

1. Harrison may also be a little like a hummingbird. He does not have an off switch, which means he might not give up. Of course, he might not ever actually do anything about the puzzles, because right now, he's telling a story—or maybe several stories—about his very large dog, Wookiee, and while he's talking, he's kicking the back of Lucy's seat over and over and over.

2. Trey might also be like an Amur tiger, which is the longest of all the big cats. He is long like the tiger, but also very quiet and watchful. If there are hidden clues, Trey might be helpful at finding them, but he's so smart that if he wants the spot on the Wildlands, Lucy's not sure he won't end up knowing the most on every puzzle and winning it!

3. Jemma could also be a little like a honey badger, because she seems completely fearless and willing to do whatever it takes to win. She's leaned forward between Lucy's and Trey's seats right now, with narrowed eyes and a super-serious scowl on her face. Lucy doesn't know what she's thinking or why she wants to win that Ambassador spot so badly, but Lucy knows one thing for sure: Jemma usually wins.

Alex drives past the part of the park Lucy is familiar with, and Lucy holds her breath when they approach the familiar turnoff to the original tryout location. Relief rushes through her when Alex drives on, taking a new road to the right. If there's one thing Lucy loves more than the idea of seeing the African painted dog and the oryx, and especially the rhinos and their dung midden,[13] it's the idea of never being anywhere near that terrible viewing platform again.

---

13 Dung is poop, and a dung midden is a giant pile of communal poop that some animal groups (like rhinos) leave to mark territory and provide important information to other animals. If you ask Lucy, though maybe it's good that no one asks Lucy about poop, it's super lucky that humans invented things like writing and smartphones.

Lucy stares out the window at an entirely new area of the park. The back part of Wildlands has been under construction as long as Lucy can remember. So, just like with the strangers[14] she's with right now, she has no idea what to expect next.

Which is why it's not even that surprising when Alex stops the truck in the middle of the road and puts it in park. "Okay, are you ready to solve this puzzle?"

Her eyes are twinkling, and everyone is very quiet as they wait. *"Our destination is impressive but not remarkable."*

Lucy jots down the new sentence, and before she's done writing, Jemma explodes.

"Okay, that's it! This isn't a puzzle. This is a bunch of stuff that's the same."

"They are similar," Alex agrees.

"Then that's impossible!" Jemma says.

"Actually, you're on the right track there," Alex says with a laugh.

"How?" Trey asks.

"I can't tell you or I'll give it away. But I'd pay very close attention to these words."

"Okay, okay, close attention to the words. Dudes, we can do this. We just need to think," Harrison says. He's

---

14 Technically, Jemma is not a stranger. Lucy and Jemma were in the same soccer camp one summer, except that Jemma was super extra serious about technique and winning and Lucy signed up for the free Popsicles and stickers. For the record, Jemma doesn't have much patience with people who aren't serious about soccer, and Lucy would know because she's been paying for her lack of seriousness ever since.

bouncing his legs now, and his shoe is still catching the back of Lucy's chair every now and then. "There's got to be some sort of twisty part. Puzzles and riddles aren't always as straightforward as they seem, right?"

"Agreed," Trey says. "And we're going to have to figure out those twists if we're going to beat the Ambassadors."

"You're right," Lucy says quietly, "but there isn't even a question here. How do we solve a riddle without a question?"

"That's a point too," Alex says with a laugh. "It is a *riddle*, but not a *question*. Again, think about those words."

"You asked a question at the beginning," Trey says.

Harrison kicks Lucy's seat and she flinches.

"Yeah!" Harrison sounds excited now. "The question is what destination we're going to, which is apparently cool but not awesome, is yellow but not gold, has blossoms but not flowers, and is impressive but not remarkable. Oh, and it's a riddle but not a question."

"That's a great memory, Harrison!" Alex says.

"Thank you!" Harrison seems completely unbothered by all of this, but Lucy is bothered a whole lot, and it's getting hard to hide it.

"It's impossible," Jemma repeats.

"Yes, I agree," Alex says, and Lucy can hear that she's close to laughing again. "It is impossible, but it's *not* unfeasible."

Something about those two words—*impossible* and *unfeasible*—makes Lucy's brain catch. The other kids are starting to argue again, because impossible and unfeasible are sort of the same thing. But Lucy doesn't pay attention. She is looking and looking at her notebook. She is thinking and thinking about those words.

And she is finally seeing something in each of the lines.

On another line she writes *impossible but not*. And then she stops. "Can someone tell me how to spell *unfeasible*?"

"*U-N-F-E-A-S-I-B-L-E*," Harrison says without missing a beat. Then he kicks the back of her seat, but this time Lucy doesn't care. She doesn't even really notice because suddenly all she can look at is the letters in *unfeasible*. And then the letters in *impossible*. And then *cool* and *awesome*. And then *blossom* and *flower*. She looks and looks and . . .

"I know where we're going!" Lucy says, and the whole truck goes completely quiet. Lucy absolutely, positively hates the feeling you get when you say something that makes the whole room go quiet and everyone in it starts looking at you. She squirms in her seat and feels her throat go tight. Everyone is just staring. What if she's wrong? She's smart about animals, but she's not a puzzle genius.

"Go ahead, Lucy," Alex says with a reassuring smile. "Tell us where we're going."

Lucy checks all the words and all the double letters twice. She double-, triple-, quadruple-checks because she definitely does not want to be wrong. But she isn't wrong. There is only one Wildlands destination that makes sense. So she tells everyone where they are going.

PUZZLE 1 – LOCATION

Our destination is (cool) but not awesome.

Our destination has (blossoms) but not flowers.

Our destination is (yellow) but never gold.

Our destination is (impressive) but not remarkable.

This riddle is (impossible) but not unfeasible.

It's a riddle, but not a question.

Our destination is the ⬭ .

"We're going to the savanna," Lucy says. And then she frowns uncertainly. "I think."

"Oh, the savanna!" Harrison says it like it's the most obvious thing he's ever heard in his life. But then he tilts his head and scrunches his eyebrows together. "Wait. Because of the blossoms thing? Or the yellow thing? Maybe it's the impressive thing, because that's where the elephants live[15] and they are pretty impressive."

"True," Trey says, and he presses his fingertips together. Lucy thinks she will add *presses fingers together* to the list of things she knows about Trey. Since neither tigers nor elephants press their fingers together (though that would be sort of awesome), she may need to think of a new animal.

Jemma sniffs. "Yeah, well, I think you're guessing."

"No, Lucy is right about the savanna," Alex says, which makes Lucy feel heaps better about everything. "But the real question is, have any of you figured out why?"

Lucy starts to explain. "It's the—"

"Don't tell them," Alex says. "I want everyone to noodle on this. Let's see how many of you can figure it out."

"Can I see your notes?" Trey asks.

Lucy isn't sure how she feels about showing everyone her notes. What if her handwriting is babyish? Or what if—yikes—she misspelled something? Her chest feels a little tight and she can feel her stomach pull back like a

---

15 The thing is, while African bush elephants do live in savannas, Asian elephants live in a variety of habitats and African *forest* elephants live in the jungles of central Africa. But honestly, can't elephants live wherever they want? I mean, who's going to stop them?

playground swing, but Harrison is already looking, so it's too late to do anything.

"Wow, your handwriting is so neat," Harrison says. "You can hardly even read mine."

Feeling a little better, Lucy tips the paper to show her notes to Trey too. Harrison is leaning up from the backseat, his sticky-up hair pointing in a lot of directions. He's drumming his fingers on the side of the seat, and there is absolutely, positively something sticky on his chin. But Lucy decides she likes Harrison.

He's very jittery and she's pretty sure she wouldn't want to hang out in his room (which she thinks might be really messy), but he's also friendly and honest. And earlier, he said he had ADHD like it's no big deal, which makes Lucy think he wouldn't look at her like a total weirdo if he knew about her panic attacks. Lucy isn't sure yet what Trey would think, and she's already 100 percent sure that Jemma thinks she's a weirdo, so knowing this about Harrison is nice.

As if Jemma reads Lucy's mind, her head pokes through the gap between the seats, her sleek black hair the exact opposite of Harrison's. "This better not count toward the individual points, because Lucy's the only one with notes."

"You're all welcome to take notes," Alex says, "and I don't track the individual scores."

"Wait, you aren't doing the scoring?" Harrison asks. "Then who is?"

"And how do we win?" Jemma asks.

"Let's just take things one step at a time," Alex says with a laugh. "First, let's remember that winning individually might not count for much unless the whole team wins. Now, what about this puzzle? Did anyone else figure it out?"

"I think I understand the answer," Trey says.

Lucy looks up, not sure how he's totally seen her notes with the way Harrison and Jemma have crowded in, but then she realizes he is so tall, he's just looking at the notebook over both of their heads. His eyes are still locked on the paper when he nods decisively and looks up at her.

He mouths something to her and Lucy doesn't quite understand, but then he tries again, mouthing the same words, but more slowly. *Double-letter words, right?*

Lucy nods, excited that someone else has gotten it. And okay, fine, maybe a bit relieved that she wasn't somehow wrong. So she's relieved-excited. Re-lited?

"I give up," Harrison says. "Can they tell me?"

"I'm over it too," Jemma says, though she sounds more annoyed at it than over it.

"You can tell them," Alex says.

"It's double letters," Trey says, looking at Lucy with a smile.

She grins too and then adds, "All of the words that the destination *is* have double-letter combinations. *Cool* has two *o*'s, *impossible* has two *s*'s, and so on."

"Oh, I get it!" Harrison says. "*Savanna* has two *n*'s!"

"Exactly!" Alex says, clapping her hands.

"So when do we get to the next puzzle?" Jemma asks, and if you ask Lucy, which no one did, Jemma looks more interested in getting to the next puzzle than she does in celebrating. Probably because getting to the next puzzle gives her another chance to win.

"Don't worry, we'll get there soon. As a team, you'll all find times where you'll be important to the puzzle-solving," Alex says. "I think one of the most important . . ."

But Alex does not tell them what's important. Lucy watches the back of her sister's head go very, very still. A shadow falls over the truck. Alex turns toward the driver's-side window and when Lucy sees the way her sister's eyes go wide, her stomach drops down, down, down. There must be something outside the window, but what?

Lucy turns so she can see. As soon as she spots the enormous, dark shape outside, she freezes.

"What is it?" Harrison asks. "Why did everyone get so quiet?"

"Shh," Alex says very softly.

Lucy wouldn't dare make a sound, because there is a very large, very gray, very wrinkly leg outside her window. She has seen elephants here before, and lots of times at the Columbus Zoo. But this time, the elephant isn't across a field or in an enclosure twenty yards away. This elephant is probably less than twenty *feet* away from the truck!

CHAPTER 6

Lucy takes a deep breath through her nose, and she can smell the sweet musty odor she remembers from the elephant barn at the zoo. The leg outside her window takes a very quiet step,[16] and Lucy spots the elephant's dangling gray trunk. Then she sees another wrinkly leg that makes Lucy swallow hard. These legs are *enormous*.

"That's . . . that's . . . It's an elephant," Harrison says. And then he takes a sharp breath and speaks again more softly. "How did we not hear an elephant and should it really be this close to our car because this feels extra close, doesn't it?"

"It does. I mean, the invitation said animals up close but doesn't this seem a little"—Jemma pauses to swallow hard—"too close?"

While Lucy doesn't agree with Jemma on many things, this is an exception. Elephants are not typically aggressive animals, but since they can weigh as much as Lucy's

---

16 Elephants walk on tiptoe, which explains why they are so quiet. Their feet look flat because there are special thick pads under the back part of their foot. So it might not look like it, but elephants spend their whole lives tiptoeing around like they're trying to sneak a cookie out of the kitchen without anyone hearing them.

school field trip van, they are big enough to cause problems.

The elephant, who thankfully isn't currently causing problems, pauses outside the truck, staying very, very still. Lucy sits up straighter and notices a familiar crisscross scar above one of the enormous, wrinkly knees. She drops her voice to a whisper. "I think it's Mwanza."

"Moo-wuh-za?" Harrison asks.

"Muh-wan-zah," Alex says very softly. "Keep your voice very low, Harrison. And keep your eyes peeled, everyone. Mwanza is not alone."

Lucy does keep her eyes peeled, because Alex is in her second year of college studying environmental science with an emphasis on wildlife conservation, so if she says Mwanza is not alone, she's probably right. Just then, Lucy sees a much smaller, less wrinkly leg, one that's attached to a much smaller, less wrinkly elephant. Tabora!

Lucy feels a different kind of stomach somersault, one that doesn't feel like a panic attack, but more like coming down the stairs on her birthday morning. Lucy loves the way her mom always leaves a wrapped birthday present beside her breakfast, but if there's one thing she maybe loves more, it's being this close to the most adorable baby elephant in the world. Tabora is right here! Right outside the safari truck, swinging her trunk in wild back-and-forth swoops.

"Hey, I can't see!" Jemma says.

Lucy winces and Tabora stumbles back, tripping over one of her mother's legs and falling sideways into the dirt.

Her not-really-that-little[17] legs go up into the air, and then Mwanza lifts her trunk. The much, much bigger elephant takes a few steps back and turns directly toward the truck, and Lucy sucks in a sharp breath.

This is 100 percent bad.

And just as she thinks it, Mwanza lets out the longest, loudest elephant sound she's ever heard in her life! This is not the sound of a trumpet; it's the sound of a truck horn, or a stuck siren, or a gym teacher with a bullhorn when it's too hot and everyone's getting lazy during kickball.

Lucy clamps her hands over her ears, but she doesn't close her eyes. Because when elephants feel threatened, especially mama elephants with babies, they sometimes decide to charge. But Mwanza doesn't charge. She stomps her giant front feet into the ground, and her gleaming white tusks glint in the sun as she bobs her enormous head to the right and then the left.

Lucy feels all her insides shrinking and shrinking into tiny little balls. This time, she agrees with Jemma. Mwanza is way too close to their truck. If she decides to charge, they're done for!

Mwanza lowers her head, and Lucy squeezes the armrests beside her seat. The giant elephant takes a few thundering steps toward the truck[18] but then abruptly

---

17 By the time elephants are a year old, they can weigh almost a thousand pounds, which is about the same weight as a grand piano, and nothing that weighs as much as a grand piano can have anything truly little about them.

18 Elephants will charge if they feel threatened or startled, especially mother elephants, and bull elephants when they are in a particularly agitated elephant state called musth.

turns to the side. She continues moving parallel to the truck, and Lucy sags back into her seat with relief. But what on earth stopped her?

"Is that a fence?" Harrison asks.

"Well, duh," Jemma says. "It's not like they can just let the elephants walk into the road."

It's a good point, and an obvious one now that Lucy can see it. Thick cables stretch out in a long line, separated by occasional sturdy-looking posts. The truck is parked between two of the fence posts, and somehow Lucy was so caught up in seeing the elephant that she completely overlooked the fencing.

Mwanza has slowed to a normal walk just behind the truck (and behind the fence, of course), but Lucy can't spot Tabora. She twists right and left. Maybe the baby elephant is hiding?

"We need to wait until Mwanza moves on," Alex says. "She's protective of her calf and might think we're a threat."

"Maybe someone should tell her she's big enough to eat anything that might look threatening," Harrison says.

"Is she going to try to eat us?" Trey asks, sounding worried.

"Elephants are herbivores," Lucy says.

"The baby is back!" Harrison says, and he doesn't even try to use a whisper voice. Lucy starts to wonder if Harrison actually has a whisper voice, but whatever she thinks about that vanishes when Tabora stops beside the truck, flapping her ears. It is completely adorable to have a baby elephant peeking into your truck's open window, but it also makes Lucy wonder if that elephant fence article she read is true.[19] Because Lucy knows lots of elephant facts, but only three seem to matter right now:

1. Elephants live in herds led by a matriarch, which means an older female like Mwanza.

2. Elephants, and in particular African savanna elephants, are the world's largest land animals, weighing up to fifteen thousand pounds, while the truck Lucy is sitting in probably doesn't weigh more than six thousand pounds, which she knows because her science teacher did a whole lesson about how much random things weigh.

3. Elephants tend to be protective of herd members that are more vulnerable because of age or size. Like baby elephants.

That last fact feels especially important, because Mwanza's calf, Tabora, is currently swinging her trunk back and forth over one of the fence cables. She is so extremely close to the truck that Lucy thinks someone could maybe toss Tabora a softball. Not Lucy, of course. Lucy is absolutely, positively terrible at throwing and kicking and

---

19 The article, which was true, discussed the fence options being used to deter elephants in Asia and Africa. The fences have drastically reduced the number of elephants strolling into villages and destroying crops. While it would be cool to see an elephant making crop circles, it's way safer to keep farms and elephants apart.

all other sports-related things. But Jemma for sure could do it.

"How strong is that fence? My braids look thicker than that cable," Jemma squeaks.

"Well, the cable is made of steel," Alex says. "I think we're okay."

But as soon as Alex says it, Mwanza turns back toward the truck, lowering her giant head. She lets out another very, very loud trumpet sound, one that feels like it rattles around in Lucy's bones. It is 100 percent the scariest thing she's ever experienced. And then Mwanza charges.

Lucy holds her breath and squeezes her eyes closed. They are about to be smooshed flat like pancakes! Like crepes! Like . . .

Lucy realizes there has been no more trumpeting. And they have not, in fact, been squashed. She opens one eye and sees Tabora running clumsily along the fence. Mwanza trumpets again, just a short little *brrreep*, but it still makes Lucy jump. Tabora startles too, moving faster in front of her mom's prodding trunk.

"I think that little guy is in trouble," Harrison says. "Boy, do I understand how he feels. I am always getting in trouble just like him."

"Her," Lucy corrects. "The calf is a girl. Her name is Tabora."

"I thought cows had calves," Jemma says.

"Lots of animals have calves. Or at least we call lots of animal babies calves," Lucy says, though her eyes are still locked on the elephant scene outside the window.

Mwanza trumpets again and bumps Tabora on her rump to keep her moving.

"Oh, right! I remember this one time in December there were all these reindeer facts at the zoo and I didn't pay much attention because the kangaroos weren't out and I was pretty ticked off about that but I'm pretty sure reindeer babies are called calves. Wait, maybe they were foals. Or is that horses? Oh, will we see horses?"

Lucy turns all the way around in her seat with a grin. She's starting to think Harrison is a little bit ridiculous, and she likes him a little bit more because of it. "You're right about calves for reindeer. Horse babies are foals."

"Well, what do you know." Harrison's smile is as friendly as his voice. "I learned something after all."

Lucy turns back around in her seat when Alex starts the engine again. The truck rolls slowly forward, moving them away from the elephants.

"Who can list other animals with calves?" Alex asks.

"Moose and buffalo," Lucy says automatically. "Camels and rhinos too."

"Hippopotamus," Jemma says. "I know that because the Cincinnati Zoo said so."

"So, that's five at least," Alex says.

"Seven, actually," Jemma corrects. "You're forgetting the reindeer and the elephant from before."

"That's true," Alex says. "You're always quick with the math, Jemma!"

"Yeah, I always get As in math," Jemma says. "In fact, I even know that we've driven a mile since we left the elephants."

"Wow!" Alex says. "Tell me how you figured it out."

"Well, we left the elephants exactly three minutes ago and you're driving twenty miles an hour if you're following the speed limit signs. You can figure out distance by multiplying speed by time."

"That's amazing," Trey says softly.

"Thank you!" Jemma sounds very pleased with herself, and if there's one thing Lucy enjoys less than Jemma when she's smug, it's thinking about the idea that if there is a whole bunch of math in this challenge, then Jemma might be the strongest team member and might win the spot on the Ambassadors.

"There are even more calves in the animal kingdom,"[20] Alex says.

"Lucy probably knows them all. You're like an animal genius, aren't you?" Harrison says brightly.

"No, not a genius. I just like animals a lot." Lucy feels her cheeks getting hot, but despite that, she feels a little bit happier knowing that her chances at making that team aren't over yet.

"Well, maybe that's because she would rather play animal fact games than hang out with other kids," Jemma scoffs, but she says it just under her breath enough that Lucy doesn't think Alex can hear.

But Lucy *does* hear, and her face feels much, much hotter now. She remembers the way Jemma and the other girls looked at her during soccer camp, when she opted to

---

20 Lucy knows more of them, including aardvark, ox, manatee, and yak, but she also knows there's a point when you stop listing things you know or you'll start looking like a snotty smarty-pants who just wants to show off.

read at lunch instead of playing a round of basketball. She wishes she had a scowl like Jemma's and a super-quick snapback ready for when people say mean stuff. But she doesn't. She mostly feels frozen and hot at the same time, and it stinks like a pair of skunks riding a musk ox.

"Jemma, are you the best pitcher on your softball team?" Alex asks brightly.

"Um, I play catcher. It's *completely* different."

"Oh, right," Alex says. And the way she says it tells Lucy that her sister 100 percent knew that fact before she asked. "So your team's pitcher isn't as good at catching as you are."

"Obviously not."

"But I bet your coach and teammates still think your pitcher is pretty important. Awfully hard to win games without one, right?"

Jemma doesn't say anything to this, and everybody else stays quiet too, even Harrison. He probably thinks Jemma is getting into trouble, but Lucy knows better.

"But they sure can't win games without a catcher either," Alex says, since no one else seems to be talking. "I guess it's great that everyone is good at different things. That's why I know you're going to be an awesome team. Lucy *is* amazing with animals. And Trey is so great with plants, oh, and Leah said you're awesome with audiovisual equipment too! And, Harrison, Leah tells me you're fantastic at problem-solving in really unique outside-the-box ways. Jemma, you're an absolute whiz with numbers and math, and I happen to know you were on the invention team at school last year."

Lucy looks at Trey and then at Jemma and Harrison in the back. Apparently there's more to them than she realized. She'll need to amend her lists with the new things she's learned, like:

1. Trey knows a lot about audiovisual equipment—which is like the projector in the school auditorium, she thinks.

2. Jemma is really good at math and maybe inventions?

3. Lucy needs to look up *outside the box* when she gets home, because she's not completely sure about what that means, but Harrison is good at it.

Alex pulls to a stop in front of a large gate and twists around in her seat to smile at everyone. Her blue hair is piled into a spiky ponytail and she has a stack of black leather bracelets on her left arm. She's 100 percent the coolest person Lucy has ever met, and sometimes it seems weird that they are related, because Alex makes friends everywhere she goes, and Lucy? Well, let's just say Jemma wasn't too far off with her animal games theory. People mostly think Lucy is weird, and Lucy mostly thinks they're right. The thing is, she doesn't mind being weird. She just doesn't love it when people point it out like it's a bad thing.

"Let's just try to remember this weekend that we are all awesome at something, and if we're going to point things out about each other, I vote for the awesome stuff, okay?"

"Definitely!" Harrison says. "All of you seem totally awesome."

"True," Trey says.

Lucy nods enthusiastically, and though Jemma doesn't say much in the backseat, she mumbles something that sounds mostly agreeable. The whole time they unbuckle, Harrison talks about all of the things his dog Wookiee is great at.[21] But Lucy is only half paying attention, because she's trying to figure out where they are.

When she gets out of the truck, she spots a sign that reads CAMP ENTRANCE on the metal arch above the gate. And right above the latch that keeps it closed, Lucy sees a big piece of parchment, like the kind you'd find at an old-timey park where everyone dresses up like pirates.

"Well, everybody, I think this is our sign!" Alex says. "Ha! Get it?"

"We should read that paper," Trey says.

"Wait, is it parchment? Or leather?" Harrison asks, tripping on a seat belt as he gets out of the truck. "Oh wait, that's not leather, is it? Because leather feels like a really weird thing to have hanging up in the animal park, so maybe we should include that on our notes to the escape challenge makers. Wait a minute, actually, are we supposed to be taking notes? If we're supposed to take notes, I vote for Lucy because she has great handwriting."

"Agreed," Trey says.

---

21 Even half paying attention, Lucy remembers that Harrison's list of Wookiee strengths is long and includes finding dropped French fries, sneaking off with entire bags of bagels, and lying right on top of a person's feet when they are cold, which might not be a great thing since Harrison also shared that Wookiee weighs 130 pounds.

"Fine by me," Jemma says. "I don't feel like lugging around a notebook, I'm going to solve this one fast. End of discussion."

Jemma doesn't totally push past Trey and Lucy, but she does rush up to the gate before anyone else can get there.

Lucy, Trey, and Harrison line up shoulder to shoulder at the gate, and Lucy spots the tops of the camp tents beyond it. The sight of them sends a squeezy feeling into Lucy's throat. Her stomach tilts, but it does not do a full loop, and she can't tell if the feeling is worry or excitement or more of that ex-wor-vous stuff she was feeling earlier.

Jemma unfolds the paper in a way that makes it annoyingly hard for anyone else to see. Then she looks up with a grin that makes Lucy think of raccoons trying to sneak into a trash can full of old pizza boxes. Of course Jemma wouldn't want old pizza boxes, but she's definitely up to something, and Lucy has no idea what that something is!

CHAPTER 7

"Oh, I don't even need help with this puzzle," Jemma says. "I have it figured out."

Lucy squints at Jemma extra, extra hard, but Jemma doesn't pay one bit of attention. She also does not share the puzzle with anyone else. Instead, she looks at Alex.

"If I tell you my answer, will I be in the lead for the individual score?" Jemma asks.

"Remember, I'm not in charge of scoring," Alex says, and then she pulls out her phone and types in a quick text. When she looks up, she grins. "Okay, Leah has the Ambassadors getting started on this puzzle now too!"

"Oh, right, we better move it!" Harrison says.

But Jemma just crosses her arms. "Not until you tell us how to win the most points. I have to know how to win the spot on the Ambassadors!"

"I already told you, I'm not in charge of that, but I can tell you that solving the puzzles before the Ambassadors will be a good start. And I bet being a good team player will probably be important too, so maybe you should share the puzzle."

Jemma hands over the parchment super quickly, but Lucy is about 92 percent sure she's only doing that because of what Alex said about being a team player. But since Lucy wants to be a good team player too, she doesn't mention her suspicions and instead leans in to take a look.

READER NOTE!

TIME TO GET OUT YOUR
PENCIL AND PAPER!

ANSWER BOTH TO OPEN THE GATE

1. CHOOSE THE HEAVIEST.

A TON OF
PRAIRIE DOGS

A TON OF HYENAS

A TON OF
AARDVARKS

2. EATING THIS WILL KILL EVERY ANIMAL IN THE PARK.

POISON IVY

POISON SUMAC

FOXGLOVE

How much does a prairie dog weigh? Does she even know? Lucy doesn't think it can be more than two or three pounds, and while aardvarks and hyenas[22] are bigger than that, how much bigger? She can't be sure. Has she even seen an aardvark in real life? So far, she has a whole lot of random questions, but she really needs to think about answers for this puzzle.

"It's all three of those animals," Jemma says. "Oh, and it's foxglove."

Jemma slides her palms across each other like she's dusting something off her hands, and Lucy has to work very, very hard not to crumple up the parchment and toss it at Jemma's nose. Jemma is really the most *ugh* person of all time.

"The goal is for you to all work together on these puzzles," Alex says. "And remember, things might not be what they seem."

Harrison begins to hop on one foot. "Well, Trey probably knew the answer to that plant thing, right? But it feels weird that all the animals weigh the same amount."

"I don't think they do," Lucy says.

Jemma crosses her arms. "They don't weigh the same thing, but a ton is a measurement of weight. A ton of anything is the same weight. And foxgloves are poisonous. My mom said so. So our answer is all three animals and foxgloves."

---

22 Surprisingly (or not surprisingly, depending on how much you know about aardvarks and hyenas), these two animals weigh close to the same, with hyenas weighing in at 90 to 170 pounds, while aardvarks weigh between 110 and 180 pounds.

"Cool!" Harrison hops from one foot to the other. "Now we just have to find out how to put in the solution?"

Lucy's neck and face feel hot again. If Jemma figures out every puzzle on her own like this, she's definitely going to win that spot on the Ambassadors. Lucy turns away, pretending she's looking for a place to put in their answers, but it's really so she won't have to stare at Jemma looking super-annoyingly pleased with herself.

"Can't you just tell us where the answer goes?" Jemma asks Alex.

"Well, I don't want to help you too quickly," Alex says. "The whole point of this invitation is to see if you guys can test the puzzles to see what's working and what's too hard."

"Excuse me, but are there slugs in Wildlands Safari Park?" Trey asks.

"Slugs?" Alex asks.

Trey nods, crossing his long brown arms over his chest. "Foxgloves are the most dangerous plant on that list, but certain slugs and caterpillar larvae can eat it without dying."

"Are slugs even really animals?" Jemma asks.

Lucy resists rolling her eyes, which feels like a thing that should earn her some sort of individual points. "Slugs are definitely animals."

"We don't have any slugs on exhibit," Alex says, "but I'm sure some do live in the park."

"But if Alex didn't think of it, maybe whoever made the puzzles didn't think of it either," Jemma says. "Didn't you make all of these, Alex?"

"No, I helped with device planning and some of the design elements, but our education team created the actual puzzles. It's possible slugs were overlooked."

"True," Trey agrees. "Foxglove is notorious. I think for the plant question, foxglove might be the right answer. Though it should be corrected in the final version of the challenge."

"Because of the slugs," Lucy says with a small smile.

"Yes," Trey says, grinning. "Slugs are animals too."

"Bluh, can you just tell us where to put the puzzle answer?" Jemma asks. "Like are we supposed to just tell you? Then we can go inside and explore at least?"

Alex checks her notes again and then shakes her head. "Nope, there's definitely a place to input the puzzle. Take a closer look at the gate, everyone."

Lucy looks at the latch on the gate. She double-, triple-, quadruple-looks, but there isn't any obvious keypad or combination anywhere. Out of the corner of her eye, Lucy notices Harrison hopscotching his way closer.

She's just about to ask where he's going when he tilts his head. But he's not looking at the large plate with the lock like she was. He's looking at one of the long metal slats, which—wait, does that one look a little thicker in one spot?

"There's something here beside the gate!" Harrison cries, and even before Lucy can close the distance between them, Harrison is pulling something slim and rectangular out of a plastic sleeve attached to one of the rungs in the gate. It was the maybe-thicker spot Lucy just spotted! Harrison holds up the item he retrieved.

"It's a tablet!"

Before being asked, Harrison presses his thumb against the glass and the screen blooms to life. Lucy moves beside him and quickly spots four boxes and six icons on the screen that match the parchment underneath. Even scarier than that, she spots the scoreboard at the top with the

Blue Team (that's them!) highlighted. Of course the Green Team must be the Ambassadors, the team she really wants to join!

"I bet we're supposed to click to move the right icons into the boxes on the screen," Jemma says, and even if Lucy is super-duper annoyed about it, she's pretty sure Jemma is right.

Jemma crosses her arms. "Well? Aren't you going to put in all of the animals, and the foxglove? And hurry, by the way."

The tablet screen suddenly flashes yellow, and the tablet gives three short low-pitched chirps.

"Did it work?" Trey asks.

Lucy doesn't feel like the sounds consisted of particularly happy or victorious tones, so when Harrison shakes his head, she's not surprised.

"I didn't even put in anything yet," Harrison says. "Wait, the score has changed! I think the Ambassadors are already winning!"

SCOREBOARD

GREEN TEAM	BLUE TEAM
1 WON	0 WON
1 COMPLETE	0 COMPLETE

"Just give me the tablet and I'll put it in!" Jemma says. "We need to go faster. We're already losing!"

"Alex didn't say it was a race," Lucy says, but it's obvious no one is paying attention.

Jemma already has the tablet, and both Harrison and Trey are leaning in to watch her tap in the answers. Even from her spot, Lucy can see her double-tap the image of the animals. One by one they disappear from the bottom of the screen and appear in the first three boxes. And then she double-clicks the foxglove and it pops up to the top too.

Jemma clicks the big ENTER button at the bottom of the screen and then . . . the boxes blink red once, and a big red X appears across the puzzle. Then, with one more red flash, each of the icons reappears at the bottom of the screen.

"Why didn't it work?" Jemma asks.

Alex starts slowly walking over. If you ask Lucy, and Alex didn't, her sister could be moving a lot faster considering that whole Ambassadors winning situation, but Alex doesn't seem to be in a hurry. When she gets there, she shrugs. "Looks like you'll have to try again."

"That's not fair! I was right!" Jemma exclaims. All the smug gloating attitude floats away now, and Lucy would be a little bit happy about it if she wasn't a little bit unhappy about the fact that the puzzle is not solved.

"I'm still not so sure about the foxglove," Trey says.

"Okay, well, it should be easy enough," Jemma says. "We'll try poison ivy."

"It's not poison ivy.[23] That's even less likely than foxglove," Trey says.

But Jemma doesn't listen. She quickly starts clicking away on the screen. The three animals pop back into the boxes, and then she clicks poison ivy, and then the ENTER button. Immediately, the boxes blink red and the X appears across the images.

"This screen thingy is completely broken," Jemma says.

"I don't think so," Alex says. "I just don't think you've put in the right combination."

"Maybe it's the order of the animals?" Lucy asks. "Try it lowest weight to highest."

"The weight doesn't matter. End of discussion," Jemma snaps.

Trey sighs. "Something's wrong. It's definitely not poison sumac. Birds eat the berries from poison sumac plants, and there are certainly birds in the park. Also, I think several animals eat poison ivy."

"They do," Lucy says, unable to resist.

"Well, it has to be one of the plants!" Jemma says. "Just give me the weight order already. We'll try that."

---

23 Trey is absolutely, positively right. Lots of animals can eat poison ivy, including deer, muskrats, and black bears, but one news story talked about a black bear that broke into a house to eat a blueberry muffin candle, so Lucy's pretty sure bears will eat absolutely anything.

Jemma is waving at Lucy, and Lucy's hands suddenly feel damp with sweat. She doesn't like the way Jemma is yelling. She seems frustrated and rude and bossy. Fr-ude-ossy. If every puzzle is going to be impossibly tricky and if Jemma is going to be scowly and fr-ude-ossy, this is definitely not going to be easy. But Lucy wants that spot on the Ambassadors, even if it's not easy. And she wants to see the new animal enclosures, and while Jemma might do whatever it takes to win, Lucy is absolutely willing to do whatever it takes to see the cool animals.

"Prairie dogs would be the smallest," Lucy says, "and I'm pretty sure hyenas and then aardvarks."

Jemma clicks prairie dog, hyena, aardvark, and then foxglove into the boxes. Everything blinks red and the X appears. Lucy shakes her head, completely confused. Jemma tries again, largest to smallest. And then tries it with poison sumac, even though Trey was certain about that bird berry thing. Jemma tries all sorts of random combinations, but every time, it's a flash of red and lots of Xs and they're right back where they started.

They're losing. A horrible feeling sinks in Lucy's chest. If they can't even win the first puzzle, how will she ever be an Ambassador? The answer is simple: She won't. And that can't happen!

"We have to keep trying. Wait, is this stupid thing broken? Can we still beat the puzzle if it's broken?" Jemma asks, looking determined.

"It's not broken," Alex says. "I have a solution list that was sent to my phone, and you haven't quite solved this one yet. I will say, it's a bit tricky, if you ask me."

"What?" Jemma looks angry and then extra, extra determined.

"Maybe we need to think outside the box," Harrison says. "We can't give up."

"Agreed," Trey says.

"But the instructions literally have us putting things *in* the boxes," Jemma says. "And the weight one has to be all three animals. A ton is a ton no matter what."

"True," Trey says.

"So it's the second thing," Lucy says, trying to think. "Something kills all the animals, but none of the plants worked."

Lucy shakes her head and gives her sister a please-help-us look. But Alex is watching Harrison, who stares at the puzzle parchment and then at the screen. Then he clears his throat and runs his finger underneath each word as he reads aloud. "Eating this will kill every animal in the park."

Then Harrison does something 100 percent shocking. He stands absolutely, positively still. His hair sticks up and his mouth stays open. And then, out of nowhere, he leaps into the air and lands with a whoop.

"What is it, Harrison?" Alex asks.

"It's nothing!" he shouts, looking more excited than Lucy's ever seen anyone look about nothing. "Get it? It's nothing! This is a big tricky trick, which is classic in escape rooms, so they're doing it here too! It's *nothing!*"

Lucy 150 percent does not get it. And when she looks at Jemma and Trey, it's pretty clear they don't get it either.

"Um . . . ," Jemma says.

"Are you sure it wasn't something?" Trey asks.

Lucy nods. "You did jump into the air."

"Oh, it *is* something! A nothing something," Harrison says.

Lucy looks at her sister, and this time she gives Alex a no-seriously-please-help-us look. But Alex just keeps smiling at Harrison.

"Why don't you try explaining what you mean by *nothing*, Harrison?" she says.

"I mean the fourth box should be nothing," Harrison says, waving wildly. "These questions are tricky. The animals are all the heaviest because of the weight thing."

"Right," Jemma says, and she stretches the word out a little, because as right as that first part sounds, it doesn't make the rest of what Harrison is talking about make any sense at all.

"Well, that's the tricky part. If you don't look at it closely, then you start trying to figure out what each animal weighs, which is totally not the point." Harrison taps the screen until each of the three animals is in a box at the top of the screen. "I think the fourth box is a trick too. It's nothing. None of those plants will kill *every* animal in the park, because slugs can even eat foxglove, but if *any* animal in the park eats *nothing*, they'll eventually die.[24] All animals need some kind of food to survive, right?"

A fluttery feeling bursts through Lucy's chest. Harri-

---

24 All animals do need to eat, but the microscopic tardigrades (also known as water bears) can live up to thirty years without food or water, which feels bonkers to Lucy, who gets cranky if she doesn't get an after-school snack.

son wasn't totally losing track of the puzzle. He was figuring it out!

"You're right," Lucy says, grinning. "It's actually one of the most important differences between plants and animals. Animals can't make their own food, so they have to eat."

"True," Trey says. "I learned that in science."

"I know! *Nothing* is the answer!" Harrison says. "Not that I know all that science stuff. I think you guys are the experts on that, but, dudes, I definitely know about trick questions, and this totally smells like a trick question. Not literally, though. Questions don't really smell at all. At least I don't think they do, but I'm not sure there's a way to check something like that."

"So what are we supposed to do?" Jemma asks, pulling back from peering at the screen.

Lucy leans closer. "I think we try to leave it blank."

"Yep!" Harrison leaves the fourth box empty and clicks ENTER. The boxes all outline in green and a short burst of musical chimes rings out! Then a sudden loud clank rings out from the gate. Lucy and the others jump, and then the slow, churning, grinding sound of metal sends them backward. Lucy watches in surprise as the gate separates in the middle. She spots a little square with a green light at one side of the gate. It's just like the lock on the front gate. And just like the front gate when Alex presented her special badge, this gate swings wide open.

CHAPTER 9

Lucy feels a rush of relief when they step through the gate. They've solved a puzzle. And maybe she didn't exactly take the lead with solving this one, but she tried to be a good team player, which Alex told them might matter.

So she still has a shot at that spot. But as much as she wants to dream of her name on the back of a Wildlands Ambassadors jersey, Lucy knows she isn't there yet.

"Wow," Trey says.

"Wow is right!" Harrison says, and then he takes off full speed around the camp.

Lucy moves more slowly, taking everything in bit by bit. There is a giant circular area behind the gate, with torches fastened at each junction of fence paneling. They look like the kind of torches you'd see in an adventure movie, but when Lucy looks closely, she notices small, rectangular solar panels at each base.

A large, round firepit sits in the middle of the camp area, with three old-fashioned green tents situated around it at a safe distance. These are the tents they saw from the gate. Lucy moves next to Alex and Jemma to check them out while Harrison runs figure eights in and out of the tents. Trey wanders right past the tents to observe a patch of wildflowers.

"They really decked this out," Alex says. "I am super impressed."

A single wooden pole and a mailbox sit next to each tent, and Lucy notices animal carvings running up each of the poles. There is a larger pole near the firepit, and Lucy realizes with surprise that it's a flagpole, one with no flag at the top.

"There isn't a flag up," she says.

"Hmm, maybe we should put one up like the other team," Alex says with a wink as she pulls a folded blue flag out of her pocket.

Jemma notices and whirls around, searching the horizon. Lucy scans the area too, and they both spot the same flag, way off in the distance. It's plain and green with white letters.

"Does that say something?" Jemma asks. "Is it a message? I can't read it."

Lucy can't read it either, but she already knows what it is. Her chest feels a little tighter and her hands squeeze into fists. She'd recognize that particular shade of green anywhere, especially with white letters in the middle. Lucy's sure those letters are a *W* and an *A*, and if you get up close enough to see it, she's also sure they'll be linked into a shield, because that's the Wildlands Ambassadors logo.

"It's the Ambassadors' flag," Lucy says. "I recognize it from their jerseys."

The same jersey Lucy desperately wants for her own.

"Oh yeah, that's right," Jemma says. And then she narrows her eyes at Lucy. "Come on. Let's get this flag up and show them we're not going to make this competition easy!"

Alex calls the boys over, and together, the four of them attach the flag and run it up the pole. And even though it's a plain blue flag and they don't have a logo, Lucy feels a rush of pride when the wind catches the fabric at the top of the flagpole, rippling it out in the air.

"Awesome!" Harrison says. "I'm going to check out the tents now!"

He zips off like a hummingbird and a mongoose and a roadrunner mixed together. Lucy is much slower to follow, taking in the details of the tents as she walks. The tent on the left has cheetahs carved in an endless loop around the pole, with feet and claws extended like they're racing to the top. The center tent has giraffes on its mailbox pole, with their long eyelashes and longer necks peeking around the edges. And the last tent on the right shows a gorgeous python carving, which is maybe Lucy's favorite. Lots of people hate snakes, but Lucy appreciates them. Most snakes seem to prefer things slow and steady and well planned, just like her.

"No way am I sleeping in the snake tent," Jemma says.

Lucy resists the urge to sigh. She's starting to think she and Jemma are the opposite person. But since they'll probably have to share a tent, that means she'll probably end up in whatever tent Jemma insists on.

Maybe she needs to add one more thing to Jemma's list.

1. Jemma is maybe a little bit like a vervet monkey—she's super clever, but she's also the kind of person that can drive you a little bananas.

Jemma looks at the snake pole at that moment and shivers. "Snakes really freak me out."

She flushes as soon as she says it, and Lucy feels a little bit bad. As much as she thinks snakes are cool, she also understands being afraid of things.

Harrison zips by, still running around the tents. "Dudes! This is amazing, and look at how many things there are. Did you see the mailboxes? Are we assigned to the tents? Can we open the mailboxes? Can we start a fire? Do we have marshmallows?"

Alex laughs. "Whoa there, let's take it one step at a time."

Lucy strides over to the center mailbox, the only one with the plastic flag raised. To her surprise, there is a letter inside. She slips it out and turns toward Jemma and Alex, who are standing near the firepit.

"Did you find something?" Trey asks, walking slowly toward Lucy. She nods and shows him the envelope.

"It was in the mailbox near the giraffe tent."

"Is one of us supposed to sleep alone?" Jemma asks, ignoring Lucy.

"Me," Alex says. "I'll stay alone in the third tent and you and Lucy can be roomies."

"Oh," Jemma says, and she looks down at her feet in the same way Lucy looks down at her feet when she's assigned to a project with Nate O'Connery, who picks his nose and calls everyone buttface.

"Did you find a letter?" Alex asks.

Lucy swallows down the lump in her throat and tries to ignore how bummed out Jemma looks. She doesn't know exactly why Jemma is like this with her, but she's pretty sure it has something to do with that soccer camp.

"These tents are so cool!" Harrison says from inside one of the tents. He continues shouting inside. "Oh man, there's a lantern! And two cots!"

He flies out of the giraffe tent and over to the cheetah tent. If you ask Lucy, though Harrison didn't, the cheetah tent seems perfect for all his racing and zipping.

"Whoa, this one has two flashlights instead of a lantern. They look like tactical flashlights! Trey, do you want a tactical flashlight?"

"Sure."

"We're the cheetahs!" Harrison emerges with two tactical flashlights and a huge grin.

Lucy and Trey both laugh, but Jemma points at Lucy. "Do you think we should read that letter?"

"Oh, right," Lucy says.

She turns the thick envelope over to read it.

To: Our Competition

From: The Wildlands Ambassadors

"It's to us," Lucy says. "And it's from the Ambassadors."

"Open it," Jemma says, and to Lucy's surprise when she looks up, Jemma gives a little bit of a smile. "I mean, don't we all want to know what they have to say?"

Lucy pulls the heavy paper out of the envelope and unfolds it. She is 200 percent sure she does not want to read out loud in front of Jemma Louise Sparks, of all people, but since she's the one holding the letter, she also doesn't feel like she has another option. So she begins to read.

Dear Team,

Welcome to Wildlands, our home turf! While we won't get to meet you until tomorrow, we're on the same mission! Here's a few tips to help you along!

* The tablet you got at the gate is linked to our tablet and to the gate locks along the escape challenge path. Solving the puzzles will unlock the gates!

* Your tablet will chime when you're near a puzzle. We aren't on the cool path (lucky you!) but are testing the puzzles at the other camp (look for our green flag). BUT we won't load the next puzzle until our tablet chimes, telling us you're starting too!

* You can see who's winning on the tablet! If we solve the puzzle before you, the tablet will flash green. If you win, your screen will flash blue. The score is at the top!

* The first team to solve all the puzzles wins their choice of a free three-day summer camp or a free special behind-the-scenes experience here or at the Columbus Zoo. And if you lose? We'll have a s'mores dance party tomorrow anyway!

That's about it. Oh! And if you want to be part of the Ambassadors, there is one open slot. Anyone interested will be scored by a special group of judges on animal knowledge, problem-solving ability, teamwork, and physical aptitude. So do your best and maybe you can join the Ambassador Team!

Good luck, and we'll see you tomorrow!

The Wildlands Ambassadors Leah Olivia Amelia
                          Emma Adam Isaac

"Okay, so there's the score," Harrison says, pointing to the top of the tablet. "They were first on the first puzzle. That's why the Green Team has a one and we have zero."

"That's still not fair. That riddle was too hard. It's like they cheated," Jemma says. "We didn't know it would be a trick question before we started the first puzzle."

"The Ambassadors didn't know either, and I did make a note that it was pretty hard," Alex says. "But let's remember, the competition is supposed to be fun."

"I don't really care about fun," Jemma says, swinging her black braids behind her back. "I care about winning. So am I winning at this point? And how many points do I have?"

Lucy immediately shoves the letter back into the envelope, if only to give her hands something to do and her eyeballs something to focus on. Because if she looks at Jemma right now, she will definitely be squinting and annoyed and it will be hard to hide it.

"I don't know if there are points, but I think you should all focus on winning as a team," Alex says.

"That's fine, but I want to win as a person most importantly."

"Jemma, I know you're eager for a chance to be on the Ambassadors, but regardless of what those points say, teamwork is super important."

"How would someone score teamwork?" Lucy asks.

"Well, if you solve a problem, that's one thing, but if you solve a problem with the help of someone on the team, that's way better in my book," Alex says.

"That doesn't make sense," Jemma says, looking frustrated. "In sports, points are points."

"It makes sense to me." Lucy really can't resist saying it. Because she doesn't want to spend the next day with Jemma pretending that the whole purpose of this challenge is to get Jemma a spot on the Ambassadors. Especially not when Lucy wants that spot too. Even Harrison said he might like it, and Trey hasn't said one way or the other.

"Fine," Jemma says. "Then I'm going to be a *great* team player, because I'm going to let Lucy decide what tent we should stay in."

"Oh, that is really nice," Harrison says, bouncing on his left foot.

"True," Trey says, but he doesn't sound 100 percent sure that it is true.

Lucy's 110 percent sure it *isn't* true, because Jemma's arms are crossed and she's wearing a smile that really isn't the kind of smile you'd think a great team player would have.

Lucy knows this is a trick question just as much as the riddles they've solved. If she picks the snake tent, then Jemma will be cranky. And if she picks the giraffe tent, then Jemma will be less cranky. But either way, Jemma still wins because she's pretending the choice is Lucy's.

Lucy squints so hard it makes her eyes hurt. Ugh, why is this girl so cranky all the time? Was she really this cranky at that soccer camp? Lucy isn't sure. But having Jemma as a roomie is like sharing a tent with an angry porcupine. One who's pretending to be a cute little koala at the moment.

"I really like snakes," Lucy says. "But we can stay in the giraffe tent."

Jemma doesn't say anything in response, not when they take in their bags or unroll their sleeping bags on the cots. Not even when they try out the lanterns above each of their beds. Finally, when they're both perched on the edges of their cots, Jemma clears her throat.

"It was nice of you to pick this tent," Jemma says.

"Sure." Lucy has no idea what else to say. It's not like they have much in common. Lucy likes puzzles and pens and notebooks. Jemma likes soccer and math and . . . Lucy isn't exactly sure what Jemma likes beyond that. But she should try to know something else, right? "So what's your favorite animal? Like the one that made you want to be an Ambassador?"

"I don't really want to talk about animals," Jemma says, and her voice sounds a little scratchy. "It wasn't about that for me. It's about my friends. I'm supposed to be with my *real* team, but they're the Ambassadors, and I'm stuck here instead."

Real team? Stuck here? Lucy feels the words like a punch to her stomach. Not only is Jemma bossy and annoying, but she also doesn't even want to be here.

"You don't think we're a real team?" Lucy asks.

"No offense, Lucy . . . ," Jemma says, but then she trails off. Which is fine, because if you ask Lucy, which Jemma obviously won't, when someone says *no offense*, they are 300 percent sure to be totally offensive.

Jemma finally takes a big breath and goes on. "I know you want to do this to be on the Wildlands Ambassadors because of animals. And even though you're really smart about animals, it just isn't going to happen this time."

To Lucy's complete and enormous horror, her eyes feel hot and prickly like she might cry. She feels so many things at the same time that she couldn't even try to make up a word that would fit all the feelings together. She stands up, hoping to shake all those feelings away.

"How do you know it won't happen?" Lucy asks.

"Because every single person on the Ambassadors is my friend. We're on like five other teams together. And I screwed up at the tryout somehow, but when you did the tower climb . . ."

Lucy shakes her head, backing toward the tent flap. "You weren't even there."

Jemma just shrugs, and she doesn't actually look mean right now, which is somehow the meanest thing she could do when talking about what happened on that awful day. "All the Ambassadors were talking about it, Lucy. It was you, right? The girl who had a panic attack on the viewing tower? They said staff members had to go get you. Is that true?"

Lucy can't answer and she can't explain and she absolutely, positively can't stay in that tent another minute. She pushes open the flap and walks as fast as she can across the camp and past the firepit. She walks until she almost bumps into her sister, who is setting up chairs around the fire.

"Whatcha thinkin', Lincoln?" Alex asks.

"I think I don't want to be in a tent with Jemma and

I know I don't really have a choice," Lucy admits quietly. One tear slips out, but she wipes it away super fast.

Alex sets down the chair she's holding and squeezes Lucy's shoulders gently. Lucy can still feel her heart beating so fast and hard. And she still feels that awful cloggy feeling in her throat like she's about to cry.

"I know you and Jemma aren't close friends, but do you think this might change that?"

"I don't know. She told me I'll never be an Ambassador."

Alex nods and makes a funny face. "You know, sometimes when people say things like that, it's not because they want you to fail. It's because they're afraid to fail themselves."

Lucy doesn't know exactly what that means, but before she can ask, a shout interrupts them, coming from across the enclosure. Lucy turns in time to see Jemma step out of their tent, but whatever they heard, it definitely wasn't Jemma. The shout comes again, and Lucy's sure it's coming from behind the tents. *Way* behind the tents.

"Over here!" Harrison's voice rings out clearer now. "We found something!"

CHAPTER 10

"**W**e found a puzzle!" Trey shouts.

Lucy tries to move fast, but Jemma is closer and she's already running. Which means she's going to get there first. Does getting there first get extra points? Lucy wants to ask Alex, but she's ahead of them, leaving Lucy last to arrive.

Lucy finds Trey and Harrison at the foot of a viewing platform. Her heart drops down through her stomach at the sight of those wooden stairs. Jemma looks right at her, and Lucy's face and neck feel so hot. But it isn't the same as the viewing tower. This platform has wide stairs leading up, while the viewing tower had a single narrow staircase that was so steep it was practically a ladder. This platform also isn't as tall and looks much larger and sturdier. But most importantly, they are not here to climb a platform; they are here to solve a puzzle.

And that's a very good thing, because Lucy is not even 1 percent interested in climbing up a platform, even one that isn't the same as the last one. Luckily for Lucy, neither Harrison nor Trey seems interested in the platform. They are on the ground, actually, crouched around what looks like a giant treasure chest in front of the staircase. Lucy really wants to touch the animal carvings that line all the edges of the chest, but the other kids are too busy checking out the strange, heavy-looking lock that holds it closed. The large lock has a green light, a lot like the lock on the gate she remembers from earlier.

"Dude, look at this! Isn't this the weirdest lock you've ever seen? Maybe there's gold inside! Do you think there's gold inside, Alex?"

"I don't think it's gold," Alex says.

"Where's the puzzle? Did the tablet make a sound?" Jemma asks, looking very eager to get to work.

Lucy steps closer so she can see too.

Harrison, who is one of those kids who probably wears hoodies every day of the year, even when it's a million degrees outside, pushes his hands into the giant pocket of his sweatshirt and pulls out the rubber-protected tablet. It's glowing super brightly in his hands. "Oh, right, I forgot! I did hear it. Look at the screen!"

Harrison tips the tablet toward the group, but Jemma grabs it before Lucy can read anything. Lucy squints over at her, feeling a little bit annoyed and a little bit frustrated and a lot bit tired of Jemma's attitude.

"Let me see that." Jemma presses the screen, which lights up at once, words blinking white against the dark background. "Did you guys even read this? We're supposed to click to start! We could be losing time!"

"We actually can't read it," Lucy says, and this time it's her turn to cross her arms over her chest. "Only one member of our team can read the screen with the way you're holding it."

Jemma's cheeks go pink and her scowl gets extra

scowly, but she lowers the tablet so everyone can see. Large, bright words march across the screen above a green START button.

**MAKE SURE ALL TEAM MEMBERS ARE PRESENT
AND READY BEFORE CLICKING START.
THE CHALLENGE IS ABOUT TO BEGIN!**

"Is everyone ready?" Trey asks.

Lucy nods eagerly, but Harrison holds up his hands.

"Hold on," he says, and then he looks up to the sky and shouts. "We're all here, okay? In case you're watching, you can rewind the video and see that we did not click past this screen until our whole team was here!"

"Why is he yelling at the sky?" Lucy whispers to Alex.

"I'm . . . not sure."

"He probably thinks we're being watched," Jemma says, looking extra grumpy again.

Lucy whirls to her sister, alarmed. "Are we being watched?"

"No! I mean, not here, anyway. Most of the park is very carefully monitored by video, but they haven't installed much around the camp."

"Really?" Harrison looks disappointed. "That's a bummer, dude! I thought there would be cameras in the sky watching us. Like in one of those survival shows."

"Sorry to disappoint, but there are no cameras in here," Alex says.

"I think we need to set the tablet down," Lucy says, looking pointedly at Jemma, who is once again holding said screen so that no one else can see it. "That way everyone can work on the puzzle together."

"Oh, right, that makes sense," Harrison says, and he pats the top of the chest. "What about here?"

Jemma hands the tablet back to Harrison, looking bored. Or maybe annoyed. Or maybe bore-nnoyed, which would be both of those things and also a really great word. To Lucy's relief, Harrison places the tablet face up on the chest.

"Are we all ready?" Harrison asks, and then he looks at each person.

Trey nods and Jemma nods and Lucy . . . hesitates.

What if she's *not* ready for this? Her throat feels squeezy and her stomach swings back and forth as she thinks about the Ambassadors' letter. She has animal knowledge and she has problem-solving, but if Jemma was right and the Ambassadors were already talking about her panic attack, maybe they think she doesn't have what it takes to be part of their team.

Which means she's going to have to prove them wrong. Lucy balls her hands into fists and nods. "I'm ready."

Harrison takes a deep breath like he's maybe been waiting his entire life to click this particular electronic button. Once he does, the words disappear and the screen goes blank. And then several numbers appear, hovering above short lines. A few of the short lines have letters, so it's a little like a hangman game, but instead of letters, there are numbers.

"Maybe there will be some directions next," Harrison says.

A few seconds pass. And then a few more seconds pass.

And soon enough, it feels like there have been more seconds than there should be without something happening. Is . . . the puzzle not working right?

"Errr . . ." Harrison trails off when something appears on the screen. And then all four kids tilt their heads to look at the numbers that have appeared. Because no matter how hard they squint, that's all that appears. A bunch of numbers and a few letters. And then seven lines at the bottom with no numbers or letters at all.

Lucy suddenly realizes what this is and where she's seen it before. The sight of it makes her insides feel squirmy. Because as much as Lucy loves puzzles, this puzzle is a cryptogram, and she's never been able to solve one of those. Not even once.

CHAPTER 11

READER NOTE!

TIME TO GET OUT YOUR
PENCIL AND PAPER!

Lucy decides she cannot afford to panic. She doesn't need to solve the puzzle on her own, anyway. She just needs to be helpful to the team. Too bad the whole team seems to be looking as clueless as Lucy feels. Trey frowns. Jemma nibbles her bottom lip. And Harrison stares at the puzzle and scratches his head, which does not help the sticking-up-hair situation. Then he stands on one pale leg before switching to the other. It makes Lucy think of a flamingo, except a flamingo that can't make up its mind about which leg it prefers.[25]

---

25 Some scientists believe flamingos stand on one leg to prevent muscle fatigue, and others suspect it protects their skin from too much exposure to the harsh water they feed in. Lucy likes to think they're having a worldwide flamingo yoga contest to see who can stand on one leg the longest.

1

6 13 18 10 6 22   11 26 7 24 19 22 8

U _ _ _ U _   _ A _ _ _ _ _

2

26 21 9 18 24 26

A F _ _ _ A

3

1 12 12   21 26 5 22

_ O O   F A _ _

_ _ _ _ _ _ _

"Dudes, does anyone know what we're looking at here?" he asks.

"A cryptogram," Lucy says. Harrison and Trey look at her hopefully. Does saying that make it sound like she's good at these? Oh man, she really hopes it doesn't, because so far not a single thing is blinking into her brain. "I'm terrible at them!"

"Me too," Trey says. "What about you?"

Lucy notices that he's looking at Jemma, who hasn't said a thing since they started the puzzle. But now she heaves a sigh. "I don't think I've ever done them."

"I do think there must be two parts," Trey says.

"Why's that?" Jemma says, and she leans in closer.

"Because there are twenty-six slots in the code, but I doubt we're supposed to type in a twenty-six-character combination on the lock."

"No, you're right, there's seven characters here," Harrison says, tipping the screen so everyone can see. Beneath the puzzle, a glowing keyboard has popped up. But there doesn't seem to be a place for notes.

"We need notes," Lucy says, and she pulls out her small notebook and her favorite pen. Green-colored ink makes all the difference, and she quickly writes down the highest number she sees, which is *26*. Even luckier, the *26* is already solved, and is an *A*.

1   10   19

2   11   20

3   12 O 21 F

4   13   22

5   14   23

6 U 15   24

7   16   25

8   17   26 A

9   18

"What if we just put in a bunch of random safari words that fit and skip the puzzle?" Harrison says.

Lucy laughs at this, but Jemma is scowling in an extra-scowly way at the puzzle. "I think the code is simple letter replacement. There are twenty-six letters in the alphabet."

Lucy's eyes catch on the last line. Two O's (number *12* on the code) sit next to a blank line, which is number *1* in the code. She writes down all the double-O words she can think of. *Moo. Boo. Coo. Zoo.* Lucy squints at *zoo*. While *moo* and *coo* are animal sounds, she's 82 percent sure that *zoo* is the word that makes sense, and she's 120 percent sure it's time to ask her team what they think.

"I think the *1* is a *Z*, because I can't think of that many words that end in O O," Lucy says, "and definitely none that make as much sense as *zoo*."

"There's lots of words," Harrison says. "*Coo* and *poo* and *loo* and *foo*, although that might not be a real word, though it is part of the name of this super-old band my dad loves. But I think *zoo* makes sense, right?"

"True," Trey says. "And if it does, then this code might not be that hard. Because *A* is number twenty-six."

Jemma brightens and crosses her arms. "And there are twenty-six letters in the alphabet. Lucy, did you write all the numbers down?"

Lucy cringes at the way Jemma closes in, looming over her notebook like she just might snatch it out of her hands. "Yes, and I already filled in the letters we know."

Jemma crosses her arms. "Well, fill in all the letters in backward order."

Lucy nods and starts writing the missing letters down,

assuming that *A* is *26*, *B* is *25*, *C* is *24*, and so on. Right away it's obvious that the code is just as easy as they thought. Excited by their success, Lucy fills in each of the letters.

"It works! The code is the alphabet backward," Jemma says. And then she actually smiles. Like a real, genuine smile.

"Are you sure?" Trey asks, his brow furrowed. "That seems so easy."

"Well, you're only done with part of the puzzle, right?" Alex asks.

Lucy is one step ahead of her. She quickly writes out the full words based on the code.

Lucy frowns. "Um . . . these don't really make sense."

Jemma leans in to read over her shoulder. "Unique patches. Africa. Zoo fave. What do any of those things mean?"

"Maybe it's another trick question!" Harrison says.

1 Z	10 Q	19 H
2 Y	11 P	20 G
3 X	12 O	21 F
4 W	13 N	22 E
5 V	14 M	23 D
6 U	15 L	24 C
7 T	16 K	25 B
8 S	17 J	26 A
9 R	18 I	

MOO BOO COO ZOO

UNIQUE PATCHES

AFRICA

ZOO FAVE

"Bluh, I hope not," Jemma says, and for once Lucy absolutely, positively agrees with her. "If everything is a trick question, then we're never going to know who's actually good at anything. End of discussion. All we'll learn is who's lucky."

"Or who's a creative thinker," Harrison says. "That's what my teacher Ms. Westwood always says. She tells me all the time that even though I don't always come up with the right answers on tests, I'm still—"

Three happy chimes interrupt Harrison's story, and Lucy's heart drops even as the screen flashes green. The Ambassadors have finished the puzzle. They've been beaten again!

"We have to put in a solution!" Jemma shouts. "We're losing!"

"You're not losing," Alex says. "You're just not finishing the puzzles as quickly so far."

"Which means losing," Lucy says, and now her stomach is swinging back and forth. "We have to finish this so we can move on."

Trey frowns. "Agreed, we should hurry. But we still don't know the seven-letter solution."

"But we solved it," Jemma says. "Those words are just nonsense. We can't solve *that*."

"Maybe we need a hint," Lucy says.

Alex tilts her head. "Are you sure you don't want to try to figure it out?"

Harrison leaps in front of Alex, waving his arms. "No! I mean yes! I mean don't tell us, because we can totally figure this out on our own. Maybe we need to read it backward?"

"Fave zoo Africa patches unique?" Jemma asks. "That doesn't make sense."

"It's also more than seven characters," Trey says.

Lucy bites her lip and looks at the word. She tries mixing up the first letters of the words, but there are only five. If she takes the first and last, then there are ten.

"What has patches in Africa? Like snakes and stuff, right?" Harrison asks.

Lucy looks up. "Wait. Is that it? Is the code revealing a clue we have to solve?"

"Don't ask me," Alex says in a singsong voice that tells Lucy she's onto something. "My job is to only be here if you're in trouble or completely, utterly stuck."

"We're not utterly stuck," Jemma says, and while she sounds annoyed and looks scowly, she also looks determined. "We need to think of things with patches that live in Africa and maybe love zoos? Or zoos love them?"

"Is it snakes? Snakes have patches," Harrison says.

Trey nods. "True."

It is true, but it doesn't feel right to Lucy. "Snakes do have patches, but there are so many varieties of snakes in Africa that would fit that description," she says. What she does not say is that most people don't like snakes, so they aren't a fave. When people talk about their favorite zoo animals,[26] it's always cute stuff like pandas or arctic foxes or giraffes or—

---

26 Interestingly, there aren't consistent statistics on zoo animal popularity, but if you ask Lucy, which someone should since she goes to the zoo every chance she gets, most visitors gravitate toward animals that are large, brightly colored, or somehow fundamentally "cute" in looks or behavior, like waddling penguins and orangutans, with all that orange spiky hair.

Wait just a minute.

Lucy thinks of a giraffe. She thinks of the fact that giraffes live in Africa. And that they are absolutely, positively one of the most popular animals at every zoo she's visited. But the real kicker? Lucy remembers reading all about how field biologists identify individual giraffes based on their unique patterns. Their patterns of *patches*, that is.

Lucy counts the number of letters in the word *giraffe*. She double-, triple-, quadruple-checks them, just to be sure.

"I think it's a giraffe," she says. "They only live in Africa. And they have unique patches."

"Are they a popular zoo animal?" Trey asks.

"They sure are," Alex says, and she is 100 percent beaming, so Lucy knows she got it right!

"Here, let me type it in," Jemma says, grabbing the lock and taking the tablet from Harrison and quickly typing in the letters in the boxes on the screen. The screen flashes green with a short chime and the lock on the chest pops open with a satisfying click. Trey pulls it off the latch, but then turns to Jemma and Lucy. "Maybe one of you should open it?"

"I'll do it," Jemma says, and Lucy flinches. Does that mean she's helpful or bossy? Because it looks a little bit helpful, but it feels a little bit bossy, and Lucy's still not sure how these individual points are going to work out.

Jemma tugs the latch open and everyone gathers around, leaning in to see what's inside the chest. And maybe there wasn't a big part of Lucy that thought there would be gold or whatnot inside, but there must have been some tiny part of her that hoped for it, because seeing the small cooler and backpack nestled inside the old-fashioned chest makes her feel like a half-deflated balloon.

Jemma doesn't wait to ask. She pops open the lid of the cooler to reveal . . . hot dogs?

Jemma pulls them out with a frown. "Hot dogs. We just solved a treasure chest puzzle and won . . . hot dogs."

"Oh good, I'm starving," Harrison says. "Do we have ketchup? I think a hot dog is just the worst thing ever until you add ketchup and then it's great, but there are other people that are mustard purists. My mom is a mustard purist, but Wookiee doesn't really have a condiment preference. In fact, one time he ate an entire package of hot dogs raw, plastic and all."

"Well, we'll skip the plastic, and look, we have all kinds of goodies!" Alex says.

Lucy squints at her sister. If you ask Lucy, which Alex definitely won't, the contents of this cooler are a little too healthy to be all that exciting. From what she can see beyond the hot dogs, there's a package of buns, a container of popcorn, a giant bag of sad-looking baby carrots, and red grapes.

"Oh, did I mention we'll be cooking the hot dogs on the fire?" Alex asks.

"Oh, I can help with the fire!" Jemma says right away. "I'd be happy to help you build it if that's okay. I learned a six-step process at Scouts."

Alex and Jemma start the fire while Harrison and Trey

help Lucy set up plates. Lucy does find a baggie of chocolate chip cookies, which makes it all a little bit better.

Trey frowns. "I still don't know who would choose to leave dinner in a treasure chest."

"Maybe the same person who thought red grapes were the right choice," Lucy says. While she doesn't feel strongly about most food-related topics, voluntarily choosing red grapes over green ones always feels like the wrong move.

"I don't mind red grapes," Harrison says. "But those dark purple grapes? Those are gross, which seems weird, you know? When you get grape jam, it's almost always purple, right? I don't think I've ever seen grape jam that was another color, so I assume those purple grapes are the ones they use in jam, and jam is pretty good all in all. But the purple grapes that aren't jam—the pre-jam grapes, I guess—are just so bleh, you know?"

"True," Trey says.

"Aren't grapes all sort of the same?" Jemma asks. She's back from the fire and looking 130 percent smug about having been the one to help build it.

"Definitely not, dude," Harrison says. "Green grapes are sort of tart but then really sweet, and red grapes are always a better size, like less gigantic, but they have these weird bitter skins and sometimes I think seeds sneak into the seedless ones.[27] I never find seeds in green grapes. And

---

27 Long-tailed macaques do not agree with Harrison's aversion to red grapes. In fact, a nature blog listed a huge number of foods the macaques would pass over to score some red grapes instead. Of course, none of those skipped foods were cotton candy or French fries from the fair, so Lucy thinks the jury is still out on a macaque's favorite food.

we've already talked about purple grapes, which really shouldn't be called grapes at all."

Lucy doesn't say anything. It's truly dizzying the way Harrison talks, his words tripping over themselves. She looks at Jemma, who doesn't seem flustered by the rush of chatter.

"Well, grapes or not, we better find something better in the next treasure chest," Jemma says. "Can you go grab the drinks, Lucy? Alex said they should be below the ice pack."

"Sure."

When Lucy lifts the cold pack, she doesn't just find six juice boxes—she also finds something flat and brown at the bottom of the cooler.

"I think there's more than dinner in the chest," Lucy says. Then she reaches down and pulls out the brown, folded square of paper she's spotted. When she unfolds it, she sees a map of the northeast section of the park, with circles hand-drawn around lots of different areas.

She looks up at three faces leaning in around her and feels a squeezy feeling in her chest. And maybe it's a little like the attacks she sometimes gets. But there's absolutely, positively something else with that scared feeling. Something really good.

"What is that thing, Lucy?" Harrison asks.

"It's a map!"

CHAPTER 12

"**O**kay, everyone," Alex says. "We're officially on dinner and camp break for the night, and the puzzles will start back up first thing in the morning. That's when you'll enter the series of locked gates! I'm going to cook up these hot dogs while you take a look at that map."

"Aren't you supposed to tell us what to do?" Trey asks.

Lucy is really glad Trey asked, because Alex is definitely the oldest and definitely the one who knows the park best and super extra definitely the one who could make sure all of this goes smoothly. But Alex is also a big sister, which means she's also pretty good at being annoying. Like she is right now when she shakes her head with a laugh.

"No way, Santa Fe! The whole point of this is to see how you guys do with these puzzles. I'm just following you and taking notes on what we might need to work on before we open the escape challenge to everyone."

"What if we get lost?" Jemma asks.

"Well, you do have a map, thanks to Lucy."

"It's really thanks to the Ambassadors," Lucy says, spotting the four names signed at the bottom of the map. They've highlighted a route that winds through the northern half of Wildlands, the half that Lucy has never been on.

"That is so cool," Harrison says, clapping his hands. "Do you think they made this map? Or wait, did they design this entire route? These kids are like animal park superheroes!"

Lucy's stomach loops end over end with every question Harrison asks. Did the Ambassadors draw this map or design their route? She's almost positive they brought in escape room experts for the puzzles, because Alex talked about that, but what about the rest of it? If Lucy needs to be a map creation expert to be an Ambassador, she wouldn't know where to start and it would leave her back where she started—teamless.

The thought is too sad to focus on. Since she was a super-little kid, she always looked at all the ribbons and trophies and team pictures her mom and Alex had. She dressed in her mom's old softball jerseys at bedtime and cut her own ribbons out of construction paper and dreamed all the time about finding a team of her own. She's always been awful at sports, but Wildlands Ambassadors felt like a real chance—and the best imaginable team—until she failed her tryout.

And now? Lucy has another chance, and she might be blowing this one too. Between the impossible puzzles, uber-competitive Jemma, and now . . . mapmaking? How is she ever going to be good enough to make it on a team like this?

"This is just a map from the visitors' center," Alex says, sitting down between Lucy and Harrison. "They just drew on the arrows for you. The Ambassadors are pretty awesome and they brainstormed some great ideas for us, but they're testing the puzzles too. They just don't have the locked gates like you do!"

"The Ambassadors must be the coolest people ever," Harrison says with a grin.

"Yeah, well, not being on the Ambassadors doesn't mean I'm not cool," Jemma says, and if you ask Lucy, which no one does, she sounds pretty angry when she says it.

"It definitely doesn't," Alex says with a nod. "I think you're all super in your own ways, and every one of you is just as cool as the Ambassadors."

Trey leans in to look at the map. "Where does the route show us going?"

Maybe Lucy can't make a map, but she's pretty good at reading them. She puts her finger on the red dot that marks their campground. "I think we start here in the savanna camp. We'll head east and north, through the ostrich enclosure and some other exhibits and the Canopy Walk. It looks like we eventually wind up inside the reptile house, which will lead us to the exit through the meerkat land."

Alex's walkie-talkie crackles with a staticky voice. She unclips it from her belt and presses the button. "I'm sorry, you didn't come through clearly?"

"Hi, it's Leah! We're at the Ambassadors' camp. How—" More crackly static with a single word popping through. ". . . camp?"

Alex presses the button. "You're still really breaking up, but everything here is great."

This time the static pops and hisses and makes terrible crunchy noises that hurt Lucy's ears. Alex holds the walkie-talkie out away from her ear, and Harrison scrunches up his face.

". . . electrical problems with some of the locks."

More terrible electric noises crackle in and out between every word, and Lucy has to fight not to cover her ears. Which she is absolutely, positively not going to do because it would make her look like a baby.

Thankfully, Alex seems to understand.

"Are you having trouble with locks?"

"The lock—camp—not—" the walkie-talkie voice says, with plenty of pops and crackles in between. Alex grabs the plate of raw hot dogs before winking at all of them. "I'm going to take these hot dogs and try to make sense of this walkie-talkie while I'm cooking."

As soon as Alex disappears, everyone looks at Lucy again.

"Well?" Jemma's voice sounds sharp on the edges, and Lucy feels her stomach slosh to one side. "Where are we heading first, and how does it all work?"

"Maybe we should spread the map out," Trey says.

"Dude, that's a great idea!" Harrison says. He starts fiddling with his pocket, snapping and unsnapping the fastener that holds it closed. "We can spread it out on a big table like we're in a spy movie and the Constitution of the United States is hidden somewhere in this camp area and—"

"We don't have a table," Jemma says, rolling her eyes.

Harrison's face falls, and something about that makes

Lucy's heart squeeze. Harrison seems extra excited, sure, but he's also extra friendly and extra enthusiastic and those traits aren't bad things to have.

"Well, we do have the ground," Lucy says. And then, before Jemma and her doom-and-gloom scowly self can change her mind, she spreads the map out and gets down on her knees right in the dirt. Harrison gets down too.

Jemma and her scowl join them, Jemma sitting cross-legged in front of the map. Only Trey remains standing. He leans over instead, his tall body bent so he can see the map too.

"I think the arrows might show our path through the enclosures," Lucy says. "We have to work through a series of gates, which I bet will only open when we solve puzzles."

"But it just looks like a path," Jemma says, waving at the map.

"It looks like there is a partially enclosed walkway that's constructed through a bunch of the enclosures," Lucy says. "So it's sort of like . . . Have you guys ever been in one of those shark tunnels at an aquarium?"

"Oh yeah!" Harrison says. "And there's glass all around you so you're like in this tube, but the sharks can swim right beside you and they're super fast and you can see their teeth, and they have like a million of them,[28] which feels like more teeth than you need."

"I think it will be fencing around us," Lucy says.

---

28 Sharks do not have a million teeth, but if you're talking about a whale shark, they do have three thousand teeth, which might as well be a million, really.

"So when do we see the kangaroos?" Harrison asks. "Alex said there would be kangaroos and they're my favorite because they box[29] and that's why I'm here. When we win, I'm choosing the special program at the zoo with the kangaroos and if I'm really lucky one might box me."

Trey frowns. "I don't think they'll let you box a kangaroo."

"You never know," Harrison says. "But I know I'm determined to win. And I want to check out this Ambassadors thing, because it sounds super cool. What about you, Trey?"

"There's a horticulture camp this June," Trey says. "That's the special program I want. And I get to see so many amazing plants here too. Do you know they have special landscape plans that are unique to each enclosure and the animals that live inside them? It's so cool."

"That is cool," Lucy says, and she can't help but grin, because Trey is almost always super quiet, but apparently plants are one subject that really gets him going!

"Of course, I wonder if they've thought about how helpful a plant specialist might be in the Ambassadors program," Trey says, looking thoughtful.

Lucy's heart squeezes. Plant specialist? It sounds like Trey might want a shot at this slot after all.

"There are elephants around here too, aren't there?" Jemma asks, gesturing at the map. "Isn't that what this big section is?"

"The elephants are around a lot of the park," Lucy says.

---

29 Kangaroos actually do box one another to assert dominance. They have strong tails and a low center of gravity, so they can really go at it. Maybe someone should create some gloves to protect them.

"They need tons of space, and some of their space is right alongside the zebras and giraffes. There are lots of large areas."

"So we have to make it through all of this to have the party with the Ambassadors, right?" Harrison asks.

Lucy traces the red line with her finger and frowns when it seems to end at the aquarium. "It looks like the party is at the aquarium, but that can't be right. We're supposed to do a campfire, which can't be inside."

"Maybe there's a park beside the aquarium?" Harrison asks.

"Or maybe we're reading the map wrong," Trey says.

"Wait!" Jemma suddenly leaps to her feet, and for the first time since she got to Lucy's house today, Jemma looks genuinely happy. "I know how we can know for sure about the map and see our route!"

Jemma pauses, and there's a very excited glint in her eyes that Lucy 100 percent does not like. Not one bit.

But before Lucy can ask what she's talking about, Jemma takes off sprinting for the wooden stairs leading up to the viewing platform. Lucy watches in shock as Jemma begins to climb, her footsteps thundering quickly up the first flight of steps.

This is not good. Lucy's face feels hot and tingly as Harrison perks up and leaps forward.

"Oh, right! The viewing platform! This is such a great idea, Jemma! Come on, everybody!"

Before Lucy can blink, Harrison has grabbed her hand and is tugging her toward the platform and up the first flight of stairs. And then Trey is right behind her and they are all moving up the stairs with fast, clomping steps.

Lucy is a little afraid of how fast they are moving, and a little afraid of how hard Harrison is gripping her hand, and a lot afraid of the fact that all she can think about is what happened on the tower during her first tryout. She tries to pull her hand free, but neither Trey nor Harrison notices.

"Oh, shoot," Harrison says. "We need the map."

"I have it," Trey says.

"Perfect! We're already a perfect team, dudes! We're reading each other's minds!"

But if they asked Lucy, and she really wishes they had, she could tell them they are absolutely, positively not reading each other's minds. If they could read her mind, they would see that she wants to stop running up all these stairs. And then, out of nowhere, they do stop.

Harrison releases Lucy's hand, and both he and Trey rush toward the railing, leaving Lucy alone near the stairs. She tells herself right away it is not the same as before. This is a platform and it is much larger and much sturdier and she is okay. But then she notices the spaces between the planks that form the floor, and then the many, many other stairs she can see through those narrow spaces under her feet.

Maybe it isn't as high as the tower from the first tryout, but it is 200 percent higher than Lucy wants. She didn't want to climb any stairs at all, but it's too late for that. Lucy closes her eyes and takes a deep breath like Dr. Kern taught her, but her face feels hot. Then her stomach swings back. Even her mouth goes dry. She knows what's coming, and she knows there isn't enough breathing in the world to stop this. She knows she shouldn't open her eyes, but she does.

In one terrible instant, Lucy knows she has made an awful mistake. Because now that she is not looking at her feet, she is looking out. And now that she is looking, she can see the park rolling out in every direction all around. And now that she can see the park rolling out in every direction, she realizes she is up much, much higher than she'd ever like to be.

Lucy squeezes her eyes shut fast, but her throat is extra squeezy and her face is hot and her stomach is slowly rolling forward. The first somersault happens, and she can already feel the next one starting up. She has to calm down! She can't have another panic attack!

"Whoa! Dudes! Do you see that giant bird over there?" Harrison asks.

"Um, yes, it's an ostrich," Jemma says.

"Wow! Ostriches are cool, but I can see four giraffes and a zebra! Oh man, do we get to go there? That's the Canopy Walk part, I bet. Where are the kangaroos?"

Harrison must start running around to look for them, because Lucy can hear footsteps. But much worse than that, she can feel every little movement jiggling the boards beneath her feet. She squeezes her hands into fists, and her breath is coming too fast.

"I see the two elephants," Trey says, and now he's moving too and the boards are moving. Everything is moving.

Lucy gasps and her stomach rolls again. And again. She can't stop it.

"Lucy, look at this!" Harrison says, and he grabs her arm, but she yanks it hard, jerking out of his grasp. But Harrison keeps going. "There's a whole path that goes through the park. And there are all these gates. I bet Lucy's right about solving puzzles to unlock them. Hey, are you even looking?"

Lucy opens her eyes to see Harrison watching her with a worried wrinkle in his forehead. "Are you okay?"

"Yes."

The word comes out of Lucy automatically, but it is 200 percent not true. Her stomach is flipping over again, and now she's breathing too fast and her heart is beating too hard and what if she dies? She could die right here!

A small voice in Lucy's mind reminds her that she has to try her grounding techniques. Dr. Kern told her that the techniques can help, so she tries to take a deep breath. It feels like it gets stuck in her throat. Is something wrong with her throat? Should she tell someone?

"You look kinda pale and pasty," Trey says.

"She always looks pale," Jemma says.

Lucy opens her eyes and sees Trey leaning down to look into her face. He is frowning and his brown eyes look very worried. "I don't think this is how she normally looks. Are you feeling okay, Lucy?"

She's not okay. She's not even close to okay, and it could be worse than she thinks. She could be sick! Her breathing technique is not working. Nothing is working. What else can she try? She remembers the senses technique and takes a breath. She can smell bubble gum. She can hear birds in the distance. Red-winged blackbirds, maybe. Lucy's stomach rolls again, and her heart is going so fast. But she has to keep trying. She looks past everyone's worried faces to see the park beyond. She sees white clouds, broccoli-top trees, and—white moving trucks?

Lucy squints because that feels like a strange thing to see in the middle of a safari park, but way in the distance she can see them, two big boxy trucks, maybe delivery trucks, off near the barns at the front of the park.

Harrison gasps, and it pulls Lucy's attention back. "Whoa, look at that giraffe! He's not even that far away!" He runs down the length of the railing, maybe to get a better look. Or maybe because Harrison always seems to be running. But whatever the reason is, it makes the planks under Lucy's feet wobble, and this time she's absolutely positively sure she's going to fall.

Her knees go limp and she crumples down to the ground, crouching into a tiny, tiny ball. She does not fall, but something even worse happens. To Lucy's complete and total humiliation, she begins to cry.

CHAPTER 13

C rying in front of a bunch of almost strangers sounds like the worst thing that could happen to a twelve-year-old person on an overnight escape challenge, but Lucy now knows that's not true. The worst thing that can happen is crying in front of two separate groups of almost strangers on two separate occasions in the same park.

Harrison tries to say something to Lucy, but she shrugs him off and keeps her face smooshed into her knees. Even curled up like a ball, she can hear the other kids whispering about getting Alex, which makes her feel even worse. Then she hears them rushing down what sounds and feels like four million stairs. All the wooden planks underneath Lucy bump and bump, and that makes her cry even harder.

She wants to go home. She wants to disappear. She wants—someone gently pats her arm, and Lucy lifts her head in surprise. She had thought everyone went to get Alex, but Trey stayed behind. He is patting Lucy's arm in a way that tells Lucy he has no idea what to do with an almost-stranger girl who is curled up in a ball crying. But it is a very nice thing to do.

Lucy puts her head back down and tries to think of a way to escape. She can't possibly finish the escape challenge. And what's the point? Ambassadors have to have the courage to lead tour groups and remind park visitors of important rules. She isn't sure she has the courage to get down from this platform. What if they have to send a ranger in to get her? What if they have to get her with a helicopter? She can't face anyone after a ranger or a helicopter or even just crying in a ball like a baby.

There's only one solution. Lucy will have to go home sick. Alex couldn't possibly ask her to stay after all this. She will have to understand. Even as Lucy thinks these things, a tiny little worry is beginning to grow in her mind. Because Alex doesn't like to quit anything. And if Lucy has to go home, that means Alex will probably be the one to take her.

As she thinks about these problems, Lucy's crying slows. And then those awful somersaults get slower. And that's when she hears Alex's soft steps steadily climbing the stairs. When she arrives, she doesn't rush to hug Lucy or make big noises. Alex actually doesn't talk to Lucy at all.

"Trey, would you be willing to help finish up those dinner plates for everyone?" Alex asks softly. "The hot dogs are ready, so it should be easy."

"I can do that."

"Awesome, thank you."

Alex and Trey both use soft voices, and Lucy feels a pang of gratitude when Trey begins his long walk down the four million steps to the bottom. Lucy is sure she's going to need that helicopter. And her stomach hurts so bad from all the somersaults that she won't need to fake being sick. She practically feels sick.

Alex plops down softly beside her, nudging Lucy's shoulder with her arm.

"Whatcha thinkin', Lincoln?"

"I'm thinking I can never show my face to any of these people again," Lucy says. "I want to go home."

"I know this really stinks, but I still believe you can do this," Alex says. "Don't you want to try to be on the Ambassadors?"

"I don't care about the challenge anymore. And I'll never be on the Ambassadors."

Lucy takes a breath, and it's one of those terrible shuddery breaths you only get when you've been crying stupidly hard.

"If we take you home right now, you're right, but if you stay, you might be surprised."

Lucy lifts her head and looks into her sister's warm, crinkly eyes. "An Ambassador should be a leader, and a leader should be brave, and I'm not brave at all."

"I'm really sorry this happened, but I definitely don't think this proves that you aren't brave, Lucy," Alex says. And then she is quiet for a few seconds. She tugs gently at her blue ponytail like she's thinking very hard. "I know you want to go home, but I think you should think about staying. I think staying after a hard thing happens is the bravest thing of all."

Staying here feels like the last thing Lucy would ever want to do. Right this second, it feels like it would beat everything in the list of top things Lucy would never want to do.

"I'm embarrassed," Lucy repeats more softly. "The only

thing I'm more afraid of than staying here is the possibility that leaving will make everyone else lose their chance at winning."

"Let's focus on the first part. The good thing is that you're doing better right now, right?"

Alex already knows the answer is yes. Lucy is feeling better now. Except for one big problem. She dares the tiniest peek out and sees the park, way, way below.

"I don't know how I will get down," Lucy says, and as soon as she says it, she realizes that's maybe the most important thing to do. She needs to figure out how to do this without Alex.

"Hey, Lucy!" Harrison's voice comes from below, and then he thunders up the stairs so fast he's standing in front of them before Lucy can answer.

Lucy doesn't even feel embarrassed before Harrison claps his hands. "Do you know there are forty-five steps to where you are right now? And I was thinking it would be super hard if we had to come up with an animal for each of those steps but that maybe you could do it and we could go down together if you want?"

Lucy isn't sure if Harrison is asking to be nice because she's upset or because he really wants to see if she can come up with forty-five animals. But what she is sure of is this: she can come up with forty-five animals, one for each step, because a good Wildlands Ambassador would definitely be able to do it, and Lucy absolutely, positively wants to be a good Ambassador.

She stands up, and Harrison grins even wider. "Dude, I

knew you'd be up for it. Can I come up with the first one? Because it has to be kangaroo!"

They take one step down together for kangaroo. And then Lucy thinks of animals that jump, and she takes one step with each animal she names.

"Grasshopper, impala, arctic hare, klipspringer—"

"That's five already!" Harrison says. "Though I've never heard of a pliksinger."

"It's a klipspringer," Lucy says, and even though her knees feel bendy, like cooked noodles, she finds herself giggling at Harrison's pronunciation. "It's kind of like a mountain goat."

"Can we count normal goats?" Harrison says, taking a step down. "And, dude, sheep and horses and pigs! The farm animals!"

Lucy nods as she goes. "Then we should definitely add chickens and llamas and alpacas too."

As Lucy focuses more on thinking up animals, she feels less wobbly and worried. She moves from farm animals to runners like cheetahs and lions and ostriches and greyhounds. After a few more of those, she moves on to climbers, and there are so many to choose from, including squirrels and black bears and ibexes and more. After that, she moves to fliers, and because she knows a lot of birds, that gets super easy. She starts with robins and cardinals but keeps going through all the birds she sees in her yard, including sparrows and wrens and finches and even Canadian geese. By the time she moves to swimmers, there is less than one flight of stairs left, so it's easy to finish up with dolphins and whales and manta rays and hammerhead sharks and even jellyfish.

By the time they get to the bottom, Lucy almost feels brave enough to stay. Maybe this won't be so bad. Maybe the others didn't even notice. And then Jemma steps in front of them with her arms crossed.

"Are you still freaked out?"

Lucy feels the heat rise in her chest and the squeezy feeling grab her throat. She even feels Harrison tense beside her, but then they are saved by the one thing on earth that could distract her from all of this.

"I'm glad you're okay," Trey says, and to Lucy's complete surprise, he's the one who looks a little freaked out. "But I think we have a problem."

"What do you mean?" Alex asks from up at the top of the stairs. Lucy turns around, because she almost forgot her sister was there. And almost forgetting is a pretty good feeling, because for a minute she wasn't sure she'd make it down without her sister holding her hand.

"What's the problem?" Alex asks as she makes her way down the stairs.

Trey swallows hard. "There's a camel in the camp."

"Wait, you don't mean inside the enclosure, do you?" Alex asks.

Jemma tilts her head to think about it. "The tents are inside the enclosure, right?"

Alex goes still all at once, and Lucy notices that her eyes have grown wider. "Yes, the tents are inside the enclosure."

Trey nods vigorously. "Then the camel is definitely inside the enclosure."

Alex's eyes go even wider and her face goes strangely blank. "Archibald."

Lucy can't even ask what that means before Alex runs down the last few steps and sprints toward the tents. Harrison leaps forward too, sprinting toward Alex. Lucy leaps forward and starts sprinting too, even though some part of her is pretty sure sprinting toward an area with a camel on the loose is probably a terrible idea.

In the clearing near the tents, they find Trey next to a picnic blanket. Lucy spots five plates complete with hot dogs, folded napkins, red grapes (ugh), cheese sticks, and cookies. Every single plate is identical, with one can of juice in the upper right corner of each place setting. Trey did an absolutely, positively perfect job putting those plates together, and Lucy would tell him that, except for the whole camel-on-the-loose situation.

Lucy hears Alex gasp. She looks around and sees something moving above the tents. She double-, triple-, quadruple-looks until she knows what she's looking at. The moving thing is a camel's head!

"Holy macaroni," Lucy says.

"There really is a camel," Jemma says matter-of-factly. Lucy hadn't even seen her standing behind Trey, but she is definitely there. And she is definitely not looking as brave as she normally looks.

"Archie, what are you doing in here?" Alex asks, and Lucy tilts her head because that name . . . it sounds familiar. She is 92 percent sure she has heard the name Archie today.

Trey and Jemma look around. "Who is she talking to?" Jemma asks.

"The camel," Lucy says at once. "I think the camel's name is Archibald—or Archie."

Trey tilts his head. "That's . . ."

"What kind of camel name is Archibald?" Jemma says with her scowl.

Lucy shrugs. Personally, she thinks it's a terrific name, but she named the goldfish in her tank at home Mortimer, Stuart, and Bartholomew, which feels like the same sort of name. And then Lucy remembers; that's where she heard that name! Mr. Swendel said something about Archie being on the run, but Lucy thought it was a person.

The giant camel head peeks around the side of the tent again. The camel has dark eyes framed with velvety lashes,[30] a long face with a funny upper lip, and small cute ears on either side of its head.

Alex stops running at the tent and begins marching around the side. "You need to go back to your paddock."

She reaches up for the halter on Archie's face, but Archie immediately turns away and walks to the other side of the tent. If you ask Lucy, though she's not sure why Mr. Swendel would, the way this camel lopes around doesn't really look like running.

---

30 A camel's long eyelashes protect its eyes from the harsh sun and blowing sand common to the deserts where it lives. But they also make the camel look like it's wearing mascara, which is undeniably adorable.

"Be careful," Harrison says.

"I think they spit!" Jemma adds.[31]

"Gross," Trey says.

"He shouldn't spit unless he's angry or scared," Lucy says. "And in that case I would be more worried about the kicking."

Archie moseys from one tent to the next, but his long legs make the moseying pretty fast. Alex follows at a safe distance, calling his name. Archie seems a little bit interested in snuffling at the tents and a little bit interested in pulling clumps of tender grass out of the ground and, sadly for Alex, a lot bit interested in staying just out of her reach.

Alex rushes closer, reaching for Archie's halter again, but the camel ducks away, moving easily between the last two tents.

Alex drops her head in disappointment. "Archie . . ."

"I thought we weren't supposed to get close to the animals," Harrison says.

Alex nods. "We're not. But Archie is an unusual case. He was raised on a ranch in Nevada, so he is a domesticated camel. He was given to us when his owner passed away. Because his whole life was spent with people, he struggles to behave like a wild camel."

As if on cue, Archibald returns to Alex, lowering his

---

31 Camels do, in fact, spit, and it's actually a bit grosser than that, because they are spitting the contents of their stomach. Essentially, they're spitting barf. Fortunately, most camels only do this if feeling very annoyed or threatened, so just don't be rude to a camel.

great head to look at her. Then he gently nudges the top pocket in her button-up shirt once, twice, and even a third time.

"He thinks you have something for him," Harrison says.

Lucy looks back at the picnic spread, searching for something that might work. "Maybe we can lure him outside the camp."

"I don't know. He's pretty stubborn," Alex says. She strokes his head, which he seems to like, but when she reaches for his halter, he jerks his head back.

Lucy glances at the walkie-talkie buckled to Alex's hip. "Maybe you should call for help?"

"Good idea!" Alex pulls out her walkie-talkie and presses the button. "Front gate, this is Alex. Archie got loose and he's back here in the camp."

When she releases the button, crackly static fills the air. Archie takes a step back, and while Lucy doesn't think of the camel as being a terribly expressive animal, something about the way Archie's ears flick and his eyes blink makes him look distinctly annoyed. Lucy takes a big step back and watches his cheeks.[32] Nothing horrifying seems to be brewing, but she absolutely, positively intends to keep a healthy distance all the same.

After a few seconds, Archie begins to snuffle at a tent again. Then he raises his head, and his nostrils flare over and over in interest. Lucy is sure he's spotted something. And when she follows his line of sight, it's clear exactly what that something is.

---

32 A camel's cheeks will puff out before it spits. Or barfs. Spit-arfs.

"Oh boy," Lucy says. "He sees our dinner."

At that moment, Archie steps around the tent and heads straight for the blanket and its neatly arranged plates. Alex tries the walkie-talkie again, with nothing but static, and Archie keeps moving toward the picnic blanket.

"Is he trying to get to our dinner?" Trey asks. Lucy thinks he sounds a little bit alarmed, and given how neatly he set everything up, she can't blame him.

"Maybe," Harrison says, but his voice is squeaky and unsure and he pulls up the end of the word like a question. "Oh gosh, what do we do?"

Archie takes another step, and Lucy immediately rushes through all the things she can remember camels eating. "Okay, I need vegetables. Or fruits. As fast as possible."

"Give him the gross grapes!" Harrison cries.

"How are grapes going to help this situation?" Jemma asks, sounding panicked.

Alex peeks around the tent where she tried to get a walkie-talkie signal.

"Archie!" Alex snaps several times, but the camel has moved in between Alex and the picnic blanket. Unless she moves toward him—which could send Archie running toward the blanket—she is trapped. Archie turns to her with mild interest, but he doesn't seem convinced to change his course.

"Maybe he just wants water," Harrison says, sounding hopeful.

"I doubt it," Lucy says. "Camels can go up to six months without drinking. I really need those grapes."

But she doesn't know how to get them. She'd have to get closer to Archie, which isn't a great idea, since she doesn't know how he might react.

"I have baby carrots from the cooler," Trey says, holding up a giant bag of baby carrots. Lucy didn't know he slipped back to the cooler so quietly, but she is super grateful when he hands the bag over.

"I'm coming around," Alex says. "Just let him have the dinner. He is gentle, but you need to give him space because he's large. He could step on your foot."

"He cannot have our dinner," Trey says. He looks a little bit serious and a little bit angry and a lot determined to keep their food safe.

Alex starts around the outside of the tent, and Archie takes another step toward them. He can't be more than ten camel steps away from the blanket. No, eight! No, seven!

Lucy tears open a corner of the bag and whistles, even though she has no idea if a camel pays any attention to whistling. Archie does stop, though, so Lucy keeps going. She pulls out a handful of carrots, and the camel's giant head swings toward her.

Archie takes another step, and this time he has shifted direction! Lucy is ready to cheer for about one second. That's when she realizes the very large camel is headed straight for her. Lucy was absolutely right about camels liking carrots, but her judgment of camel steps was way, way wrong. Archie is definitely not ten, or eight, or even seven camel steps away from her, because after he takes four camel steps he is *right* in front of her, and he is much,

much taller than she realized.[33] She takes a breath and smells an earthy, sweet smell that reminds her of hayrides and horse barns.

And then Archie is stretching his long neck and reaching forward with his enormous head.

"Dude, is the camel going to eat Lucy?"[34] Harrison's voice is a squeak that feels a lot like the noises that want to come out of Lucy too.

"Archie, stop!" Alex says, and she breaks into a jog toward the camel.

But it is too late. Archie is already opening his lips and leaning closer. Lucy closes her eyes and waits for the worst.

---

33 While she was aware that male camels were over six feet tall, Lucy did not realize this meant six feet to the top of their hump. You'd have to add another couple of feet to get to the top of their heads, so Archibald isn't the height of their science teacher, Mr. Lawry, who is pretty tall. He's more like a professional basketball player. A professional basketball player who just might spit barf on you.

34 Camels do not eat people. They are generally vegetarians.

CHAPTER 14

Lucy keeps waiting for the worst, but it does not happen. Generally speaking, how long does the worst take? Ten seconds? A minute?

Since she isn't sure, Lucy cracks open one eye just in time to see Archie's strange lips gently pluck the whole pile of carrots out of her palm. His furry lips are soft and tickly, and most importantly, not bitey.

Archie leans back then, his mouth moving in an odd back-and-forth motion. The orange tip of a baby carrot disappears in the valley between the left and right parts of his top lip.

"Did he bite you?" Harrison asks.

"No," Lucy says softly. And then she remembers feeding horses when she was younger. She retrieves more carrots from the bag and carefully holds her hand flat, keeping her fingers away from the carrots[35] as Archie leans in again. His furry lips move quickly, grabbing three baby carrots this time. One drops to the ground, but he leaves it while he munches the other two, his large brown eye watching her.

---

35 Horses also love carrots. Carrots and apples and boxes of cereal that seem too stale to eat, that is.

"Good job, Lucy," Alex says. And then she's right beside Lucy, taking the bag of carrots. "You guys go ahead and eat."

"What are you going to do?" Lucy asks, watching Archie eat another two carrots Alex is offering.

"I'm going to try to get Archibald out of the enclosure, and I'm going to try to call the front staff again."

"Maybe they turned their walkie-talkies off?"

"Maybe they went home," Trey says.

"No, there are always security guards here," Alex says. "Even when the park is closed."

Suddenly, Lucy remembers the white trucks she saw from the platform. "Do you guys get deliveries on the weekends?"

"No, deliveries always come on Tuesdays and Fridays," Alex says.

Lucy frowns. "Are you sure? I thought I saw trucks."

Alex shakes her head, looking distracted. "Must have been on the road outside the park. Part of my job is checking in deliveries, so I always receive notifications when they're coming. Trucks really aren't allowed in the park other than delivery days."

Not allowed? Lucy frowns and feels all of her insides go a little twisty. Mom always says that's intuition and Lucy should pay attention to it, but sometimes intuition just means worry. Still, if the trucks aren't supposed to be here, then why are they around?

"Come on, Archie," Alex says.

Archie's focus shifts to Alex and the carrot bag. This time, he seems happy to follow her as she walks slowly away from the picnic. Which Lucy is 100 percent sure has everything to do with the carrots and nothing to do with his commitment to being obedient.

"Okay, let's eat," Harrison says.

Lucy turns to the group and suddenly remembers that they all know she was crying at the top of the platform less than fifteen minutes ago. Now that she's thinking about it, her eyelashes still feel damp and clumpy from that crying, but apparently, there are some benefits to having a rogue camel wander into your camp. Namely, everyone seems to forget the super-embarrassing thing that happened a few minutes earlier.

"Lucy can't eat dinner," Trey says. "Not yet."

Lucy cringes. Maybe the camel troublemaker wasn't as distracting as she hoped. She slowly turns to Trey, who is holding out his brown, long-fingered hand with a very serious expression. Is he going to remind everyone that she cried like a baby and shouldn't be part of the escape challenge?

But instead Trey shows something small and clear that he's holding in his hand.

"What's that?" Jemma asks.

"Antibacterial gel," Trey says. "If you could wash your hands, that would be even better, but since Alex hasn't shown us the bathrooms yet, this will help with the worst of the germs."

Lucy cleans her hands and doesn't say a word. If she opens her mouth, who knows what might happen, but if everyone is willing to ignore the whole platform crying debacle, then she is more than happy to ignore it too.

Alex returns to camp a few minutes after they finish dinner, but she doesn't look too happy.

"Is everything okay with Archie?" Lucy asks, because if there's one thing she likes less than Alex looking concerned, it's not knowing why Alex looks concerned.

"I think so. He ran off, and usually he ends up back in his enclosure."

"Did anyone check?" Lucy asks.

"No, I couldn't reach anyone. The walkie-talkie isn't really working. I could drive up to the gate, but I'm not too worried. Our cheetahs and lions are in secured enclosures on the other side of the elephants, and Archie steers clear of them. He's an escape artist, but he tends to lurk around the human areas and the Ambassadors know him pretty well."

"But why can't you get in touch with anyone on the walkie-talkie?" Harrison asks. "Did you double-check your batteries? Sometimes batteries like sort of die but they don't totally die and then electronics get all messed up."

"True," Trey says. "But I think this is a signal issue. You probably have a signal booster, and it might not be working right."

Alex shakes her head. "It happens sometimes out here. There's a lot of hills and sometimes it messes with the signal. Plus, this is a newer area in the park. We probably haven't figured out all the dead spots in service."

"What about your cell phone?" Jemma asks.

"My cell phone is in the truck, but nothing is going through. I'm trying to charge it up to see if that helps, by some miracle."

"Is that normal for the walkie-talkie not to work?" Harrison asks. He's sitting on the ground, his dinner abandoned. Now he's pulling all the laces out of his left shoe. "I mean, is it always staticky and now there's extra static, or is there some sort of massive scientific laboratory nearby that causes disruptions to the frequency?"

Alex laughs. "Well, there's no laboratory, but this seems worse than usual."

Lucy doesn't like the sound of that. But she likes looking nervous even less, so she is extra careful to sound unconcerned when she asks, "Do we need to do anything now?"

"I'm not too worried. We have everything we need. And if we do need anything, we'll just hop in the truck and head to the front."

Right. They have the truck, so they aren't cut off. Lucy relaxes and then flinches when Alex claps her hands. "Okay, everybody. I'll clean up the picnic blanket and you guys can finish unloading the truck. I'll show you the restrooms too. After that, we can set up our tents, have some s'mores, and start thinking about sleeping."

"How late is it?" Harrison says.

"It's only seven-thirty now," Alex says, "but by the time we're all cleaned up and cooking s'mores, I bet it will be close to nine p.m."

Lucy doesn't like anything that's coming next. She doesn't like it when she follows Trey, Harrison, and Jemma to the truck and she doesn't like it when they're walking back. She definitely doesn't like it when she's alone in the tent with Jemma setting up their sleeping bags on their cots without saying a word. Lucy feels squirmy and miserable thinking of the last time they were in this tent. What will Jemma say this time?

But she doesn't say anything.

The tent stays quiet for one minute. And then another. And then another.

Finally, Jemma puts down the lantern she's been fiddling with and clears her throat. "Can I ask you a question?"

"Sure," Lucy says, though she's only about 15 percent sure she actually means it.

"Why do you want to be on the Ambassadors so much?"

"Because I love animals and I like the idea of helping other people learn about them," Lucy says, surprised that it comes out so easily. Maybe it's easy because it's the truth.

Jemma nods and then looks at her feet. "But it's also about being a leader, right? Showing people how to climb the platforms and the zip lines in the play center."

Lucy isn't sure how much of these things the Ambassadors do, but she is sure about one thing. If Jemma thinks those things would scare her, she's right. But Jemma doesn't even seem to like animals, and that's confusing.

"Jemma, why do you want to be on the Ambassadors?"

Jemma shrugs. "Because I'm supposed to be on the team already."

An invisible weight is pressing into Lucy's chest, making it hard to breathe. She doesn't want to hear any more of what Jemma is saying, but some part of her can't help but ask. "What do you mean?"

"I mean my whole Mathletes team tried out together.

Emma, Olivia, Isaac, and Adam? We've been on the same academics teams since first grade. We have six pictures of the six of us in different jerseys and it's like a joke with our moms now—we're the forever team."

"But someone named Abigail made it on the Ambassadors. I take it she's not on your other teams."

"Yeah, I know. She is a total stranger, from a private school I've never even heard of. And don't you think that would be weird for her? Being on a team where no one else knows her and everyone is already friends? I mean, seriously, Lucy, does that sound fun to you?"

It doesn't sound fun. To be honest, it sounds scary. But the real question is: Does the scary part seem bigger than the exciting part of being able to work with animals? This morning Lucy would have said working with animals outweighs everything else, but now? With the idea of platforms and being an outsider and everything else? Lucy isn't sure. And not being sure is making her feel a little like a balloon that's losing its helium, droopy and saggy and sad.

"I'm really not trying to be mean," Jemma says. "I just know that I'm supposed to be with the rest of my team so when we're all finished, that's what will happen. End of discussion."

Usually when Jemma says *end of discussion*, it's with a hard voice and a very determined face. But this time her voice is quite soft and her eyes are almost kind, but the sort of kind that people feel when they feel sorry for someone.

Lucy is very, very quiet as she thinks about Jemma's

words. Jemma really believes that she's supposed to be on the Ambassadors. Is she right? Is it true that things are all supposed to happen in a specific way no matter what? Lucy just isn't sure she believes that.

"What if it's not the way it's supposed to be?" Lucy asks, her voice small and worried. "I mean, you can't really know for sure that you're going to be put on the team, can you?"

Jemma suddenly goes very still, and her scowl turns into a flat line. "What did you say?"

"I said that you don't really know that they'll pick you for the team. You probably thought they'd pick you when you tried out, right?"

Lucy is genuinely curious, but she has a bad feeling that all of her words are coming out wrong. Because Jemma isn't answering. Instead, her face turns very red and her eyes look very glassy. Then, out of nowhere, she leaps back to her feet and shouts at Lucy. "Why don't you mind your own business, Lucy Spagnola?"

Jemma storms out of the tent before Lucy can even blink, leaving her wondering what on earth went wrong.

CHAPTER 15

Normally, Lucy loves s'mores, but tonight if she could stay ten miles away from the firepit and from Jemma, she would 100 percent do it. But about ten minutes after Jemma storms out of the tent, Alex starts calling for Lucy.

At first, Lucy ignores her sister, hoping Alex will get distracted and she can continue doodling flip cartoons in the corners of her notebook pages.[36] But Alex doesn't give up, so eventually, Lucy puts down her notebook and slips out of the tent. She searches for Alex and notices Trey and Harrison sitting on small folding chairs near the fire. Lucy can tell by the way Harrison is squirming and wiggling that Alex must have told him not to move from the chair. Which makes a lot of sense. All that jittering[37] can't be safe near a fire.

Lucy doesn't risk moving too far from the tent until she finds Jemma. It doesn't take long. She's standing by the far

---

36 Lucy draws ostriches in most of her flip cartoons because they're easy and fun to draw and make really funny flip cartoons, thanks to their long legs and neck.

37 Harrison is not the only thing on earth that moves all the time. Sharks and manta rays, for example, have to constantly move forward in order to obtain enough oxygen underwater to stay alive.

edge of Alex's tent, with her arms crossed and her scowl looking extra scowly. Just looking at Jemma makes Lucy feel jumpy.

Has she ever had another kid yell at her like that? Lucy is 87 percent sure it's never happened in her life, and she's not about to risk letting it happen again. Lucy finally spots Alex emerging from behind a bush. She's carrying a tray of marshmallows and roasting skewers, and Lucy wishes with all her might for some sort of sister telepathy to kick in so Alex will see her over here and realize she desperately needs to talk to her alone.

But instead of telepathy, Alex just looks up with a big smile and a wave. "Oh, there you are! Hurry over here and get a marshmallow! We've got to wrap this up, because tomorrow is a super-big day. We want to get an early start!"

Lucy positions herself as far away from Jemma as possible while they roast marshmallows. She sits next to Trey, who does not seem happy about touching the marshmallow and tries to eat it with a fork. She remembers him not sitting on the ground with the map earlier too and decides she should add another small thing to Trey's list:

1. Does not like to get dirty or sticky.

After marshmallows, Alex claps her hands and informs them that it's after nine o'clock and they should head to their tents soon.

"We have to be up by seven," Alex says, covering the itinerary as the fire grows dim. "The keepers will be here for an hour to check food and water right at sunrise, and then we've got to get moving on those puzzles by eight a.m. sharp!"

"Maybe we can ask the keepers about the walkie-talkie?"

"We probably won't see them," Alex says. "It's rare to have the park closed on a weekend, so they'll probably be as quick as they can. Plus, three of the keepers have to come back at three o'clock to meet us for the special activities."

"What are the special activities?"

"They're going to help present the prizes and help with the selection of the newest Ambassador."

Lucy is very careful to not look at Jemma without looking like she's not looking at Jemma. But when she dares a peek, she can see that Jemma is watching her with narrowed eyes. How is she supposed to sleep in a tent with someone who is currently looking at her like a cockroach that's eating her birthday cake?

"Trey and I don't care that much about the Ambassador part," Harrison says. "Do you think the keepers can tell me if bathing one of the kangaroos is part of the behind-the-scenes kangaroo tour in Columbus? Because I really, really want to give a kangaroo a bath."[38]

"Sorry, Harrison, the kangaroos don't get baths."

"Well, still. I'll get to hang out with them. And we get

---

38 Lucy was pretty surprised when she read that kangaroos are fantastic swimmers and will occasionally hop in the water to cool down too. That said, their coats don't require specialized grooming, so baths are infrequent at best.

to see some tomorrow. Dudes, for the first time in my life, I want to go to bed so we can wake up already."

Lucy suddenly feels like her last bite of marshmallow was coated in glue or got stuck halfway down her throat. She takes a drink from her water bottle, which doesn't help very much.

"Good idea," Alex says. "We'll meet here for breakfast and hot cocoa at seven a.m. sharp! You have to finish the last puzzle by four o'clock, so we need to get started on the path right away."

Everyone agrees and starts saying their good nights, but to her surprise and relief, Alex calls her name.

"Can you help me clean up these marshmallows really quick?"

Lucy takes one look at her sister and realizes that maybe the sisters telepathy thing worked better than she thought. Because it's crystal clear that Alex either overheard what happened with Jemma or at least knows something is wrong. Though she has no idea how everyone doesn't know. Lucy barely spoke throughout the marshmallow eating, and Jemma looked at every single person and thing in the camp *except* Lucy.

When she slips into her sister's tent, Lucy is ready to tell her every detail. But to her surprise, Alex does not ask if she's okay and she does not tell Lucy how terrible it is that Jemma yelled at her. Instead she sits down on her cot and pats the space beside her. When Lucy sits, Alex heaves one of those sad sighs again.

"Do you remember when you first started having panic attacks?"

Lucy nods. Remember? How on earth could she forget? At first, she thought she was just feeling a little queasy out of nowhere. And it kept happening day after day at school. For a while, that was her big worry, that she was going to get sick in the classroom, right in front of everyone.

"You were going to the restroom a lot at school then, but it wasn't really because you needed to use the restroom, and as far as I know, you never actually got sick, right?"

"Right." Lucy says the word slowly, because she's not sure what Alex is getting at.

Alex nods. "Well, if you remember, your teacher started to think you were faking feeling sick to skip class. But that's not what was happening. You were leaving class a lot, which isn't the best thing, but because of the situation you couldn't help it."

Lucy squints at the ground and then squints at her sister. She's pretty sure Alex isn't just talking about the bathroom-breaks mess of last year. Lucy is 91 percent sure she's talking about Jemma yelling at her. But she's 100 percent sure that unlike panic attacks, people *can* choose to not yell.

Alex reaches for Lucy's hand and gives it a squeeze. "I'm really sorry that Jemma yelled at you. She shouldn't do that, and she is being rude. I will talk to her if you like, but first I want to see if you'd like to try to talk to her about what happened."

"I definitely wouldn't."

"I'd like you to think about it first."

Lucy opens her mouth to argue, but Alex holds up

a finger and keeps talking. "I'd like you to sleep on it. I promise you there's another side to all of this with Jemma. And even though she's not very good at showing it, I think she could really use a friend, someone who understands what it feels like when things are hard."

Lucy is tempted to tell Alex she doesn't have any intention of being Jemma's friend, but something about that feels just as mean as all the stuff Jemma is doing to her. So she hugs her sister and heads to her tent with the fake torches on the camp fence flickering to light the way.

Inside the tent, Jemma is already in her sleeping bag, turned away from Lucy. She has left the lantern on very low, which feels pretty nice on a Jemma scale. Lucy puts her jacket on top of her duffel bag and slides into bed. There are shadows in the tent, and she can hear spring peepers outside, and normally this would keep her up all night. But instead of all the normal things to keep her awake, she's mostly worried about what Alex meant.

What is wrong with Jemma? And if she needs a friend, does Lucy have to be that friend? Would she even want to?

"Lucy?"

Jemma's voice is so small and soft that Lucy isn't sure at all it belongs to the same scowly girl who yelled at her two hours ago. She can hear Harrison and Trey talking in the tent next to theirs. Their voices are too quiet to make out clearly, but they're also quiet enough that Lucy knows it was absolutely, positively Jemma who called her name. Finally, because she feels too weird about pretending to be asleep, she responds, in an even quieter voice than Jemma's.

"Yes?"

"I'm sorry I yelled at you earlier."

Lucy doesn't know what to say to that. And she doesn't know what to think, but she knows that the right thing when someone offers an apology is to respond kindly. "Thanks, Jemma."

And then a few minutes later, because there's something so sad and small about the way Jemma is lying on her bed, Lucy adds, "Is there anything I can do to maybe cheer you up?"

But Jemma doesn't answer. At first, Lucy is sure she's being ignored. But then she hears the soft sounds of Jemma breathing. It isn't quite a snore, but it's something close enough to tell Lucy she's asleep.

Lucy is pretty sure she'll never fall asleep, but at some point she does. She wakes up to sunshine in the tent and the sound of Harrison shouting outside.

CHAPTER 16

As soon as Lucy steps out of the tent, Harrison runs over. "Lucy, I'm so glad you're awake. When I woke up this morning, I was really hungry and wishing I had chocolate milk because I love chocolate milk in the morning and sometimes I put it on my Froot Loops, which Mom tells me is way too much sugar, but anyway, I walked toward the firepit and then saw . . . Well, look!"

He waves wildly toward the camp gate where Alex parked the safari truck yesterday. But now there is more than the giant, shiny black safari truck—there's a tan keeper van!

"That's a zookeeper van!" Lucy says. "I saw them parked outside the animal barns during—" She cuts herself off, because she doesn't want to explain that she saw them at the Ambassador tryouts when everything went wrong. But before Harrison can ask what she's talking about, Jemma and Trey emerge from their respective tents.

"What's going on?" Trey asks.

"Why is that keeper van here?" Jemma asks, and Lucy realizes she must have seen them at her tryout too.

Jemma turns back to the gate, where the van door is opening. A tall, wiry woman emerges, wearing bright green glasses and carrying a cooler. Lucy notices the woman's khaki shirt with the Wildlands logo, and her tall, rubber boots. Most of all, Lucy notices the coils and coils of dark shiny hair twisted into a cool design at the nape of her neck. This woman is absolutely, positively a zookeeper!

The absolutely-positively-a-zookeeper woman sets the blue cooler just outside the gate and then gives them a big wave and a grin.

"Good luck on the path today, team!" she says. "Say hello to the ostriches for me!"

"Thank you!" Harrison says, and the woman gives another wave before hopping in the van and tootling away.

Lucy feels a fluttering in her chest that makes her bounce up and down a little bit like Harrison. Like maybe she's part hummingbird too, because she can't stop wiggling. But that's because it's finally really here! The big challenge day is happening now!

Harrison is already flying toward the gate, and Lucy rushes after him.

"Is there breakfast in that cooler?" Jemma asks.

"I'm super hungry," Trey says.

Harrison pulls open the gate, and Lucy is right behind him. She reaches down for the lid of the cooler and pulls it open, spotting the breakfast Trey was hoping for . . . and something else.

"There is food!" Harrison says.

"Yes, but there's something better," Lucy says with a grin, pulling out a rolled-up parchment. "I think this is it, you guys! Our first puzzle for the path!"

Lucy moves closer to the other kids, and they all form a circle around her. She feels like a pirate getting ready to find a treasure when she unrolls it for everyone to see.

READER NOTE!

TIME TO GET OUT YOUR PENCIL AND PAPER!

"It's a crossword puzzle!" Harrison bounces on his feet. "Lucy, I think you're going to solve the whole thing, because it's all about animals!"

Lucy puts up her hands quickly. "I don't know everything about animals."

"What's going on?" Alex asks, and Lucy sees her sister standing in the doorway of her tent with bear slippers on. She's yawning and her blue hair is in a sloppy bun and she still looks so cool. Lucy wishes, not for the first time, that she had a little bit of her sister's cool factor.

"Looks like our keeper friends were here, huh?" Alex asks with a grin. "Well, you'd better get to it, everybody! It's already seven-oh-five a.m., and now that you have the puzzle, I better let the Ambassadors know so they can get started too. Your tablet actually should tell the Ambassadors when you approach a puzzle."

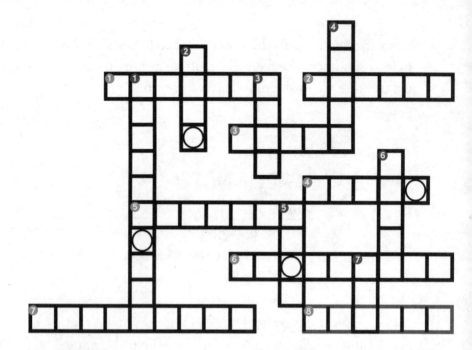

ACROSS

1. Savanna feline with tufted ears

2. Night-blooming trees with large trunks

3. Both male and female giraffes have two ossicones, which most people think are these _____

4. Striped herbivore

5. Females of these big cats live in solitude while males are social

6. Largest savanna in Africa

7. Two million animals search for better water and grazing each year in the Great _____

8. Termite colonies build _____

DOWN

1. Savannas are found on all but this continent

2. Body parts that keep an elephant cool

3. This feline will have spots when young that disappear as they mature

4. Most common plant type in a savanna biome

5. Group of elephants

6. A group of lions

7. Another name for wildebeest

"Okay, dudes, let's do it!" Harrison says. "Do you know a savanna feline with tufted ears? It's seven letters long."

"Tufted ears?" Lucy tries to scan her brain in case there are any other creatures she can think of that fit that description. "I think it's the caracal."

"See?" Harrison is positively beaming. He begins walking toward the chairs near the tents, when a ping sounds from his tent. Harrison rushes inside and brings the tablet out.

Alex crosses her arms and winks. "You know what that sound means, right?"

"We have walkie-talkie signal again, right?" Jemma asks.

"Oh, actually, no," Alex says with a frown. "I tried my phone and walkie-talkie this morning, and they were much worse than normal. I wish I'd been awake to talk to the keeper about it."

"The tablet probably works on a local connection, like wireless headphones," Trey says. "It pings when we are physically close enough to the puzzle for the connection to happen."

Alex nods. "That's probably it."

"I think the sound means the Ambassadors are working on the puzzle," Lucy says.

"Then let's keep going," Jemma says, but as she looks over the crossword, she shakes her head and looks uncertain. "I don't think I know these for sure."

But Lucy does know them, some of them at any rate. A few of answers jump right out, like the Great *Migration*. But others could be a few things.

"I think I know some of them," Lucy says, pointing at the clue with a nine next to it. "Like this is *migration*, but we have find out where they all fit and how they fit together."

Jemma does her Jemma scowl. "How will we know if you're right?"

"I'm sure she'll be right," Trey says.

Harrison waves his hand wildly. "We have to hurry if we're going to beat the Ambassadors!"

Lucy's not 100 percent sure she'll be able to solve them all. She's maybe 86 percent sure, but the more Jemma and the others look at her, the more 86 percent doesn't feel like enough. "I think I know a lot of this, but I could be wrong on some things."

"It's okay, dude," Harrison says. "We'll write them down to see what fits."

"Oh, I've got one," Trey says, pulling a small notebook with lined paper out of his back pocket. "I keep it for plant observations."

Jemma reaches for the notepad Trey is holding. As soon as she has it, she starts writing. "Okay, so *migration* would go here at the bottom, right? What's next?"

Lucy nods. "And the elephant group is a *herd*. I'm sure of that one too."

"Great, that one's a four-letter word. We have at least one spot for those, so put it on the side," Harrison says. "Keep going, Lucy!"

Lucy nods and keeps working. She can feel the funny way Jemma is looking at her, with her eyes very narrow and suspicious. Maybe Jemma doesn't think she can do this, but she's wrong. Lucy might not be good at volley-ball or really any sports-related things, but there are some things she's great at, and animal facts is at the top of that list.

Lucy goes line by line, calling out answers while Jemma tries to write them in. She has to skip the one about the solitary females and the one about the night-blooming trees, but Trey knows that one right away, so Jemma writes *baobab*[39] and they keep moving. In just a few minutes, they have an answer or at least a good guess for almost every clue.

Jemma helps Harrison try to find ways to arrange them. They count the number of letters in each word and then try to put them in the right boxes. It's slow going, but it's not terribly difficult, and it's absolutely, positively better than sitting around watching Jemma solve a puzzle pretty much on her own.

Before they know it, the boxes are full and all the letters line up perfectly. They stand back and grin at each other. And then Lucy looks around with a frown.

"Wait. What happens now?"

"Well, now you'd better find the gate," Alex says. "Check the map."

Jemma grabs the map before anyone else can get to it, which is only 63 percent annoying this time, because Lucy knows she did the lion's share of solving for the puzzle.

---

39 Trey doesn't just know what a baobab is either! He tells Lucy that there are nine varieties of them, and six of those varieties only live on the island na-tion of Madagascar. Makes you wonder what's so baobab-friendly about that island.

ACROSS

1. Savanna feline with tufted ears

2. Night-blooming trees with large trunks

3. Both male and female giraffes have two ossicones, which most people think are these _____

4. Striped herbivore

5. Females of these big cats live in solitude while males are social

6. Largest savanna in Africa

7. Two million animals search for better water and grazing each year in the Great _____

8. Termite colonies build _____

DOWN

1. Savannas are found on all but this continent

2. Body parts that keep an elephant cool

3. This feline will have spots when young that disappear as they mature

4. Most common plant type in a savanna biome

5. Group of elephants

6. A group of lions

7. Another name for wildebeest

Jemma nods. "You guys can follow me. I know where we're going."

If you ask Lucy, which Jemma would clearly never do, it would have been just as easy to point the way or show everyone the map. But everyone else is following Jemma, so Lucy falls in line. She's a little breathless by the time they get there. And *there* means the farthest edge of the camp, at least half a football field behind the tents. Lucy spots the tall, sturdy-looking fence that marks the border of the park. The other three kids gather in a semicircle around the gate that lets them into the escape part of their challenge!

The gate looks like it has been there for a thousand years. Lucy also thinks it looks a little bit like a prison door, which she does not care for but also does not mention. Instead she steps back and takes in all the details. The gate is maybe eight feet tall and made of iron, with vines curled around the black metal bars.

"It looks like it's been here a million years," Harrison says quietly.

Lucy isn't sure she totally agrees with that, but she is 200 percent sure there will be at least one spider lurking in the shadows of those vines. While she can appreciate the important role spiders play in the world,[40] she doesn't want to shake hands with one. She also can't see a latch or a lock. Those vines that seem to be covering every metal

---

40 Spiders do play a critical role in controlling the populations of smaller insects and keeping entire ecosystems balanced. Still, they are a little spooky when they're hiding in a place where you're about to stick your hand.

bar in the gate also appear to be crawling up and down the tall fence that rises on either side of the path, and she can't see—

A clanging interrupts Lucy's thought. Jemma is holding out a clunky-looking metal lock.

"How long has this lock been here?" she asks. "Because it looks like centuries."

"Ivy grows quickly. It could do this in two years," Trey says.

"Would they really plant ivy in an animal park?"

"I think yes," Trey says. "Climbing plants would probably offer shelter and food for small animals and insects."

"Okay, animal lessons aside, I think we need those weird circled letters in order because this is a combination lock with letters instead of numbers."

Harrison stops balancing on one foot and checks. "The letters are *S*, *A*, *T*, and *R*."

Jemma rotates the dials for the lock, and suddenly the tablet begins to chime and chime and chime. Harrison's eyes go wide, and he holds out the tablet, which sounds exactly like a fairy wand when a spell is being cast in a cartoon. The screen is flashing too, not green but blue, over and over. There is a loud electronic click and Lucy notices a tiny green light on the strange lock just before the gate unlatches. Their team is going inside the escape challenge path!

CHAPTER 17

"The lock was just a fake," Jemma says. And then she grins. "The tablet is connected and it's all electronic. That's cool."

"That's not the coolest part," Lucy says, because now she's leaning in to see the tablet again. She points to the scoreboard at the top, where the Ambassadors still have two wins and two puzzles completed. But now the Blue Team has a win too!

SCOREBOARD

GREEN TEAM	BLUE TEAM
2 WON	1 WON
2 COMPLETE	3 COMPLETE

"We won," Lucy says, pointing at the screen. "We beat the Ambassadors!"

Footsteps behind the kids tell them Alex has returned. She's smiling from ear to ear. "Amazing! You guys found the lock."

"Yeah, we did more than that. We finally won a puzzle!" Jemma says.

"We won! We're amazing! Well, at least Lucy and Trey are amazing, because they knew all this stuff," Harrison says, hopping in a circle on his left foot.

Trey nods. "True. Also, the electronic lock on the gate unlocked, so the gate is open."

"Perfect! I know the designers wanted as many digital elements as possible so we could change combinations in the future."

"So we aren't going to have any giant old keys or whatever?" Jemma asks.

"You'll have real elements like the parchment, but the locks themselves are electronic. It's more secure that way."

Lucy follows the others through the gate, trying to let her eyes adjust to the shadowy path. The gate closes behind them with a similar electronic click.

"This is so super-high-tech," Harrison says. "Oh wow, are there going to be lasers? Dude, I love lasers. Oh, what about robots? Safari robots!"

"Sorry, no lasers or robots, but I think there will be some fun surprises. Go on in. This section of the path leads us through the ostrich enclosure."

"I thought safari parks had all the animals together," Jemma says.

"Wildlands exists to support rescue and rehabilitation

efforts, and often rescued animals can't fully integrate into a natural setting. We try to provide the closest-to-natural environment that our animals can thrive in."

"Are animals together in this new section?" Lucy asks, because she knows from earlier visits that animals are often placed together if they would naturally coexist or are well suited to coexistence.

"Yep! The animals in the Canopy Walk area live together and are often allowed into the larger grazing area with Mwanza and Tabora. But sometimes, like this weekend, they're placed in their own areas. Other animals need more support. Our tortoise Leonardo is blind, so he lives in an adjacent enclosure. Our ostriches and a few other animals were part of a petting zoo, and you've met Archie, of course."

They slow down, and Lucy notices the fence on either side of the path now. Through the spaces in that fence, she can see a wide stretch of grass in either direction. There are signs here and there, but no one else seems very interested in reading them. Jemma, who is in front, is marching along as if her entire goal is to get to the next puzzle.

"According to the map, I don't think we're more than two hundred yards from the next gate," she says.

"Okay, we can get there fast!" Harrison adds, jogging to keep up with her.

But Lucy pauses by the grass, peering around the enclosure beyond their pathway. It's mostly grass, with a few trees dotted here and there. She sees what looks like a feeding station and a large bare dirt circle off to one side,[41] but no animals at all.

"I don't see an ostrich," Trey says.

Lucy leans in close, scanning the grassy slope slowly. She scans a cluster of slender trees, some low scrubby flowers, and another short tree behind a brown leafy bush.

Wait a minute. Did that shorter tree just move?

The shorter tree moves again. And that's when Lucy sees that the tree she has spotted is not a tree at all. It's a neck! The neck bends down again, and then she sees that the shrub was not a shrub either. It was an ostrich body!

"Trey," she whispers. And then she slowly points. "The ostrich."

"Her name is Penelope," Alex says softly. "The male has a mostly black body. I'm not sure where he's hiding."

"Wow," Trey says. "I've never seen an ostrich before."

Lucy has seen an ostrich before, and she's drawn tons of them. Even last night, she was working on her ostrich flip cartoon. But still, Lucy isn't sure she'll ever get tired of watching Penelope. She is so close! The ostrich is peering here and there, her long, slender neck[42] swiveling back and forth. Penelope is too far away for Lucy to see her face, but if she could, Lucy knows the ostrich would have watchful dark eyes framed by long, velvety lashes.

---

41 This circle is almost certainly an ostrich nest, which isn't too fancy but is probably safer than a two-hundred-pound bird climbing a tree.

42 An ostrich's long neck provides important temperature control. And it does look a little bit like an old-fashioned thermometer coming out of a giant ball of feathers.

Lucy knows lots of things about ostriches. Here are the ones she can think of:

1. Ostriches can make a shocking roaring sound.

2. They have powerful bare legs that are super good at kicking.

3. The males practice elaborate courtship displays or dances.

Lucy is sure that if she stands here long enough or reads some of the signs, she'll learn even more. But she won't get the chance, because at that moment, there is a faint and familiar electronic ping. The tablet! Then Jemma whistles and the ostrich startles, trotting off to the farthest corner of her enclosure. Lucy's not sure if it's possible to lose points in the individual portion of the competition, because scaring the animals feels like the opposite of what an Ambassador should do.

"We found the next puzzle!" Jemma shouts.

Lucy, Trey, and Alex head in the direction of Jemma's whistle. They find her at the next gate, and sure enough, there is a puzzle beside her. This time, it doesn't look electronic. There is a giant scale with two big plates. And there is a pile of wooden blocks carved with various words.

"I do a lot of puzzles in books and online and stuff, but this isn't like anything I've seen before," Lucy says.

"Well, if it's about stacking blocks, I'm awesome at this," Jemma says, rubbing her hands together.

Lucy starts reading the blocks she can see, all of which have writing carved into the wooden sides.

READER NOTE!

TIME TO GET OUT YOUR PENCIL AND PAPER!

Lucy is 100 percent sure some of these are facts, but she's 94 percent sure some of them are just myths. For one, she knows beyond a doubt that the ostrich is not the tallest land animal; that's the giraffe. Harrison hops in front of Lucy before she can read much more. He starts reading the tablet screen aloud.

"Okay, dudes. It says to start the timer on your screen. Place the true blocks on the correct side. Be sure the rest are left behind."

"Wait, what timer?" Lucy asks. "There aren't supposed to be any timers. Right?"

Lucy looks at Alex, who 100 percent makes an *oops* face. "Shoot, I forgot about this one," she says.

"There weren't supposed to be timers," Lucy says again. What she does not say is that a race between the two teams for the finishing time feels like a sort of timer too. But even though she doesn't say it, she squints her eyes at Alex in a way that probably makes her feelings clear.

THE OSTRICH

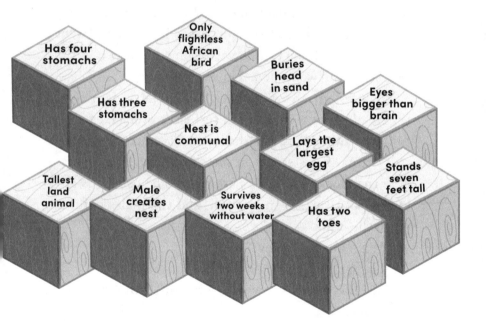

Has four stomachs

Only flightless African bird

Buries head in sand

Eyes bigger than brain

Has three stomachs

Nest is communal

Lays the largest egg

Tallest land animal

Male creates nest

Survives two weeks without water

Has two toes

Stands seven feet tall

"Well, there definitely is one. And we have forty-five seconds left," Harrison says.

"Forty-five seconds?" Jemma shouts. "You already started it? We aren't ready for this!"

"It told me to push the button, so I did. . . . We have thirty-eight seconds left now."

"We need to pause it!" Jemma shouts. "We don't even know what we're doing."

Lucy's throat squeezes and squeezes. If there's one thing she's starting to hate more than this stupid timer, it's the way Jemma is shouting right now. Harrison jabs at the screen and then shakes his head.

"Well, I can't pause it," he says, sounding about 110 percent calmer than Jemma. "I think we're just going to run out of time. What happens then? Because unless we can put all the blocks in the right places in the next twenty-eight seconds, I don't think we're going to make it in time. Oh, actually, twenty-five. No, twenty-four."

Lucy's stomach swings back and her face goes hot. She thinks of every terrible math test she's ever taken. Every time the other kids put their pencils down but she was still sitting there, stuck on the third page. She rushes to grab the blocks she knows are right. The ostrich is absolutely, positively seven feet tall, and the males definitely make the nests.

"What are you doing?"

"I'm grabbing the right blocks."

"We don't even know where to put them yet," Jemma complains.

"I imagine the correct blocks go on the right," Trey says. He hands her a block that says *Has three stomachs* and smiles. "I read that one on one of the signs on the fence."

Lucy thinks it's awesome that Trey managed to read this, but she can't say that because there's no time. She puts her two blocks on the right plate beside the stomachs fact. The scale creaks and shifts to the right.

"Seven seconds left," Harrison says.

"Hurry up!" Jemma says.

Between the timer and the yelling and the blocks, which are hard to read super quickly, Lucy's throat squeezes and squeezes and her cheeks feel hot.

"You're going to make us lose!" Jemma says.

"Why are you so angry?" Harrison asks.

"Because we're going to run out of time!"

"We did run out of time," Trey says. "Just now."

Lucy looks at the SORRY—YOU'RE OUT OF TIME! message on the tablet and then the block in her hand, the one that didn't end up on either of the plates. She doesn't actually know where it goes, but it doesn't matter. Time ran out and they didn't solve the puzzle! Does that mean they just lose? She doesn't see anything about a second chance, so if they didn't do this in time and they don't get to keep going with the challenge, then she isn't going to be part of the Ambassador team.

Lucy curls her hands into fists. She's sure her stomach will start somersaulting over and over. Except it doesn't somersault over and over. It doesn't somersault at all.

Still, just like the tablet says, they're out of time. Part of Lucy wants to ask if this means they're going home, and another part of her wants to know if they're in some kind of trouble for not finishing it, and maybe the smallest part of Lucy of all wants to know if they could maybe try it one more time.

"Ugh, this is all stupid," Jemma huffs. "They should have given us more time!"

"It's okay, Jemma," Harrison says. "Every team loses

169

sometimes. You probably already know all about it because of your other teams. Now you'll have to teach us about it, because we're your new team—"

"You're not my team! Don't ever say you're my team again!"

Jemma's shout is every bit as loud and shocking and awful as it was last night in the tent. Except this time, the other kids are there to hear it too. Lucy notices that Harrison's eyebrows are arched high with surprise, and Trey's forehead has that crease that Lucy thinks he sometimes gets when he's thinking. Even Jemma looks shocked by her own outburst, or at least Lucy thinks she looks shocked. She can't be completely sure, because Jemma runs past them super fast. Like ostrich-and-cheetah-combined fast. And Lucy is about 92 percent sure that she's crying.

Lucy realizes three things very quickly:

1. No one else on the Blue Team seems interested in following Jemma.

2. Jemma is clearly too upset to come back on her own.

3. Lucy may be the only one who knows enough about what's going on to go after her.

Lucy doesn't know that Jemma will want to talk to her, but no matter what, she feels like she has to try. "I'll be right back. I need to talk to Jemma."

CHAPTER 18

It is easy to find Jemma in the ostrich enclosure. It's not a big enclosure, after all. The hard part is, now that Lucy's close enough to see her, she is absolutely, positively afraid to ask what's wrong. She's generally reluctant to ask Jemma about the weather or what time it is, so feelings seem 100 percent out of the question.

But she is a little worried about Jemma, especially now that she can see her sitting on the path with her knees pulled up to her chin.

"What do you want?"

Jemma's voice snaps at Lucy like a rubber band right between the eyes.[43] Lucy knows the very best thing in this situation is to not take things personally. She knows she should ask calm, kind questions. That's what Alex would do. That's what Mom would do too. But Lucy has had just about enough, and when she opens her mouth the truth comes out.

"What I want is for you to stop yelling," Lucy says. "You're scaring the ostrich[44] and probably half of the other

---

43 Lucy was shot between the eyes with a rubber band when she was riding home on the bus in the third grade and it really stung.

44 Ostriches have very sensitive hearing to alert them to predators, so Jemma's yelling is probably quite upsetting.

animals in the park." Lucy realizes she is dangerously close to shouting herself, but even though she tries to quiet her voice, she can't seem to stop the stream of words coming out. "I also want to know why you're always scowling and why you dislike me so much. But mostly I came here to check on you."

Jemma lifts her head, and her eyes are red and swollen. "You came to check on me?"

"You seem very upset."

"Well, of course I'm upset. I don't like to lose! And I'm already a loser here."

Jemma lets out a little hiccup breath, and Lucy's heart aches a little. She really *is* upset. Crying and everything.

"Do you want to talk about it?" Lucy asks softly.

Jemma huffs and scoots around to face her. "I'm the only one who didn't make the Ambassadors team. The five of us have always been together. Remember the pictures?"

"The pictures with the jerseys," Lucy says with a nod. She feels a little sting, thinking of all those pictures and all those jerseys. She'd do anything for one jersey, from one single team.

"I tried so hard. I did good at all the stuff like building fires and climbing and even the obstacle course. I don't think you got to that part," Jemma says, and Lucy's face burns. But she nods for Jemma to go on. "Anyway, I didn't do great at some of the animal questions. But who cares about that? There are signs and stuff all over."

"I think most of the Ambassadors care about that," Lucy says. But when Jemma gives her a look, Lucy winces. "I didn't mean that to be snotty."

Jemma doesn't respond to that, and instead keeps going. "So, after the tryout, we were all texting. We have this group text because we're always on the same team. We text constantly, so of course we were texting after try-outs. And they were all getting phone calls that they'd made it, but I didn't. And at first they were all waiting for me to get the call. But I didn't."

Jemma's voice is so very, very small when she finishes. Lucy's chest hurts as she thinks of how Jemma must have felt waiting for that call. She knows exactly how it feels to not get called to be part of a team. But she can only imagine how much worse it would be if all of her friends were on a team *except* her.

"Were they . . . were they mean to you?"

"No, they were *so* nice. And that was almost worse, because after a while, the group chat got really, really quiet."

"Maybe they didn't know what to say because they felt bad," Lucy guesses.

"That's not what it was. They created another group chat. An Ambassadors Only group chat so they could be excited and talk Ambassador stuff without hurting me." Jemma takes a snuffling, shaky breath. "That's why I have to fix this. I have to be an Ambassador like them."

Jemma's face is blotchy and her eyes are full of tears[45] and Lucy feels something she's never, ever felt for Jemma before. Sadness. She can't shake the feeling that Jemma

---

45 Of all the animals in the world, humans are the only ones who cry when they are sad or upset.

really needs a hug. If she wasn't half convinced Jemma might punch her in the nose if she tried, Lucy just might give her one.

But instead she tries to use the most gentle words and voice she can. "I'm really sorry, Jemma. That sounds terrible."

"It is terrible," Jemma says, and her blotchy face seems a little bit less scowly in that moment. Jemma looks over to the fence and winces. When she speaks, she keeps her voice extra soft. "I didn't mean to scare the ostrich. Do you think he's okay?"

"She," Lucy says. "Alex said her name is Penelope. We don't know where the male is right now. Want to see if we can find Penelope, though?"

Jemma doesn't answer, but she does walk quietly over to the fence to peer through the holes between the ivy. The sky is bright blue overhead, and a breeze is shifting through the grass. For the first time she can remember, Lucy isn't worried about Jemma being so close. Instead of wishing she'd go away, Lucy wishes she could find the ostrich to make Jemma smile.

And then, as if Penelope somehow knows an ostrich sighting would be super helpful, Lucy hears a soft, high-pitched sound, somewhere between a chirp and a gobble.[46] Jemma and Lucy look at each other and break into wide grins.

---

46 Ostriches make a variety of sounds, including a very unique booming that they produce by expanding air in their throats.

Lucy looks back at the fence and the enclosure beyond, and then, in the same place where she spotted Penelope earlier, she sees the slender curving neck, this time even closer than before. Lucy slowly and quietly points at the ostrich, and Jemma's eyes narrow as she searches and searches. And then, all at once, Jemma's eyes and smile both widen. She's seen Penelope!

They watch the ostrich quietly for a few minutes until the giant bird settles down on the ground behind a bush in her enclosure. Lucy feels a strange gnawing feeling inside her chest. Because as sad as she is for Jemma, it doesn't change one important fact. She still wants to be part of the Ambassadors too.

Jemma lets out a little breath and turns back to the path. "I guess we should get moving."

Back at the puzzle area, Harrison is bouncing on the balls of his feet while he tosses a rock into the air and catches it. He does it over and over in a way that tells Lucy he's done a lot of tossing and catching rocks in his time. But when he sees Jemma approaching, he immediately tenses, dropping the rock altogether.

"Hi! Are you feeling better?"

"I don't really want to talk about it," Jemma says, but Lucy notices she doesn't sound like a jerk about it. She just says it.

"Oh, that's cool. Maybe we can talk about the puzzle."

"But we failed the puzzle," Lucy says. "We're out of time."

"Nope." Alex smiles a lopsided smile. "I checked my

notes because I was confused too. There isn't a clear message on the tablet. But once you take all the blocks off the scale . . ."

Alex waves at Harrison, who takes two blocks off the scale. Lucy realizes now that most of the blocks had already been removed. One of them must have put those two back on, but why?

"The tablet resets the timer with a button that says 'try again.' See?"

Harrison turns the screen so they can see the TRY AGAIN button in the center of the screen.

"What happens if we can't finish it this time?" Lucy asks.

"The same thing," Trey says. "We've already let the timer run out twice."

Alex nods. "It's a really good note for the puzzle team. It would sure help if there was a clear message to remove the blocks to try the puzzle again."

"I really thought we lost," Jemma says.

"Me too," Lucy agrees, and then they do an absolutely, positively weird thing. They share a smile.

"Well, I'm glad you didn't," Alex says. "The escape challenge isn't about making people lose. It's about trying to solve puzzles while you learn about animals. It's educa-fun!"

"No offense, Alex, but that sounds like something a teacher would say," Harrison says. "And they'd probably say it before they gave you some sort of game that isn't really a game but is just a different way of learning multiplication tables or something."

"Well, I'm cool with it, because teachers are great. Now, are you ready to try again?"

"Hold on," Trey says. "We need time to strategize."

"That's a great idea," Harrison says. "Sixty seconds isn't a very long time."

"The timer doesn't start counting down until the first block is on the scale," Alex says.

"Dudes, we can totally do this. We just need to go really fast the second we throw that first block on. Of course, I guess we need to know where the blocks go. The correct ones go to the right, which makes sense, but what about the ones on the left? Shouldn't the wrong ones be left off the scale altogether?"

"The sign says they should be left behind," Jemma says. "I think that means they go on the left plate."

"Me too," Lucy says, and then she looks at Jemma and thinks about how sad she was. The whole trip so far, Lucy has tried to keep her distance from Jemma, but maybe she should try something else. "I have an idea. Jemma, you're super fast, right?"

Jemma looks surprised. Her voice is quiet when she responds. "Yeah, I am."

"Okay. Harrison, I think you're pretty fast too. I know some of these facts for sure, but we might need to check the signs for the others. We can separate the blocks into two piles before we place a single one on the scale. Trey and I can work on separating the piles and you and Harrison can run back and look for any answers we need."

"And that should give us plenty of time to finish before the timer runs out," Jemma adds.

They start to separate the blocks, adding the ones Lucy knows for sure to the pile. She puts a few on the left pile, because she knows ostriches aren't the tallest animal on earth and she's sure there's at least one penguin that hails from South Africa, so ostriches can't be the only flightless African bird.

They place even more blocks toward the right side of the scale. Trey starts with the three stomachs fact, which reminds Lucy that the four stomachs fact can go on the left pile. Then they add facts about the ostriches laying the largest egg, and standing seven feet tall, and surviving up to two weeks without water. But then Lucy steps back.

"I don't know if the nests are communal," she says.

"Maybe there's something about it in the enclosure," Harrison says. "I can run back there and yell back up to you."

"No, don't yell," Jemma says. Then she flushes a little. "I think that scares the ostriches."

"Okay, we just need to run and check a few facts about how nests are built. And then a couple of other things." Lucy hands two blocks to Harrison, who dashes down the path into the enclosure. She hands two more blocks to Jemma, who reads them aloud.

"Buries head in sand. Has two toes.[47] Got it!" Jemma heads out, and Trey picks up one of the remaining blocks.

"Nest is communal," he says.

"I think that's right, but I'm just not sure," Lucy says.

---

47 Two toes doesn't feel like enough for a seven-foot-tall bird, but nevertheless.

Then she grabs the last block, which reads "Eyes bigger than brain."

As she's dusting off her palms, she feels Alex's hand on her shoulder. When she looks up, her sister is absolutely, positively beaming at her. "Lucy, I'm super proud of you. I knew you'd be great at this."

Lucy doesn't know exactly what to say, but before she can think of anything, she is interrupted by the loudest, most endless series of elephant noises she's ever heard. It echoes on and on, a trumpeting roar that makes Lucy's insides turn cold. Even Alex's smile vanishes as the startling noise goes on and on and on. And it's not just an elephant. For just a second, Lucy's sure she hears something slam, and then a very distant human shout.

The other kids run back to the front, and everyone's face looks as worried as Lucy feels. And then, all at once, the sounds stop. Everything feels strange and eerily quiet.

"Was that the muh-whah elephant?" Harrison asks.

"Mwanza," Alex says. She still looks very worried. "Yes, that was definitely her."

"Do elephants normally make those noises?" Jemma asks. "Because she really sounded . . ."

"Upset," Lucy says. She can't make other words seem to come out. She already knows that elephants are noisy, but she also has seen enough documentaries to know that the noises they just heard weren't part of ordinary elephant small talk. Something is happening up toward the front of the park, something that has Mwanza very, very upset.

CHAPTER 19

Lucy can tell Alex is worried, and Alex being worried is worrisome. "Why would Mwanza be upset, Alex?"

Alex hesitates but then shrugs. "I don't really know, but I'll check with the front to make sure someone looks in on the elephants."

Alex tries her walkie-talkie again, but it is purely fuzz and static now. She even tests the second walkie-talkie she picked up in one of the tents, but nothing works.

"You could still call 911," Lucy says. "There's the SOS feature, right?"

Alex hesitates and then shakes her head. "I left my phone at camp, since service doesn't work at all in this part of the park. Maybe she's scolding Tabora for something."

"Scolding?" Harrison looks surprised. "Baby elephants get into trouble?"

"Sometimes, sure. Since we don't hear her now, it's possible that's all it was," Alex says, but Lucy isn't convinced Alex believes that.

"So what should we do about the walkie-talkie?" Lucy asks.

"Well, we should see about getting this puzzle solved. I'm sure everything is fine," Alex says. But Lucy doesn't think she looks 100 percent sure about everything being fine. Maybe 75 percent sure, which is not as sure as Lucy would like.

Still, Lucy doesn't know what they can do about a scary elephant noise that isn't happening anymore. So she and the other kids go back to searching the enclosure to find out how ostriches nest and whether or not they bury their heads (they don't). When the kids gather at the scales again, they quickly separate the remaining blocks into the proper piles.

"Are you ready?" Lucy asks, holding one block over the right side of the scale.

"Totally ready," Harrison says.

She places the block, and the digital timer on the tablet quickly begins to tick down. With each block Lucy adds, the scale creaks down or up. The metal plates look old and rusted, and part of her thinks this whole puzzle must be a hundred years old. Except that everything is linked to the tablet and the small gray lock with the red light that holds the gate closed.

"Twenty seconds left!" Harrison says.

"Here," Jemma says, handing over the four stomachs block.

Lucy places it carefully on the metal plate to the left, which is quickly getting full. One of the blocks threatens to topple off the edge, but Lucy saves it just in time, pushing it gently back into place.

"Only twelve seconds left," Harrison says.

"All the blocks are on there," Lucy replies. "It isn't working."

"Wait, there's one that's shoved mostly off the left plate," Jemma says.

"It could affect the weight," Trey says. Together they gingerly tap the block until it's not hanging over the side of the left plate.

Lucy feels her insides crunching into a tighter and tighter ball, almost like she expects that same SORRY—YOU'RE OUT OF TIME! message. But instead, the timer freezes. The puzzle is complete!

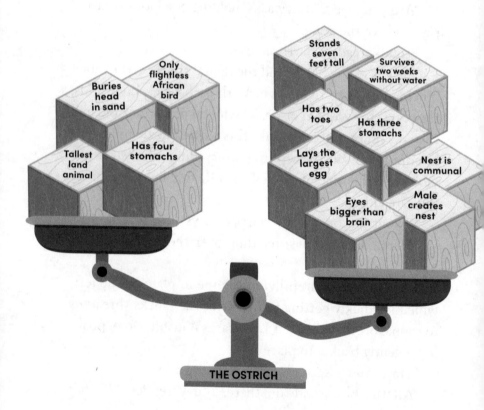

THE OSTRICH

Lucy crosses her fingers and looks at the tablet screen. The timer has stopped with two seconds remaining!

All four kids lean in around the screen as *Congratulations* scrolls across the now-frozen timer. The screen flashes blue and then the chiming starts—and it's the same happy fairy-wand song from the last time, and the screen is flashing blue over and over again.

Lucy raises her hands in victory just as Harrison leaps into the air with a shout.

"We won again!"

"We did it!" Jemma cries.

All of the kids are whooping, and Lucy feels like her insides are bubbling, but then she notices something in Alex's expression, something beneath her sister's smile. Alex checks her watch. Discreetly, but she does it, and all at once, Lucy knows why.

Lucy grabs the forgotten tablet as the gate unlocks with a click. The other kids are gathering around as it creaks slowly open, but she is looking at the numbers at the top of the screen.

SCOREBOARD

GREEN TEAM	BLUE TEAM
2 WON	2 WON
3 COMPLETE	4 COMPLETE

The Blue Team is up to two wins, so the teams really are tied, but something about that feels off. This puzzle was all about animal facts, and specifically animal facts that could be found within the exhibit. In their letter, the Ambassadors said Wildlands was their home turf. And they probably did not have a team member like Jemma who ran off upset over not making the team, which means that even if it took them a little longer to finish the crossword puzzle, this puzzle should have been super easy for them. But the Ambassadors still haven't finished it.

Lucy looks up as Harrison peeks through the now-open gate. "Come on, Lucy!"

She follows slowly, looking at the number 2 under the Blue Team one more time. Lucy is 92 percent sure the Ambassadors would have solved this puzzle in half the time it took the Blue Team. Which means they should have solved it first. So why didn't they?

CHAPTER 20

Lucy shivers the minute she steps through the gate. She can't tell if it's because of the small fenced area they seem to be trapped in, the stark black gate in front of them, or the fact that she still can't shake the idea that the Ambassadors should have solved that last puzzle first.

"Why is there another gate?" Trey asks.

"Why isn't there another puzzle?" Jemma asks.

Lucy spots the sign above the second gate that reads PLEASE, ONLY ONE GATE OPEN AT A TIME, and she knows exactly where they are. "We're in a safety section. Zoos and parks create these spaces anytime there's a possibility of an animal escaping through a human entrance.[48] We just need to close the last gate before we head into the kangaroo zone."

Harrison whirls around to look at Lucy. His eyes are absolutely enormous. "Did you say kangaroos?"

Lucy laughs and points at the signs for the red kangaroo carved around the frame of the gate. Alex tries to close the first gate, the one that leads back to the ostrich domain. It creaks and scrapes and—sticks.

---

48 Animal escapes do happen. One late-night Google search by Lucy revealed stories about cheetahs, penguins, and an octopus (!) that escaped their enclosures through entrances intended for humans.

"Do you need help?" Lucy asks.

She joins Alex before she can even answer, and they both push from one side and then pull from the other. It's no use. The other kids join them, and now it's like piles of hands pushing and pulling. It should be enough, but the gate is 150 percent stuck halfway open. Really it's more partway than halfway. Definitely not enoughway for anyone to squeeze back through.

Alex wipes her hand across her brow. "Well, that's not awesome. We'll need to call about this as soon as the walkie-talkie is working. Lucy, can you take a note?"

Lucy pulls out her notebook and pen and jots down a few details about the broken ostrich gate. But making the note does not change the fact that they can't follow the rules at this point. They can't open the gate ahead without both gates being open at the same time.

"What should we do?" she asks.

"You guys go through the next gate there," Alex says. "Once you're in the next area, I'll follow you. I just want to be sure nothing gets in or out when all of you are heading inside."

"But there's no way a kangaroo can fit through that gap."

"We have brown kiwis in there too, though. Don't worry, I'll come right after you guys get in."

"Okay, we can do that," Harrison says. "Dude, I love kangaroos. I hope we see some. Do you know they have pockets and their babies are called joeys?[49] Oh, and al-

---

49 Some other adorable animal baby names include puffling (baby puffin), cria (baby alpaca), porcupette (baby porcupine), and puggle (baby platypus).

most all of them live in Australia, though some of the tree kinds live on an island. I don't know a lot about animals, but this one time I watched a whole documentary on kangaroos about a hundred times."[50]

Lucy walks through the gate, in hopes of getting Harrison to follow. It's kind of ridiculous and fun (ridi-fun?) the way Harrison chatters on and on, but right now, Lucy just wants to get through the gate so Alex can get in here too. When they're through the gate, the second gate slams shut behind them, and Lucy watches her sister double-check for stray kiwis.

"No kiwi escape artists here," Alex says with a grin. "You guys watch and make sure nothing is approaching on your side of the gate."

Lucy turns around to see a narrow dirt path surrounded by scrubby grassland on either side. The enclosure is pretty large, and a kiwi could definitely be hiding in the grass, but nothing is approaching the path or the gate. "I think we're good."

"Awesome, I'm coming in," Alex says, but when she tries to pull the kangaroo enclosure gate open, it doesn't budge. She twists and tugs and then frowns. "Maybe you have to let me in from your side?"

Lucy grabs for the gate handle and tries to open it. It's locked. A tiny flicker of worry flares inside her chest. She checks the gate and notices a small red light glowing above the lock. It's the same light she's seen on the other gates.

---

50 Lucy saw the same documentary a couple of times, so she knows that the island with tree kangaroos is actually Papua New Guinea.

She pushes at it again, and then pulls for good measure, but it's no use.

"It's locked," Lucy says.

Jemma joins Lucy at the gate. "This is one of those electronic locks, so we must have missed a puzzle."

"I don't think there was supposed to be a puzzle here," Alex says. "I really should have brought my phone to check."

"There wasn't," Harrison says. "I mean, not because I know about the puzzles, but because I know there is a pinging noise when we run into one and the tablet is right here."

"Good point," Alex says. "Can you check the tablet to see if there's a message about the lock, though?"

Harrison powers on the tablet, but the screen is white except for a plain text message scrawled across the top. *Proceed to the Next Puzzle.* Harrison tries to power the tablet off and on, but the message does not change.

"Maybe we missed it. Is there something in the safety zone where you are?"

"I don't think so," Alex says, but she dutifully looks around the small enclosure anyway. "Nothing here but me and a sign about only keeping one gate open. I guess they meant it, huh?"

Alex laughs, but Lucy is absolutely, positively sure this is a no time for jokes. Her sister, who is also their chaperone, is trapped on the wrong side of a locked gate!

"What should we do?" Lucy asks, and her voice cracks just a little bit.

"I'll check the gate that let us into the ostrich enclosure. Maybe I can squeeze through?"

"What about emergencies?" Lucy asks.

"Every gate has an override button, but I'm not sure they're connected, because this one isn't working. I already tried. It's a new area, so there are still kinks to work out."

"Should we wait for you?" Lucy asks. Her chest feels a little tight at the idea of being locked away from Alex, but her sister quickly shakes her head.

"You guys should go find the puzzle and get started on that," Alex says. "It's possible that the next puzzle will fix whatever glitch is happening here and I'll be able to get right in when you unlock the exit gate."

Why is she so calm about this? Lucy is 180 percent the opposite of calm.

"Okay, we'll do it," Harrison says, "and I'll tell you if we find kangaroos. I haven't seen any, and that's a disappointment." Lucy notices the way he is hopping back and forth on the path,[51] his eyes scanning the horizon. But there is no kangaroo in sight. Not a single one in any direction, or any other Wildlands animals, though Lucy does spot a brave chipmunk sneaking around one of the feeding stations for some abandoned treats.

"How many kangaroos are there at Wildlands?" Lucy asks.

"Three, but they don't always hang out near the path,"

---

51 It makes sense that Harrison would love kangaroos. After all, Harrison loves to hop and kangaroos move by hopping instead of walking.

Alex says. "They could be in their little shelter. Kangaroos aren't very active this late in the morning."

"But it's still possible for us to see them, right?" Harrison asks.

"Yes, definitely! And if one happens to cross the trail, just let them move across. Ours are pretty shy, so it isn't likely, but you never know. Oh, and wait!"

Alex reaches into her pocket and retrieves the second walkie-talkie she picked up earlier. She feeds it through the fence until Lucy grabs it. She doesn't offer it to anyone else. Teamwork or not, if there's going to be a way to talk to her sister, Lucy would like to be holding that way.

"I thought the walkie-talkies weren't working," Lucy says.

"The long-range channels aren't working, but if we're close we should be able to reach each other on the short-range options. Let's test it."

Lucy walks twenty steps away and turns on the walkie-talkie.

"We're testing this, Annapolis!" Alex's voice crackles through extra clearly, and it makes Lucy feel a lot better.

With the walkie-talkies working, Lucy is ready to keep going. She follows the other three kids. Jemma has the map again, and Trey is busy looking out for clues or puzzles. Harrison is far too distracted looking for kangaroos to be doing anything else at all.

"I can hear you," Lucy says, and secretly, even if Lucy never likes being separated from her sister in a situation like this, she has to admit it's pretty cool to use a real walkie-talkie.

"I can hear you, *over*," Alex says, and Lucy can hear the smile in her voice.

"Oh, right." Lucy laughs. "I can hear you, *over*."

"Okay, I'm going to go try to shove that gate a little wider. You enjoy the kangaroos and find the puzzle, over and out!"

Lucy joins Harrison, Jemma, and Trey on the path. Grasslands roll out in either direction, and there aren't many trees around. It's amazing to be out here with no other guests. It feels like she can see for miles and miles, like she's on a real safari with nothing but blue sky and animals doing all the wonderful things animals do.

Except . . . there aren't actually many animals, aside from the chipmunk, of course, and a couple of long-billed kiwis, which to Lucy's surprise are about the size of an ordinary chicken. The kiwis are cute, but they aren't kangaroos, and Harrison seems to be taking the lack of marsupials especially hard.

He looks left and right and sighs. He looks left and right again and scuffs his sneaker in the dusty path. But all the sighs and kicking and searching don't seem to encourage any kangaroos to show themselves. If there actually are kangaroos in the enclosure to show themselves, which Lucy is beginning to doubt.

"Do you think they're all asleep?" Harrison asks.

"I don't think so," Lucy says. "Kangaroos are more diurnal than nocturnal."[52]

---

52 Technically, kangaroos are mostly active at dusk and dawn, and the word for those animals is *crepuscular,* which is a super-icky-sounding word, so Lucy avoids it unless absolutely necessary.

"What does *diurnal* mean?" Jemma asks.

"It's the opposite of *nocturnal*," Lucy says. "Animals that sleep at night and are awake during the day are diurnal."

"But if that's true, they should be out there, right?" Jemma asks.

Trey nods.

Lucy nods too. She stops and listens. She doesn't think kangaroos are particularly noisy animals, but shouldn't she hear something? Or see something? A twitching ear or a shifting tail—just some evidence of one of the three kangaroos that are supposed to live here.

"Wait, is that a fence in the back?" Harrison asks.

"I think so," Trey says.

"If that's the fence for the back of the enclosure, then we should be able to see the kangaroos," Jemma says. "It's not that far away."

"Maybe," Lucy says. "It's possible they provide them with a shelter that's outside the viewing area. Alex said something about that, and there are some trees hiding part of the fence."

But even as she says it, something feels wrong about this. About these missing kangaroos, and the way Mwanza was trumpeting earlier, and the fact that the Ambassadors didn't win that last puzzle before the Blue Team. Lucy can't put her finger on why, but it doesn't feel right.

Lucy keeps walking, noticing how very quiet and still the kangaroo enclosure is. It doesn't just look empty, it *feels* empty.

"I think they should be here," Harrison says softly.

He looks at Lucy, and she knows she should say something reassuring. She even wants to, but what would she say? The truth is, she thinks Harrison is right. The kangaroos should be here. And she doesn't know why they're gone.

"**M**aybe we should check the enclosure a little more carefully," Harrison says. "There isn't a fence keeping us on the path or anything."

Trey points at one of the signs on the edge of the path. LAND DOWN UNDER is at the top of each sign in a fun yellow font. And beneath that in a plain font: DO NOT LEAVE PATH.

"Okay, you're right." Harrison sighs and kicks the dirt again. "I'm just really bummed, you know. Kangaroos are my absolute favorite. Did you know they can box? I probably told you that, but did you know they can hop eight feet in a single jump?"

"Careful!" Jemma laughs. "You're starting to sound a lot like Lucy."

"Good," Harrison says with a grin. "Lucy is supersmart and cool."

Lucy's chest feels tight and her neck feels warm, but there aren't all the swirling, squeezing terrible feelings that come with one of her attacks. She mostly just feels nice that someone would say she's cool. Nice and a little embarrassed, maybe. Nice-arrassed?

Lucy shakes her head, ready to change the topic. "Come on. We really need to stop looking for kangaroos so we can get to the puzzle. Alex is still stuck back there."

Lucy does want to get to the puzzle, and she is worried about Alex, but despite what she said, she absolutely, positively does *not* stop looking for kangaroos. And if you ask Lucy, though no one would ask anyone about this, she doesn't think Harrison gives up on finding one either. Trouble is, they don't find one. Not an ear or a tail or even a wisp of fur floating through the air. It's like the kangaroos just hopped away.[53]

"We must be close to the gate," Jemma says, consulting the map again. "This section is only supposed to be a quarter of a mile long."

The path curves to the left, and before anyone can answer, the gate appears in the distance.

"I think you're right about the map," Trey says. "This is the gate."

When Harrison approaches, the tablet gives a soft ping and begins to glow. It's the signal that tells them another puzzle is about to appear!

Lucy steps up beside Harrison so they are shoulder to shoulder at the gate. Metal letters at the top spell out THANK YOU FOR VISITING THE LAND DOWN UNDER, but other than that, she doesn't see anything noteworthy at first. Then she notes a large dull green rectangle attached to the middle of the gate.

"What is that green thing?" she asks.

"Whoa, I almost didn't see that," Harrison says. "It's like that green they use at Disney World so that people in

---

53 Interestingly, kangaroos can only hop forward or from side to side. Their anatomy, and especially their large, powerful tails, don't allow for hopping backward.

the park don't notice behind-the-scenes stuff and can just enjoy the fun things."

"Like that shade?" Jemma asks.

"Oh, sort of like camouflage!" Lucy nods. "Animals use that too!"

Harrison stops. "Wait, animals use go-away-green paint so people won't notice behind-the-scenes stuff?"

"No, no, but I think it's the same concept. Like, an octopus will change its color and texture to blend into parts of the ocean floor so that predators don't look at it. Chameleons do that too."

Lucy moves a little closer to the gate, where she spots a familiar lock with a glowing red light. "This must be it. I found the electronic lock."

"I think that thing has hinges. Is the puzzle inside?" Jemma asks.

"Yes, we're supposed to open the cover," Harrison says. "Sorry. I didn't look at the tablet, but it does say to open it."

He turns the tablet toward them, and words are now blinking on the screen. *Remove the green cover.*

Jemma steps forward to unfasten the small latches, but then she frowns. "Well, this is a problem. They're stuck."

Trey leans in close and squints at the latches. "I think they might be rusted."

"Um, that's not great," Harrison says. "The tablet already pinged."

Lucy tenses. He's right. The Ambassadors' letter said they would start each puzzle as soon as the ping alerted them that Lucy's team had found the puzzle. But this time they haven't found the puzzle. Or they've found it, but they can't get to it.

"Can we work them back and forth? Try to loosen them maybe?" Lucy asks. She moves closer and tries to demonstrate, but she can't even get a fingernail under the latch.

"Okay, we need to think of another way. How long has it been since the timer pinged?"

"Two minutes and twenty-four seconds," Harrison says. "There's a timer at the top."

"Bluh, this is a nightmare," Jemma says. "Maybe we should just pry it open." She tries to tug at the cover too, and she does manage to get her nails underneath the bottom. But after it moves a fraction of an inch, she pulls her fingers loose and it snaps back into place.

"What about the other hinges?" Trey says. "Maybe we can unscrew them."

Lucy shakes her head. "We don't have any tools. How long now, Harrison?"

"Three minutes and twelve seconds."

Worry stabs through Lucy's middle. They can't lose their lead. They have to get this puzzle open, and fast. She paces a few steps in one direction and then a few in the other. Then she shakes her head. "We have to think outside the box."

"Ha!" Harrison says. "Outside the box. That's pretty good since we're currently trapped outside a box. Oh, that's what I'm good at! Leah always says I have a different way of looking at things, which I try to tell her is because

I have ADHD and I can barely sit still for enough time to actually look at anything for very long but—"

Harrison cuts himself off and tilts his head like he's heard an interesting bird or maybe like he's had a flash of inspiration. Before Lucy can ask, Harrison snaps out of it with a big, hard exhale of air.

"I think I know what to do. But I'm going to need some ChapStick. And this is going to ruin my toothbrush, so somebody has to explain it to my mom."

Lucy has no idea how a toothbrush and ChapStick are going to help, and she doesn't know why Harrison even has his toothbrush on him, but when she checks the tablet, the timer is now at four minutes and twenty-six seconds. The Ambassadors have been working on this puzzle for almost five minutes and they haven't even seen it yet!

Lucy searches around in her pockets, finding a tube of lip balm. "Will this work? It's more squirty than sticklike."

"That's even better!" Harrison says. He's already handed the tablet to Trey, and now he's rooting through his backpack.

Lucy is absolutely, positively sure she's never seen such a messy backpack in all of her life. There is a wadded-up sweatshirt and a granola bar wrapper and a crumpled math worksheet that she's pretty sure looks like one from the unit two months ago. Finally, Harrison pulls out a red toothbrush. He blows some bits of paper off the bristles.

"Got it! Now I need the lip goop," he says.

Lucy tosses over the tube and then watches in horror as Harrison squirts a ton of the balm onto his toothbrush and then more onto the latches.

"Um, I'm not really sure how this is going to help," Jemma says, but Lucy is actually starting to see a plan.

"You're going to try to break down the rust layer!" Trey says. "Like on the Cool Science videos!"

"You watch those too? They're totally awesome," Harrison says, and he starts to scrub the hinges with his toothbrush. The angle is awkward, and Harrison has to stretch his arm up to reach the higher hinge. Lucy can tell pretty quickly that he's getting tired.

"Here, I can take a turn," she says.

"Try the hinge again," Jemma says. She looks very, very worried now. She's standing by Trey and staring at the screen, and Lucy feels her stomach drop. She doesn't want to know how much time has passed. She knows it can't be good.

Lucy checks the bottom hinge, prying with the tip of her thumb, pushing until it hurts her skin and it—

Pop!

The bottom latch pops open.

"It's working!" Lucy shouts, and then she checks the top latch, but it's still rusted shut. A little flame of panic flickers in Lucy's chest. It's taking too long. They're going to lose.

"Here, let me try," Trey says, handing the tablet to Jemma.

Lucy gratefully hands over Harrison's now totally rusty, grody toothbrush. It's much easier for Trey, who is almost a foot taller than Lucy. He just reaches out and starts to scrub. He can probably see things perfectly because they're at eye level, not over his head.

And sure enough, before Lucy thinks it will work, Trey moves the toothbrush and reaches for the latch. At first, it doesn't look like anything is happening. Lucy watches the line form between Trey's eyebrows. She can tell he's working so hard, and she feels hope building and building in her chest. It has to work. It has to work. It has to—

Pop!

The second latch is loose! Trey pulls the lid and tugs the cover open.

"It's been almost nine minutes," Jemma says. She sounds like she might cry, and Lucy knows that feeling. She feels a little bit like that too. But she also feels like a person who isn't about to give up.

"Come on. We can do this," she says. And then she steps closer to the green box to see the puzzle inside.

What she sees is even more complicated and intricate than the ostrich blocks. Lucy takes a deep breath and squints at the scene in front of her. Eight circular metal discs are fitted into tracks on a slotted maze. Four sit on the top and four sit on the bottom, with tracks connecting each one to a central channel that connects each of the tracks. To make things more complicated, each of the discs has a different number of mixed-up letters that seem to be set into a similar track system on the discs.

READER NOTE!

TIME TO GET OUT YOUR PENCIL AND PAPER!

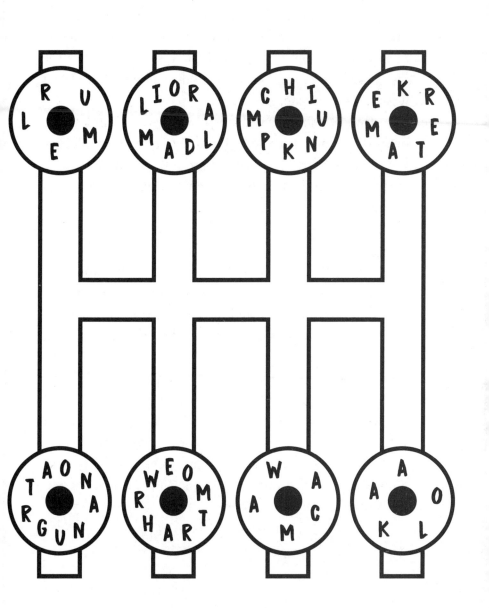

"I have no idea what this is," Trey says, but Lucy is pretty sure she's seen something a little like this before. She checks the grooves behind the discs and checks the discs themselves. And then she nods, feeling relieved that it isn't a total mystery.

"I think I know what this is," Lucy says. "I think this is one of those puzzles where you have to move each piece in the right order to get everything into the right slot."

"So the circle things can move along those slots?" Jemma asks.

"It looks that way to me," Lucy says.

"Agreed," Trey says.

"Oh, right!" Harrison reaches up to the puzzle and grabs one of the discs, shifting it down the track. He pushes it down and over a notch and moves it to a different vertical channel, so that it's stacked on the disc that's already there. "Okay, I think I get it. If I wanted to move this one here to the far bottom right, I'd have to move this other one out of the way first, and so on."

"Makes sense," Jemma says. "But how do we know which circle or disc or whatever goes in which slot?"

Lucy's heart drops and her face feels suddenly cold. Knowing what this puzzle is, is one thing. But solving it? She doesn't even know where to start.

CHAPTER 22

"It must have something to do with the letters on the discs," Trey says. "Those letters have to spell something, right?"

"Oh, sure," Harrison says. "The one on the top right definitely spells *meerkat*. Or at least it could spell *meerkat*. I guess it could also spell *mat reek*. Or *meek rat*. Or maybe lots of other things, but since we are in an animal park, *meerkat* seems like it might work."

Harrison is already shifting and spinning the letters on the bottom left disc. "Dudes, this is completely awesome. This whole thing is like one of my fidgets. The most enormous fidget ever."

"Okay, if the first one is *meerkat*, then maybe they're all animals," Lucy says. She looks at the other discs, but nothing jumps out at her. If there's one puzzle Lucy is worse at than cryptograms, it has to be word scrambles, but she's not the only one working, and the other three kids are figuring it out fast.

"There's *koala*," Harrison says.

Lucy tugs out her notebook and sketches out the puzzle quickly, just the lines and circles. Then she writes out *koala* above the disc in the position Harrison points at.

"That's *lemur*, maybe?" Trey says, pointing at another one.

Lucy nods and writes it down too.

"Oh, I see *orangutan*!" Jemma says.

"Keep going!" Lucy says, writing that one down too. She's getting excited now. They're already halfway there. "You guys are doing amazing! Only four left!"

Jemma smiles and calls out another one. And then Harrison. And then Trey. And then Harrison again, and Lucy realizes that all eight animals have been solved. Lucy helps Harrison rearrange the letters on each disc until they're in the right order to match the animal names. Then she stands back, feeling practically giddy. The animal names are all complete!

Lemur
Armadillo
Chipmunk
Meerkat
Orangutan
Earthworm
Macaw
Koala

"Okay, we got it!" Jemma says, clapping her hands. Then she turns. "Wait. The lock is supposed to turn green. There's supposed to be chiming. End of discussion."

"True," Trey says, looking uncertain.

Lucy looks at the puzzle again and touches the track. They haven't moved any of the discs on the track. That has to be part of it. "I think the animals are in the wrong places."

"Of course!" Jemma says. "That makes sense! So how do we figure out where they go?"

Lucy's chest feels heavy when she takes her next breath, and it comes out in a sigh because she is 150 per cent stumped. "I have no idea."

Everyone goes very quiet, and Lucy looks carefully at each disc and then at each animal name. This time there aren't any clues at all. So are they supposed to move them into order from smallest to largest? Or alphabetical order, maybe? Even if one of those is right, it doesn't explain what order they should follow.

"Should we just try to start arranging them?" Harrison asks. "I could just keep moving stuff around."

"We can't do that. It would be tens of thousands of possible combinations," Jemma says. "There are eight possible positions."

"Agreed. It wouldn't be reasonable to guess," Trey says.

"Besides, most of the other puzzles are about animal facts," Lucy says. "It's supposed to be educa-fun, right?"

"Oh, right!" Harrison says. And then his grin fades. "Only, what facts for what animal?"

Lucy has no idea. And she can feel that everyone is waiting for her. Because this is her part of the puzzle. She's the one who knows animals. Lucy takes a breath that feels a little tight in her throat. And is her stomach feeling a little twisty? It definitely is.

"*Lucy? Come in, Lucy?*"

Lucy startles at the noise coming from the walkie-talkie

clipped to her belt. Alex! Alex can help them! Lucy unfastens it and brings it closer to her mouth. "I hear you, Alex. Over."

"Did you get through the ostrich gate?" Harrison asks.

"I have to push the button," Lucy says. When she holds the button down, Harrison speaks again, practically screaming the words.

"DID YOU GET THROUGH THE GATE?"

"Well, I don't think the kangaroos will come back anytime soon," Trey says.

Jemma laughs. "I agree with that."

"I was able to get back into the ostrich enclosure, but the first gate that let us in is locked and the override isn't working. And there's more news. Over."

"What's the news? Over."

"Archibald got into the ostrich enclosure. That's a whole different gate system through the behind-the-scenes part of the park, so I think something is wrong with the electricity. It might be the same thing that's been wrong with the walkie-talkies, because our signal amplifier might not be working, which limits our range. Over."

"We'll come back to get you." Lucy turns to start walking, and then remembers, pressing the walkie-talkie button again. "Over."

"Solve the puzzle first. We need to see if that resets it. Over."

Jemma leans in and presses the button on the walkie-talkie. "We did find the puzzle. It's the one with the wheels and the scrambled-up animals."

"Oh, cool, I wish I could see it. Over."

"Except we can't figure out what to do now that the animals are unscrambled. Over."

"Okay, would you all like a hint? Because I still have my notes on me, but everyone should agree. Over."

Lucy looks up and Harrison and Trey nod, but Jemma's eyes look squinty and unsure.

"I don't like getting help on stuff," Jemma says. "But maybe a little teeny-tiny one."

Lucy nods and presses the button on the walkie-talkie. "We all agree to a hint, but we only want a small hint. Over."

"Like coaching, not like cheating!" Jemma shouts.

"Okay, one tiny coaching hint. Hmm." There is one hissy soft moment that tells Lucy that Alex is thinking. And then her voice comes back, bright and Christmas-morning excited. *"I got it! Four of these animals live in one general area and the other four live in another. Over."*

"Okay, two groups of four," Lucy says. "We'll call you when we solve it. Over and out!"

But Lucy's excitement fades quickly. "This might be harder than I thought. Koalas live in Australia and macaws are in South America, but orangutans only live on islands[54] in Asia."

"Could it be island and nonisland animals?" Harrison asks.

Lucy shakes her head. "No. Most of the animals live in lots of different places."

---

54 Sadly, orangutans are only found on two islands in Southeast Asia: Sumatra and Borneo.

Lucy looks with a sigh and sees the THANK YOU FOR VIS-ITING THE LAND DOWN UNDER sign at the top of the gate. Her eyes pause on the word *under*. She looks back at the puzzle and at the dividing horizontal line. There are four discs above this line. And four discs *under*.

"Wait, I think I might have something," Lucy says softly.

She looks again at the sign above the gate, the one that reads THANK YOU FOR VISITING THE LAND DOWN UNDER. And just like that, all the lightbulbs in Lucy's brain switch on at once. She lets out a breathy laugh. "I think I know exactly where the animals need to go."

CHAPTER 23

"It's above and under!" Lucy shouts.

But to Lucy's disappointment, the other kids don't offer high fives and fist bumps. They look at her with blank stares.[55] So much for the team mind-reading stuff Harrison claimed earlier.

"What's above and below?" Trey asks.

"The animals," Lucy says. "Some of them live below-ground. Earthworms, meerkats, armadillos, and . . . um, chipmunks too, I think."

"Definitely chipmunks," Harrison says. "Last summer we had a chipmunk living under our porch and he was digging out this huge pile of dirt and leaving this big hole and Mom was super ticked off because she kept sweeping the front sidewalk and she didn't know where all the dirt was coming from and then one day the chipmunk flew out of that hole and across the yard."

"Did it leave?" Trey asks.

Harrison waves his hands wildly. "No, no, it was a whole thing. It ran around the backyard and Wookiee was outside, so he started losing his marbles, running around

---

55 Lucy had a guinea pig named Gertrude who seemed to stare like this, but Lucy later learned that guinea pigs, along with many other small mammals, sleep with their eyes open, so she decided not to take it personally.

and barking like there was a murderer in the yard, but it was just this chipmunk and eventually he chased it into one of those downspout thingies on the house and bit the whole downspout shut and we had to call a repairman and everything."

"What happened to the chipmunk?" Lucy asks, and she's absolutely, positively sure the horror she's feeling at this story is showing all over her face.

Harrison just blinks. "Huh. I don't really know. Anyway, Lucy, what were you saying?"

Actually, Lucy has no idea what she was saying. Harrison's story wound in and out and up and down long enough to twist her brain into a confused little knot. She shakes herself to remember her train of thought. "Sorry, right. So, chipmunks, earthworms, meerkats, and armadillos all make homes in underground burrows. The other four animals live far above the ground, actually in treetops. They're considered canopy dwellers."

"Wait, what about orangutans?" Jemma asks. "Aren't they too big to be living in trees?"

"No, they definitely live in trees, but probably pretty big trees," Lucy says. "They live on jungle islands and their whole bodies are perfect for tree life. They have superstrong arms and a powerful grip in their hands and feet to help with swinging."[56]

In the distance, a small, excited elephant noise interrupts Lucy's orangutan speech. She pauses, and another

---

56 Male orangutans are so strong they can lift around five hundred pounds. This means they could pick up a fridge and a stove at the same time.

noise drifts across the park. Lucy smiles. It's too high-pitched to be Mwanza, so it must be Tabora. She trumpets over and over, like she's singing a song. Or maybe trying to drive her mom up a wall.

"That elephant sure is noisy today," Harrison says. "At least it sounds less angry. Earlier, I thought it was a lion roaring. Or maybe a dinosaur. Okay, I knew it wasn't a dinosaur, but still."

"The elephant we heard earlier was Mwanza. Her voice is deeper and louder because she's so much bigger," Lucy says. What Lucy doesn't say is that it's strange to hear Tabora *without* Mwanza. Especially since she heard Mwanza so clearly earlier. It's starting to feel like a whole lot of things aren't quite right at Wildlands.

If Lucy had a list, it would include:

1. An angry mother elephant.

2. Missing kangaroos.

3. Broken locks.

4. The Ambassadors not solving puzzles.

Lucy stops her mental list because she suddenly realizes how very wrong that last item is. The scoreboard at the top still shows the teams in the same places. If the scoreboard is right, the Ambassadors haven't even solved the scale puzzle, which was back with the ostriches. Have they really not solved anything in the last hour or two? Or is it like the cell phones and the walkie-talkie range and the Ambassador scores just aren't registering? The locks work like cordless headphones, but the tablets are too far away from each other for that, right?

"So what order should we put the treetop animals in?" Harrison asks.

Lucy shakes her head, trying to forget about her worries about the Ambassadors and what they're doing right now. "I'm not sure about the order."

"Well, why don't we try just putting them on the correct sides of the dividing line?" Jemma says. "Like, we'll put *orangutan* and *macaw* at the top. What are the others again?"

"*Lemur* and *koala* too," Lucy says, but she's only half paying attention because somewhere out there in Wildlands, Tabora is still making a lot of noise. Is she trying to get someone's attention? Lucy knows deep down how silly that is, but she's starting to feel a little bit worried and a little bit paranoid. Wor-anoid? It feels like the right word.

While Harrison lines up all of the animals, moving them along the tracks to the correct locations, Lucy listens to the elephant sounds that are continuing to fill the air. She can tell that Tabora is moving. Her little elephant trumpets are traveling back and forth, like she is running giant laps. Maybe because she's excited. Or maybe because she's in trouble.

The last thought comes in unexpected and unwelcome. Lucy tries to shake it off but notices Jemma looking into the distance with a frown.

"Is the baby elephant crying or is she playing?" Jemma asks.

The question leaves a prickle of fear running up Lucy's back. Is it possible that something really is wrong?

Lucy reminds herself that Wildlands is a protected animal sanctuary, and elephants living here are much safer than they would be in the wild. There are fences and security guards and cameras. Too bad all those reassurances do not remove the little wiggling worry that makes her face feel prickly and hot.

"Got it!" Harrison shouts. When Lucy looks, she can see that the four canopy-dwelling animals are on the top and the burrow builders are on the bottom.

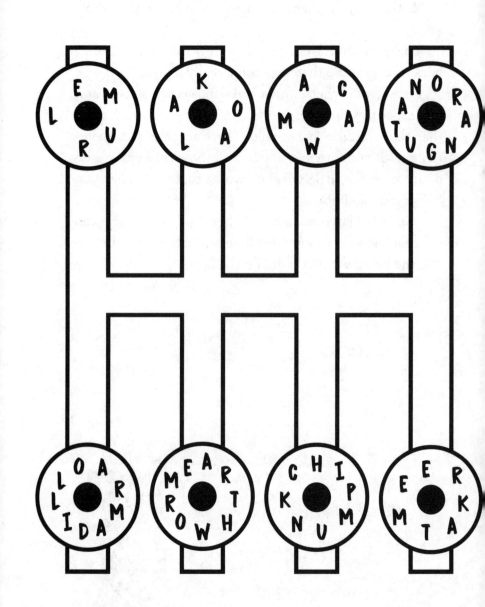

The screen flashes blue, blue, blue and the song chimes, chimes, chimes. But this time, when the other kids whoop and high-five one another, Lucy takes the tablet and looks at the finish time for their puzzle. Sixteen minutes and twenty-two seconds from the first chime.

"We're winning! We're totally beating them!" Jemma cries.

But Tabora is still crying in the distance, and Lucy feels like something is stuck in her throat. Maybe it is just a weak signal that's causing the Ambassadors' score to stay unchanged. Maybe they aren't actually winning at all.

But Lucy is pretty sure about one thing: Something is wrong at Wildlands, and whatever that something is, it's happening to Tabora.

The gate has clicked open and Harrison has wedged his messy backpack into the space to make sure it doesn't close. And now Lucy is trying to figure out how to explain her worries to a group of kids who might think she's losing her marbles like Wookiee with the chipmunk. Because "Hey, guys, I think the missing kangaroos and the Ambassadors not finishing puzzles might add up to some sort of mysterious terrible thing" feels a little wacky.

"Lucy, are you going to call Alex?" Jemma asks. "To see if the gate unlocked for her?"

Alex! Of course! Alex will definitely not think she's losing her marbles. Or even if she does think that, she will take Lucy's worries seriously. Lucy nods and pulls the walkie-talkie out, calling for her sister: "The gate is unlocked. Over."

After a brief delay, Alex's voice comes back through the walkie-talkie. *"That's awesome! I thought I heard you guys cheering, but I just checked the entrance gate in the ostrich enclosure and it's still locked."*

Lucy's stomach sinks even as she hears Alex walking on the other end of the walkie-talkie. *"Let me try the gate that opens into the kangaroo enclosure. Over."*

Lucy looks around and feels that wiggling worry begin

216

to grow. Her sister is still trapped, and now she can't hear Tabora. Ever since Jemma put the thought of the baby elephant being scared into Lucy's head, she can't shake the idea that Tabora did sound worried. Or scared. Or maybe both of those things. Like she's sca-rried. Though Lucy knows she might be thinking that since she's feeling pretty sca-rried herself.

The walkie-talkie crackles again. *"Well, everybody, it looks like I'm really stuck. Both of the gates are locked, and I'm trapped here in the middle."*

"We're coming back to you to strategize," Lucy says, and then she cringes because she knows she's supposed to act like part of a team, which means deciding together. But she didn't do that. And now that she's seeing everyone standing around the walkie-talkie, she feels a pang of regret.

"Um, is that okay with you guys?" Lucy asks.

"Sure, that's cool," Harrison says. "Alex will probably know what to do."

"But let's hurry. It looks like we're going to need to get through this whole escape challenge faster. On top of winning, I think we need to find help," Jemma says.

"True," Trey says.

Lucy moves fast with the rest of her team close behind. When she makes it to the gate where Alex is trapped, her sister waves with a big grin. "You guys are doing amazing!"

Lucy tries to smile, but it doesn't seem to stick. Her insides feel wobbly, like at any moment the dumb stomach somersaults might start again. She tries to speak, but she's breathing super hard from practically running the whole way.

"Whoa there, little cheetah."[57] Alex laughs, and even though she looks completely calm, Lucy feels super worried.

Something could go wrong! Someone could get hurt! And if either of those things happens, they are literally locked away from the only adult they can talk to. Lucy looks at her sister and tries to convey her panic without saying a word, because even though she's pretty freaked out, she's not so freaked out that she wants anyone to know she's freaked out (which is really the dumbest thing about freaking out).

Somewhere out there in the park, Tabora cries again. It's like the little elephant is trumpeting out all of Lucy's worries in the distance.

"I think Tabora sounds scared," Lucy blurts. "And the kangaroos are missing and the Ambassadors haven't won or even finished either of the last two puzzles even though they had way more time."

"Maybe they're not as good as us," Jemma says, puffing out her chest.

Lucy watches Alex's face very, very carefully. She can't be 100 percent sure that her sister hesitates before grinning, but she is 200 percent sure that Alex pulls out her walkie-talkie awfully quickly.

"I bet it's just the signal. But let's try to check in with everyone again," Alex says.

---

57 Lucy doesn't correct Alex, but it's not a great comparison. Cheetahs are made for sprinting and don't tend to run for longer distances too often. Then again, the length of two enclosures probably isn't a long distance in cheetah terms.

And she does try. She tries the security channel and the channel for the other camp, calling out to see if anyone can read her. She double-, triple-, quadruple-checks, and when no one answers, Lucy is sure that Alex's next grin is a little bit forced. Her sister is worried now too. And that makes Lucy feel like there's a lump in her throat again.

"I think you should keep going," Alex says. "Since I'm stuck and the walkie-talkie isn't working, that's the fastest way for us to get help for these gate issues we're having."

"What about the missing kangaroos?" Harrison asks. "I definitely feel like someone should know about those."

"The kangaroos are probably just hiding," Alex says. "They've never run off before. The gates are the real concern here. I think it might be related to our power grid somehow. I'm worried that's how Archibald got out."

Archie suddenly lifts his head. Lucy hadn't even noticed him before, but just like Alex said, he is in the ostrich enclosure, on the other side of the fence that keeps humans on the path and animals in the enclosures.

A new and scary thought roots into Lucy's mind. "If Archibald got out, could other animals get out?"

"It is possible," Alex admits. "But all of the more dangerous animals, like the elephants and the predators, have both electronic and physical locks, so I think things are mostly okay."

Lucy squints at her sister because she doesn't like the *thinks* and *mostlys* in that sentence. She'd really prefer more *absolutelys* and *definitelys*.

"What about cell phones?" Trey asks. "Is there signal anywhere in the park?"

"There is sporadic signal near the gate, but I left my phone back at the camp. That was a boneheaded move, I admit."

This situation is looking scarier by the minute. Lucy swallows hard and tries to understand. She doesn't know why some of the gates are working if others aren't. She doesn't know why Tabora is scared. And she doesn't know that she believes they're going to be able to get through all of this.

"We are in a bit of a pickle," Alex says with a sigh. And even though she looks a little bit worried, she forces a bright smile. "But I have all of you on the case, so it's going to be fine!"

"Tr—" Trey stops himself with a frown. "Are you sure that's true?"

Alex nods. "Absolutely."

Lucy notices that Jemma looks worried too, with eyes that are super wide and round.

"So you really think we should keep going?" Harrison asks. "By ourselves? My parents don't even let me stay home when they go to the grocery store. Though I think that has something to do with the time they went on a date and I made a smoothie in the kitchen without the lid on the blender."[58]

"I think you can do it," Alex says. "And I also think we

_____

58 Weirdly, Lucy's mom says Alex did something similar when she was little, but in that case she was trying to make one of those frozen fruit punches in a blender. According to Mom, Alex plopped the ice part in and filled the blender to the top with water and at some point the lid flew off. To this day there are a few reddish-purple stains on the kitchen ceiling, which Mom points out anytime someone asks for juice.

might as well try. Otherwise we're all stuck here until the zookeepers come at dinnertime. But the whole team has to agree. What do you say?"

"Let's do it," Jemma and Harrison say together.

"I agree," Trey says.

Lucy feels her stomach tumble over in a single, slow somersault. If there's one thing Lucy likes even less than having to do this without her sister, it's the idea of being the person to say no. Because the truth is this: If they don't get help, the animals could continue to find broken locks and open gates. Really bad things could happen. And Lucy has the chance to stop them.

"Yes, let's do it."

Alex reaches through the gate and touches Lucy's hand. "I know this isn't the escape challenge we expected, but you're going to beat it in no time! And then we'll stop for ice cream on the way home tonight."

"Ice cream sounds like the perfect way to end this weekend," Harrison says.

"Can I get a banana split?" Trey asks.

"Ew." Jemma frowns. "Fruit and ice cream do *not* go together. End of discussion. Now come on, let's get going."

Jemma and Harrison start walking, with Trey just a few steps behind. Lucy moves to follow but stops at the gate. Harrison is snapping and unsnapping again. Snapping and unsnapping. And every snap makes Lucy flinch. Her face feels hot and her stomach is swinging back, back, back.

"Uh-oh," Jemma says. "She's going extra pale again."

"I don't think it's a choice she's making," Harrison says.

Then he walks over to her with all his sticky-up hair. "How are you feeling, Lucy?"

Lucy takes a deep breath and looks back down the path. She can see Alex there, and she doesn't want to act like a baby, but she doesn't want to do this without her sister. How is any of this even happening? Why is everything going wrong?

But wait. What if it's not only going wrong for them? Something is happening in this park, and even though it's scary, they know how to get out and how to get help. They even know help will be coming by dinnertime at the latest.

But what about the animals?

Lucy hears distant elephant cries again and worry fills her mind. The Wildlands animals might be hearing strange noises from the broken gates or rumbles from those trucks that shouldn't be here. They could freak out or run or . . . Lucy tries to stop herself midthought, but her brain won't slow down. If the animals get scared and try to run, they could discover that the locks are broken. Which means they could escape. And then Lucy remembers the kangaroos!

Lucy rushes to the other kids. "You guys, I think we have a really big problem."

"What do you mean? Of course we have problems! Our chaperone is literally locked in an animal enclosure!" Jemma looks worried, and Lucy understands, but she shakes her head.

"It's a bigger problem than that. Something is wrong with the power at the park, right?"

"Right," Trey says.

"Well, if the power isn't working, then some of the gates might not be working either. There might be some places where animals could escape."

"Right," Jemma says slowly, looking uncertain. "But we don't really have a reason to think that's happening, do we?"

Suddenly Harrison, who has been very, very quiet, especially by Harrison standards, takes a loud, sharp breath. "The kangaroos are missing. The kangaroos could have escaped!"

CHAPTER 25

Lucy hurries to meet the other kids and tries to ignore the faint baby elephant trumpet noises coming from somewhere in the park. The only thing worse than Alex being trapped inside an ostrich enclosure and the possibility of escaped kangaroos is the fact that it's all happening while a baby elephant is crying desperately in the distance. It's very unsettling.

"So . . ." Jemma holds out her hands awkwardly. "What do we do now?"

The thing is, Lucy isn't quite sure what they should do. But before she feels the need to figure it out, normally quiet Trey gives a solemn nod.

"I think we need to go through the next gate. I think we've got to try to find help."

"Me too," Lucy says.

"Yes. A thousand times yes or a million times. Whatever lets us save those kangaroos!" Harrison says. "I'm worried about them because I'd be worried about any animal, but you guys know that kangaroos are my absolute favorite and all I've wanted all day . . ."

Harrison trails off, and Lucy can tell he's looking into the distance, toward the kangaroo enclosure. His mouth falls open.

"What is it?" Trey asks. "Do you finally see a kangaroo?"

"No. But I do see that camel."

Lucy follows Harrison's gaze to the fence at the back of the kangaroo enclosure. She does not see the kangaroos who should be there, but Archibald is wandering past just like Harrison says. He's getting in and out of enclosures on the behind-the-scenes side!

"The gates in the back definitely aren't working right," Jemma says.

"That could be bad," Trey says.

"What should we do?" Harrison asks as Archie steps through an open gate Lucy didn't notice earlier at the back of the enclosure. Harrison twists his hands, and his voice is sharp and high. "We can't just leave this random camel in here. What if he hurts the kangaroos?"

"Uh, didn't you say kangaroos can box?" Jemma asks.

Harrison straightens. "Oh yeah. They can."

"I don't think there's anything we can do anyway," Lucy says. "We couldn't catch him earlier, so I don't think it's going to be different now."

"Why do they even have gates back there, Lucy?" Jemma asks.

"Keepers usually have nonpublic entrances into animal areas for care and feeding."

"Really?" Harrison looks delighted by this news.

"That makes sense," Jemma says. "They wouldn't want entrances in areas that guests could use, but that means there have to be keeper gates on all the back fences."

"And apparently those locks are messed up too," Trey says.

"Wait a minute," Harrison says. "If the gates are messed up all over the park, how do we really know dangerous animals can't get out?"

That's just the thing. Even though Alex said it should be okay, she didn't sound sure. Lucy tenses, imagining cheetahs and rhinos breaking free of their fences to wander the park. The idea sends a creepy-crawly feeling up her neck. Having a stray camel running around is one thing. But Wildlands has lions and elephants. Even snakes! How many of the locks are broken?

Lucy shakes her head to push away the thoughts. She's sure there aren't any predators running loose. Then again, she was certain the emergency overrides would work, and they didn't. So, really, she doesn't know anything for sure.

Archie bends down to tug another clump of grass from the earth.[59] He looks right at them while he chews and chews, and Lucy imagines a lion in that grass right now, low down on its belly, watching the camel eat without a care in the world. Lions are masters of camouflage. If there's a lion out there right now, Archibald won't know until it's too late.

"I think we need to call Alex," Lucy says, and her voice squeaks.

Lucy isn't sure how Jemma got ahold of the walkie-talkie, but she has it now and is already pushing the button on the side. "Are you there, Alex? Over."

---

59 Camels chew cud, or half-digested food, over and over in a circular motion. It helps to mash the food for digestion, but it also looks incredibly silly.

Lucy counts three whole seconds before her sister's voice comes through. *"Hi there, how's it going, team?"*

"Well, it could be better," Jemma says. "We have Archibald here."

"Wait, you broke up there a little. Did you say Archibald is there? Where exactly are you?"

Lucy moves closer to the walkie-talkie with the others. "We're getting ready to leave the kangaroo area. I think he must have gotten in through one of the keeper access gates."

"But those are all locked by keeper keys, unless . . . Maybe they upgraded the locks on the back entrances already too." Alex trails off for a minute, and then her voice comes through smaller. *"Guys, we could have a real problem on our hands if they're all glitching out."*

Lucy's stomach swings back and her chest tightens. "A problem?"

"I know we're all going to be okay, but I think some of the animals might be in danger."

Lucy wonders if Archibald can hear Alex talking and if he somehow understands what she's saying, because he pauses midchew, watching with his large, dark eyes. Then his mouth begins to move again in that endless circular motion.[60]

"Okay, team," Alex says. *"I'm going to try again to reach*

---

60 Camels (and cows) actually eat twice, chewing and swallowing food and then regurgitating it to chew it again for easier digestion. This didn't sound too bad to Lucy until she learned that *regurgitate* means *barf.* Now the whole camel eating situation makes her a little queasy to think about.

security. But I need you to work on solving these puzzles fast. You're our best chance right now of getting help."

"What about Archibald?" Trey asks.

"Don't worry about Archie," Alex says. "He's pretty good at taking care of himself."

But Lucy can hear that there's something in the silence that follows Alex's words. Maybe Archie can take care of himself in another animal's enclosure. But Lucy has a bad feeling that not every animal would be so lucky.

CHAPTER 26

L ucy pushes open the gates, and the other kids gather around behind her. They might gather because they aren't sure what to do, or they might be doing it because she freezes the second she sees the next section. This is the brand-new Canopy Walk. Alex has been talking about it for months, about how visitors will climb several sets of staircases and will then walk through the tops of the trees to see the world from the view of a canopy dweller.[61]

After Alex went on and on about the Canopy Walk, Lucy told her it sounded completely awesome. And it did sound awesome. Before she flipped out on top of that viewing tower. Now completely awesome feels more like absolutely terrifying. She swallows hard and stares up at the giant, steep staircase directly in front of them on the path, one that leads up and up and up.

Lucy hesitates, because it's scary. But Alex is stuck, animals are missing, and locks are broken all over the park. Oh, and something might be wrong with Tabora, so she is absolutely, positively going to figure this out.

---

61 Canopy dwellers are animals that live in the treetops, like birds, tree snakes, and several species of monkeys. Interestingly, Wildlands does not have these animals, but a canopy walk is still a cool way to see savanna animals.

"You guys, listen to this," Harrison says. He's found a sign near the stairs and reads it aloud to everyone. "The Canopy Walk took almost a year to construct. It spans the width of the largest enclosure in the savanna area where herd animals have space to roam and graze much the way they would in the wild. Instead of interrupting that space or keeping visitors at a distance, the Canopy Walk allows guests to see the animals without disrupting their space. From the walkway, visitors can see giraffes, zebras, gazelles, and wildebeests as they graze, play, and rest in the enclosure below."

"Cool," Trey says.

"*So* cool!" Jemma says, sounding genuinely excited.

Lucy takes a deep breath and feels her insides curling up on itself. Her breath squeezes in, but her throat is growing tight. She stares at the steps leading up to the path and the beautiful carved wooden sign over the top that reads CANOPY WALK.

Jemma's eyes gleam with excitement. She claps her hands. "All right! Let's get a move on!"

Harrison doesn't even wait for her to finish. He sprints up the stairs, and Jemma is quickly on his heels. Trey starts to follow too, and naturally, Lucy does the only thing that makes any sense at all. She turns away from the stairs and tries to figure out a way to magic herself out of this enclosure and this park and this whole challenge altogether.

Sadly, none of those things happen. Lucy listens to the other kids thunder up the steps and crosses her arms over her middle. If Alex were here, she would tell Lucy that she can do this. She would remind her of all the things Lucy knows. Facts like:

1. The walkway is very safe. It's wide and sturdy, with high railings on either side.

2. When Lucy, Alex, and Mom go hiking in Hocking Hills, they are often on trails much higher than this, so really it's nothing new.

3. If Lucy doesn't try this, she'll always wonder what it's like to gaze down on a giraffe.

The last one makes her really want to try. She looks up, hearing Harrison and Jemma continue to thunder up the steps. But Trey has stopped.

"Aren't you coming too?" he asks.

"I . . . don't really like heights," she says. But that's not it. She's okay with flying and being up in skyscrapers and hiking in high-up places. It's just the idea of walking on small, wobbly-looking things. Like high ropes courses or viewing towers or . . . Well, or canopy walks.

"Okay," Trey says. Then he pushes his hands into his pockets and waits.

It's pretty obvious he doesn't know what to say, but he isn't leaving her behind or poking fun.

"Thank you for waiting for me," Lucy says, even though she can't imagine that another two minutes or two hours or two years is going to be long enough to convince her to do this. Except she has to do it for Alex. And maybe for Tabora. And maybe just a tiny bit for a chance to prove to herself and to the Ambassadors that she can do this.

"I'm going to try in a second," she says, even though she's not entirely sure that's true.

"Okay."

Lucy looks up at the top of the platform, where she can see sturdy handrails on either side of the walkway. And then she hears a strange, snorting *moo* sound. On the path at the top of the stairs, she hears Harrison gasp.

"Oh my gosh they're right there," he whispers. And this time, it isn't a Harrison whisper; it's a real whisper. Like he's seeing something truly magical that deserves a very soft voice. His feet move overhead, taking him from one side of the path to the other.

"We were looking on the wrong side," Jemma says softly. "They are so beautiful."

"Dudes, come quick," Harrison says quietly. "There are giraffes and zebras and little deer things and, um, maybe cows? Like big cows with horns?"

"Those are wildebeests," Lucy says automatically, and a fluttery feeling in her middle pushes her to put one foot on the stairs. She wants to see the wildebeests. And the giraffes. And all the animals he's talking about.

If she goes up there, she'll get to see them like Harrison and Jemma. This is her chance to see herding animals living the way they might live in the Serengeti. What if she doesn't get another chance like this for years? Shouldn't she try? If Alex or Mom were here, she would try.

And then she remembers . . . Alex needs her to try. They have to keep going, not so Lucy can be on the Ambassadors, or win the safari escape challenge. She needs to do it to tell someone about the gates, and about the noises she's hearing Tabora make. Even if she's never, ever an Ambassador, she will do whatever it takes to keep the animals of Wildlands safe.

Lucy's stomach feels like a swing moving back and forth, but she takes one step and then another. She keeps going until she's halfway up the first flight of stairs, and she thinks of animals each step of the way, the black rat snake and the giant tortoise in the reptile area. The eastern gray kangaroo that's missing and the dromedary camel who's wandering all over the park. When she pauses, she's surprised to spot Trey on the stair right beside her.

"You don't have to wait for me," she says.

"I think we're supposed to go together. That's what teams do."

Lucy feels a rush of gratitude when she nods.

Having Trey beside her helps her to keep going. Her knees shake and her palms feel sticky with sweat, but she thinks of other hikes she's done, like Delicate Arch in Arches National Park. She got through that. Though she was scared earlier on the platform and during that awful day on the viewing tower—even those terrible moments turned out okay. This will probably turn out okay too.

Lucy doesn't even know if she 100 percent believes that, but she 120 percent knows if it means helping her sister and Wildlands' animals, then she is going to try.

"I think you're doing really good," Trey says.

Lucy takes a deep breath and tries to smile. "Thanks, Trey."

And she keeps going. She takes it step by step, holding on to the handrail and feeling scared. But mixed in with that fear, she also feels pretty excited, so she's really just scare-cited. And the closer she gets to the top, the more sounds she hears from the enclosure below. Animal sounds.

At the top, Lucy's stomach instantly tumbles into a somersault. She squeezes her eyes shut and feels her face going hot and tingly.

"This is pretty high," Lucy says, and by *pretty high* she means *way too high* and by *way too high* she really means *get me off this thing right now*. But instead of saying that, she just holds the handrail extra, extra tight.

"True," Trey says beside her. When she opens her eyes, she sees that Trey is not holding the handrail and he does not look scared. Maybe she could feel less scared this time too.

Lucy looks out, and it feels like she can see forever, which is not a great thing when one is afraid of being high on a wobbly thing. Technically, this isn't that wobbly, but—

Lucy's thoughts are cut off by a barking, laughing sort of sound. A laugh-ark? What kind of animal makes that sound? She opens her eyes and looks down just as a zebra passes underneath the walkway. And then a second. She has never been so close to a zebra. She's never heard their strange laugh-arks or seen how lovely and warm their brown eyes are. They are so much closer than Lucy dreamed they would be.

She looks down to see more animals a few yards farther away. Zebras and wildebeests peacefully graze, and gazelles dart around the edges of the herd. But when Lucy spots a giraffe, she gasps out loud. The giraffes are by far the largest, almost comically tall as they strip leaves from branches in the high feeders with their long tongues.[62] Despite their size, they move slowly and gracefully, and while they can make plenty of noise, they are currently very quiet.

By contrast, the wildebeests are sending up a symphony of soft snorts and moos and the zebras are yipping back and forth at one another. It's like being inside one of those amazing African documentaries, only it's not TV. It's really happening and it's happening right here, thirty feet below them.

"Isn't it amazing?" Harrison asks. "I've never seen a giraffe up close like this. Except one time at the zoo but we were up high too and there were like twenty bazillion people around."

"It is cool," Jemma says. "I wish there was a ninja course or something. Or—ooh—a zip line like the one on the other side of the park."

Lucy does *not* wish there were a zip line here, but otherwise, she agrees with both of them. It's completely beautiful, and so surreal to see animals like this. She can

---

62 Giraffe tongues are eighteen to twenty inches long, which is the same length as Lucy's old cat, Noodles. Incidentally, a spaghetti noodle is around ten inches long, so a giraffe's tongue is also two spaghetti noodles long.

almost convince herself that she's in Africa right now, maybe in Tanzania on the real Serengeti.

"This is like a little tiny piece of Africa right in Ohio," Lucy says.

She looks at the zebras, and then the giraffes, and then two creatures hopping out from behind a large bush maybe a hundred yards from the rest of the animals.

Wait a minute—what was that?

Lucy looks again, sure she's confused. She examines all the pieces and parts. Large pointed ears, dark eyes, and that thick, powerful tail behind them. And then one of the creatures bounds forward in a single, unmistakable jump.

"Um, do you see that?" Lucy asks.

"See what?" Harrison asks.

"The kangaroos. I think I found them."

CHAPTER 27

Lucy points to the bushes where the kangaroos are happily nibbling on leaves in what is supposed to be the Serengeti savanna. Great for giraffes and zebras, but it's not really the right place for animals that exclusively live on islands six thousand miles away from the Serengeti.

"Oh, sheesh," Jemma says. "This is probably not good, right?"

"Nope," Lucy says.

"Are you kidding?" Harrison all but squeals. "I've been looking for these kangaroos all day. This is amazing! Oh wait. Do any of those animals eat kangaroos? I mean, are there kangaroo-eating things in the world? Or is there going to be some knock-down-drag-out kangaroo-zebra fight, because if so, the kangaroos are going to win. They box, you know."

"You may have mentioned it,"[63] Lucy says, and whatever worries she had before about being on this platform feel distant and small compared to the worry she has for these kangaroos. "This is really not a great situation. We've got to get in touch with security."

She tries to determine how far they can see from this

---

63 Harrison had indeed mentioned the boxing fact at least three times.

vantage point. She can definitely see the fence running along the back of the enclosure. It has to be the access fence the keepers use for care and feeding. At least one of those gates, the kangaroo gate, is not working. Well, and the camel gate. Unless Archibald is the Houdini of camels, he has a defective gate too.

Lucy wonders how many more gates might be broken and how many more animals are running loose. And then she spots something far beyond the fence that concerns her even more. Gray ears, long trunk. Small, stumpy body. Lucy takes a deep breath.

"I think I see Tabora. Back there beyond the fence."

"Oh yeah," Jemma says. "I see her! She is so cute."

"Shouldn't her mom be with her?" Trey asks.

Lucy searches the area for Mwanza, because she obviously can't be far. Elephant calves stay very close to their mothers.[64] But maybe they just can't see Mwanza? The enclosure Tabora is in is at least a football field away. She looks pretty tiny, perched where she is on top of the hill. So maybe Mwanza is hidden?

Except how would you hide a giant African elephant? Lucy watches Tabora wandering in circles on that hillside, her trunk swinging wildly. The baby elephant stumbles, looking a lot like a giant, clumsy puppy. It is one of the cutest things Lucy has ever seen, but it does not make her smile. Because Mwanza should be close. She would not let Tabora wander off.

---

64 When Lucy was in preschool, she had a friend named Grace who used to hide behind her mom, sort of clinging to her legs at all times, and every time Lucy sees a baby elephant, she thinks of Grace and all that clinging.

"Is it weird that she's by herself?" Jemma asks, and her voice is small and worried.

Lucy's heart feels small and worried in that moment too. She nods, because she doesn't trust her voice to stay strong, but she agrees with Jemma. Mwanza should be there, and she isn't. Not in the field or on the hill or even grazing somewhere farther away.

"Maybe she just wandered off on her own like the kangaroos," Harrison says.

"I don't think so," Lucy says. And her worry is growing stronger. "Can everyone look with me? Mwanza should be out there with her baby. Does anyone see her hiding?"

"Can you hide a ten-thousand-pound elephant?" Jemma asks.

"Female elephants only weigh around seven thousand pounds,[65] and believe it or not they can blend in when they aren't moving," Lucy says. What she doesn't say is that no, she doesn't think you can hide an elephant, regardless of their weight.

"Well, my eyeballs are searching all over that part of the park," Harrison says, "and I don't see anything but the little one."

"Me either," Trey says.

"She'd go to her mom, wouldn't she?" Jemma asks, and then she turns to Lucy with a frown. "You said baby elephants stay close to their moms, so why is the mom not here?"

---

65 Which is about the same weight as a large pickup truck, so maybe smaller than a male African elephant but certainly big enough not to be messed with.

"I don't know," Lucy says. "This could be super bad. We really need to get help."

"Would that truck be large enough to hide the big elephant?" Trey asks.

"What truck?" Lucy asks.

"It's way in the back. Behind the hill."

Lucy's throat feels extra tight and her hands suddenly feel extra cold. Her shoulders tense as she remembers way before. "Is it a delivery truck?"

"One of the boxy ones?" Trey says, and when Lucy nods, he nods back. "Yes, there is a white delivery truck out there in the field."

CHAPTER 28

Lucy's heart is dropping down, down, down into her stomach. She saw delivery trucks yesterday, and Alex specifically said trucks aren't allowed on nondelivery days.

Could these trucks be connected to the problems with the broken gates and missing animals? Lucy isn't sure, but she has that twisty intuition feeling again. There's something not right about a truck being inside the enclosure. Especially if it's one of the ones she saw earlier.

"I need to see that truck," Lucy says.

"I'll try to look," Jemma says, and then she climbs up on the first rung of the railing.

Lucy's heart gives a double thump as she watches Jemma. "Be careful."

"Relax, I won't climb any farther."

"Can you pick me up?" Harrison is asking Trey, and he's bouncing on his feet while he does it. "Like piggyback style? I only weigh like seventy-two pounds. Or maybe seventy-one? I can't remember, but it's not very much."

"Sure," Trey says, and then he's picking Harrison up and Jemma is climbing up another rung, and Lucy knows her heart is too young and healthy for a heart attack[66] but this is making her chest ping and cramp like she would imagine a heart attack would feel.

Jemma cranes her neck, searching the field where Tabora is still doing loops. Then her eyes go wide. "There! I do see it! That white one!"

Harrison leans this way and that on Trey's back. "Oh yeah, I see it! That is totally a delivery truck, dudes. Are they sending us like a whole, whole lot of pizza?"

"Why would they deliver pizza in the middle of a field?" Trey asks.

"They wouldn't," Lucy says.

"What's HTF?" Harrison asks. "Is that like Home Town Foosball? Or Henry's Taco Factory? I like tacos too, so that could be cool."

"It's not pizza or tacos," Jemma says, and she leaps down from the railing rung with a thump that makes Lucy's heart skip three beats. "Those things don't come in delivery trucks."

Lucy doesn't add anything to the pizza-taco conversation, because she's too busy trying to figure out what those two trucks she saw are doing, especially the one that might be in a field with Tabora. A field where Tabora is away from her mother.

Lucy's heart drops like she's swallowed a very heavy rock. A giraffe moves into her view, and it is shockingly close to the Canopy Walk. She stares as it turns its giant

---

66 Lucy was so worried about this for a while that Dr. Kern actually ran a test to assure her that her heart is in tip-top shape.

head, its dark lashes so delicate on its long, pale face. It is maybe the most beautiful animal she's ever been close to, and Lucy knows she has to figure out how to fix these locks to make sure this giraffe stays safe. To make sure all of the Wildlands animals stay safe.

Which means finding out what's happening with the one she knows is in trouble.

The beautiful giraffe turns away, its long bluish-grayish tongue[67] wrapping around leaves that have been threaded into a tall feeder. The zebras flick their tails and the kangaroos (who should not be here but are worth protecting all the same) happily munch on whatever they've found in the corner. And then Lucy takes a deep breath and steps up to the rail.

She is not tall enough, but she will be if she steps up on the bottom rung like Jemma did.

"Trey?" Lucy's face already feels hot and she hasn't even asked anything. "Could you stand here with me so I don't fall?"

"You won't fall," Jemma says kindly.

Harrison says, "But if you do, you might get to ride a giraffe, which would be cool."

Trey doesn't say anything, but he does step closer, so Lucy wedges her feet into the lowest slat in the railing. She can see Tabora, of course, and the hill, but nothing else. She stretches up to her tiptoes, feeling her heart pounding and pounding. And there it is, just like they said. A giant

---

67 Giraffe tongues are not blue because of a recent blue-raspberry snow cone snack but because of extra melanin in the front portion of the tongue. The back of a giraffe's tongue is a fairly standard pink color.

white delivery truck is parked in the field. She spots bright green letters on the door, an *H*, a *T*, and an *F*.

Lucy turns her attention back to the truck that she's 94 percent sure should not be in an animal enclosure. Then the truck starts moving, and that changes everything. Even if there is a reason for the truck to be there, Lucy is 1,000 percent sure it should not be driving toward a baby elephant. But that is exactly what the truck is doing.

"The truck is driving toward Tabora," Lucy says.

"What? Why?" Jemma asks, sounding alarmed.

"Does the driver see her?" Trey asks.

It's a good question, and Lucy can't imagine a way you wouldn't see an elephant, even a baby one. The truck slows and then lurches to a stop. Lucy watches, reporting every single thing she sees.

"Two men got out," Lucy says. "They're looking at Tabora."

"Oh, maybe they are zookeepers. Wave so we can get their attention!" Harrison says.

"They aren't keepers," Lucy says. "They aren't wearing uniforms. Remember, the keeper earlier had the khaki shirt, and they have special keeper vans. These guys are in sweatshirts."

"Then who are they?" Jemma asks. "Do you think they might be here to help?"

"I wish I did, but I don't," Lucy says, even though she knows she can't be 100 percent sure. The men stop walking in front of the truck. They point at Tabora, who is a little bit stuck in a corner behind the hill. At the base of the hill, the men bend down to examine the ground.

"They're looking at some mud," she says. "It doesn't make sense."

"Is the truck stuck?" Trey asks.

"I don't think so."

"Maybe they're worried about it getting stuck," Harrison says.

"Let me see," Jemma says, and she climbs up on the railing beside Lucy, except she doesn't go slow and she doesn't stay on the bottom rung. She stares out at the scene with the truck and the men and the baby elephant, who seems calmer, but that might be because there's a shrub between her and the truck. Maybe Tabora thinks she's hidden. Or that the truck is gone.

"They're getting back in the truck," Jemma says. "Maybe they just want to help Tabora. They could be vets, right? Or maybe Alex sent someone."

"Alex doesn't have her phone," Lucy says. "And Mr. Swendel said it's just him and us and the Ambassadors, and the Ambassadors are kids like us," Lucy says.

"Except for Leah," Harrison says. "She's with the Ambassadors team, right?"

"But they could be vets, right?" Jemma says, sounding desperate.

Lucy knows it's possible, but she can't imagine the keepers leaving a sick baby elephant away from its mom. Phoebe would be here with them, wouldn't she? Wouldn't lots of keepers be nearby? Before Lucy can ask any of those questions, the men start the engine again and the truck trundles forward, forward, forward.

"They're getting really close to that bush," Lucy says,

but as soon as she says it, she cringes, because they're not slowing down. They're speeding up! Lucy and Jemma gasp as the truck runs right into the shrub, sending branches flying. Tabora hurries backward, but she's running straight into a corner. There's a fence on two sides, a steep, steep hill on the third side, and a truck speeding right at her.

"Oh no!" Jemma cries.

Lucy's hands fly up to her throat as the truck rolls closer and closer. And she is too far away to stop it, too far away to do anything at all.

And just like that, a list counts itself off in Lucy's mind. All the things she knows about these men:

1. They do not work at Wildlands.

2. They are not here to deliver a pizza or anything else at all.

3. They aren't just driving in that field; they are *chasing* Tabora for a reason and Lucy's sure that reason can't be good.

CHAPTER 29

Tabora tries to get up the hill, but it's too steep. She stumbles back to the bottom and makes the most pitiful and frightened sound.[68] Lucy's heart squeezes and her whole body feels cold. And then she remembers! The walkie-talkie!

"We need the walkie-talkie," she calls. "We have to reach Alex!"

"I'm on it!" Jemma says, hopping down.

In the field, Tabora backs into the fence, and the truck lurches and then slows. And then . . . stops. Lucy holds her breath and waits one Mississippi, two Mississippi, three Mississippi. The truck doors open and the men hop out again.

Lucy sags in relief, knowing that Tabora might be stuck but she isn't going to get hit by a giant truck. Lucy hops down from the fence and turns to see Jemma fumbling the walkie-talkie out of her pack. "What do I tell her?"

"Just that Tabora is in trouble. Those men are not with

---

68 Elephants are highly intelligent, and baby elephants learn quickly that making certain kinds of noises will get them lots of attention. Some elephant babies will cry as if in danger to get their mothers to come running. But after a few episodes, those mama elephants can figure it out, and then the babies will be in big trouble.

the park. I don't know where they are from, but it definitely isn't good."

Jemma twists the volume knob on the walkie-talkie and then freezes. Lucy sees her eyes go very, very wide. Then her black braids shiver.

"Jemma?" Lucy asks. "Are you okay?"

"That's not the volume knob." Jemma's voice cracks and squeaks. "That was the channel knob. What channel is your sister on?"

Dread fills Lucy's heart. She has no idea. "I don't know. We'll have to try them all."

"There are like twenty channels," Jemma says.

"We'll just try them one by one," Harrison says. "Twenty won't take very long. But we should hurry, because this truck situation sounds like bad news."

"True," Trey says, and then he frowns. "But I think the truck is stuck."

"Stuck how?" Lucy asks, rushing back over to the railing to see.

"They stopped again. It rained most of the week, so the ground is probably really soft."

Lucy's hands feel shaky and her insides feel even shakier, but when she climbs back onto the bottom rung, she sees what Trey is talking about. The truck isn't moving. The men are still outside, and now they're squatted down near one of the tires.

Behind Lucy, Jemma calls Alex's name three times on channel 1, and then she switches to channel 2 and tries again. Lucy doesn't hear anything but a static hiss before Jemma moves on.

A long, whiny cry startles Lucy. She turns to see the giraffe who'd watched her earlier nudging into another giraffe near the Canopy Walk. Are they nervous because they sense how upset the team is? Lucy doesn't know much about giraffes, but they make strange sounds—a rasping-roaring-mooing kind of sound. A rasp-oar-oo? Then the same giraffe lets out a low, motoring snort.[69] If you ask Lucy, though the giraffe doesn't seem interested in asking any questions, she'd swear the giraffe was telling them to get moving.

Out in the field, Lucy spots Tabora rushing along the fence. The man on the left side of the truck shouts, and Lucy is 100 percent sure his voice sounds mean. Tabora bursts into a run, her trunk smacking hard into the man's outstretched arm. She flies right past him, her little elephant legs carrying her around the truck and out of the corner she'd been stuck in!

"She's out!" Lucy says. "She got away from them!"

Jemma and Lucy look at each other and share a huge grin.

"Dudes, that's totally awesome," Harrison says, but Lucy can tell he doesn't feel totally awesome about it. "The thing is, she's still in an enclosure, isn't she? And trucks can get unstuck."

Lucy's body goes colder and colder. Harrison's question is a good one. And it means the baby elephant is still in danger. They've got to get help fast.

---

69 Giraffes are often considered gentle and quiet giants, but in actuality they are very noisy animals who chirp, snort, and make sounds that are similar to moos. Sounds like they've got some tall tales to tell. Get it?

"We need to keep trying those channels," Lucy says. "And we've got to keep moving."

"You're right," Harrison says as they start down the Canopy Walk. "The faster the better. I just wish I knew what's in that truck."

"I don't think there's anything in that truck," Lucy says, and even though it scares her, she shares the rest of what she's thinking. "I feel like it might be here to pick something up."

"Like a baby elephant?" Trey asks.

Lucy does not want to admit that Trey's words are exactly what she's most afraid of. But she doesn't want to lie either. So she looks at Trey and nods, and Trey looks at Harrison and nods, and Harrison looks at Jemma and nods. And then Jemma smacks her fist right into her palm like she means business.

"Come on, you guys. We are not letting those men get away with this," she says.

"No way," Lucy says, and now there is a new heat in her chest and neck, one that feels a whole lot like anger. "They are not stealing baby Tabora on our watch!"

They race quickly down the walkway, and toward the end, Lucy has to step over a wide crack between planks. She still hates being up this high, and the idea of getting down is 100 percent ugh. Those stairs make her insides feel topsy and turvy at the same time. But Lucy doesn't have time to be afraid right now. Saving Tabora is the only thing that matters.

Lucy keeps on marching, and it works! She passes the giraffes and the zebras and then heads under the shade of a tree with a couple of wildebeests grazing below. Lucy keeps jogging behind her friends, and then, out of nowhere, the Canopy Walk narrows.

Everything feels shaky. Her knees tremble and her heart feels like it's beating too fast, but she knows she can't stop. She can't even take it slow and list a different animal for each step. Not this time. Tabora needs her. So this is what she has to do:

1. Take one step.

2. Feel absolutely, positively terrified.

3. Take another step anyway.

She keeps doing it over and over and over. Even though her hands are getting sweaty and her stomach is definitely doing lots of loop-de-loops, she is proud that she is moving. Lucy goes much, much more slowly than Harrison and Jemma, of course, but before she knows it, the narrow terrible part is over and she is stepping off the bottom step of the Canopy Walk.

Harrison's tablet pings from somewhere ahead.

"Dudes! Hurry!"

"Come on," Jemma says, and she isn't panting or red. She barely looks like she's been running at all, which is probably from all of the soccer running she does. "The gate should be just ahead."

"What about the walkie-talkie?" Lucy asks. "Have you reached Alex?"

"Oh shoot, I forgot after channel seven." Jemma hands the walkie-talkie to Lucy, who twists the channel knob to 8 and tries again.

"Alex, it's me, Lucy! Are you there? Over!"

More low, hissing static. Lucy hears a hollow ringing of something hitting metal and keeps walking quickly behind Jemma. She tries channel 9, which is more of the same, and then channel 10, which is when she almost smacks right into Jemma's back.

"Whoa!" Lucy says, looking up from the walkie-talkie, surprised that Jemma stopped.

The tablet chimes and Jemma just points. Lucy steps around her and freezes. The puzzle is directly in front of them, and this one is huge. Lucy immediately pulls out her notebook, because whatever this puzzle is, it looks like the most complicated thing they've seen all day.

CHAPTER 30

Lucy takes a step back. "Why does this puzzle look like the tub of cords in the back of my technology class?"[70]

Harrison laughs. But then he leans forward. "Wait a minute. My neighbor is a DJ and he sometimes does music at parties and weddings and stuff and those cords look kind of like his cords, which I know because Wookiee stole a whole bunch of them out of the back of his van when he was unloading one night and dragged them into my yard and it was a whole thing."

"Um, that's interesting," Jemma says, blinking. "But what are we supposed to do?"

Lucy nods, thinking the exact same question. She nods toward the screen, which Harrison has angled in a way that makes it hard to see. "Is the tablet giving instructions?"

"Oh yeah. It says: *Make the right connections.* That seems easy enough."

Lucy kind of agrees. The puzzle in front of them shows ten animal names and ten animal facts. Draped over a hook below the puzzle are ten old-fashioned connection cords with metal tips on each end. Now that she's closer,

---

70 Lucy's technology classes always seem to have tubs of random cords. Sometimes these are for teaching, but sometimes they're just all the left-over cords from old laptops and tablets that will never work again.

she can see that the cords look like giant old-fashioned headphone jacks.

"What even are those?" Jemma asks. "Why do DJs use them?"

"Those are audio connection cables," Trey says. "They're used to connect large speakers to sound systems, among other things."

"So is it going to play music or something?" Lucy asks.

Trey shakes his head. "I don't think they're using it for sound here. It's probably been coded so that only two matching inputs and outputs will work. And once the correct combinations of input and output connections are complete, the electronic lock will open."

Lucy stares at Trey, completely shocked. Her list for him might have been really wrong. She quickly revises it to:

1. Uses the words *True* and *Agreed* a lot.

2. Knows practically everything about plants.

3. Is very calm and patient, especially when others are feeling extra scared.

4. Apparently knows everything there is to know about sound cords.

"Let's hope you're right about the electronic lock," Lucy says, feeling like there's a knot forming in her chest as she stares at the red light on the lock. "This whole escape adventure isn't having the best of luck with the unlocking part today."

Lucy turns then to Jemma, who has stepped a few feet away and is back to trying to get ahold of Alex. It feels like they should have found the right channel by now, but when Lucy catches Jemma's eyes, Jemma shakes her head sadly.

"How many have you tried?" Lucy asks.

"Sixteen," Jemma says. "I think there are only twenty. But I can try again."

"Let's just keep trying them," Lucy says. "The rest of us will work on this puzzle."

Lucy faces the board and quickly jots down the facts on the right and the animals on the left. Now she's just got to figure out what goes with what. It sounds easy, but it's pretty clear it's going to test her animal knowledge to the max.

READER NOTE!

TIME TO GET OUT YOUR PENCIL AND PAPER!

Nine-banded armadillo

Chameleon

Grizzly Bear

Camel

Hippopotamus

Koala

Polar Bear

Giant Pangolin

Doesn't usually drink water

Can drink 50 gallons in 1 min

Can swim for days at a time

Rolls into a ball in defense

Bite can crush bowling ball

Tongue is as long as body

Usually has quadruplets

Closest relative is dolphin

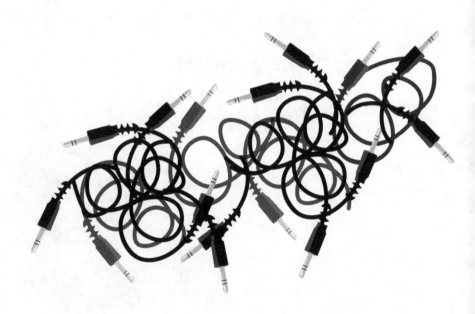

"It's lots of animal facts, but I don't think any of us stopped to read the signs along the Canopy Walk," Harrison says.

"It's okay," Lucy says. "I don't think all of these facts are on the signs anyway. Let's see what we know together. Maybe we've already learned more than we think, or maybe we know some stuff already."

"I bet you know stuff," Harrison says. "You know a ton about animals."

Lucy cringes at some of the facts. "I don't know all of them, though."

"It's okay, we'll use deduction," Trey says. "That's how Leah taught us, right?"

"Oh yeah! In any multiple-choice question, there are usually two answers that are sort of obviously wrong.[71] So remove those and then just look at the other two. Even if you have to make a guess, you have a fifty percent chance." Harrison hops twice, clearly happy to have remembered all of this. "Leah told me it's actually Alex's strategy."

"It is. And don't forget a fifty percent chance is always better than leaving it blank," Lucy says with a grin.

"And if you aren't sure, it's best to go with your first instinct," Jemma says with a smile.

It's obvious they've all heard the same lesson from Alex in one way or another. Lucy's proud that it's her sister's words sticking with all of them. She wishes she could tell Alex that it worked and that the strategy helped them win

---

71 This is a proven fact, which is why most multiple-choice tests feel easier and why teachers always make you do those ugh short-answer questions too.

the puzzle. But to tell her any of that, Lucy has to get her out of the stinking ostrich enclosure.

Also, she should probably solve the puzzle before bragging about solving it.

Lucy looks at the puzzle again, searching for the easy ones so they can start eliminating answers more quickly. "Okay, so I know the chameleon one. They have famously long tongues,[72] sometimes even longer than their bodies."

"Cool," Harrison says, and then he hunts around in the mess of cables, finding and plugging in the two ends to match up the fact with the animal.

"Is it the koala that doesn't drink?" Jemma asks. "I thought I remembered something like that about all the eucalyptus they eat."

"You're right!" Lucy says. "That's a great memory! And that means the drinking fifty gallons one is the camel, I'm pretty sure."

Lucy stands back to let Harrison untangle and do the actual plugging. She works with Jemma and Trey to figure out the animal facts, which are pretty easy now that a few are removed, except for the pangolin and armadillo, which everyone swears can both roll into a ball.[73] Lucy solves that

---

72 Chameleon tongues are super fast too. If they were cars, they'd go from 0 to 60 miles per hour in less than a second, which is a heck of a lot faster than Lucy's family minivan, which Lucy is sure takes about ten minutes to get up to 60 miles per hour.

73 Three-banded armadillos are actually the only armadillos that can roll into balls. But all armadillos have tough, shell-like armor that makes them look like little adorable animal knights.

one, though, when she remembers that the giant pangolin at the zoo gave birth to a single baby.

The remaining facts are easy because:

1. Polar bears *do* swim for days at a time, and if you aren't careful about which documentaries you watch on polar bears, you'll end up bawling your eyeballs out because sometimes those swims don't end well.

2. A hippo's closest relative is a dolphin, which Lucy remembers because she was so sure it was a manatee and was surprised to learn otherwise.

3. The grizzly bear has to be the one that could crush a bowling ball, because it's the only animal left. And also, did they have to use a clue that used something that's vaguely the same size and shape as a human head? Yikes!

Harrison inserts the final input and the connections are complete. Lucy stands back with an enormous sigh. But nothing happens. There is no chime and no light and absolutely, positively no clicking of a lock opening up on the gate.

"Did we get it wrong?" Lucy asks.

"Maybe we should switch that one we weren't sure about," Jemma asks.

Lucy shakes her head. "I don't think so. I'm like ninety-eight percent sure we're right on everything."

"True," Trey says. And then his brows pull together. "One of the connections must be loose. Did you check each of the inputs and outputs to make sure nothing jiggles?"

"They didn't seem loose," Harrison says.

But just to be sure, Lucy double-checks them one by one. And then she triple-checks them and checks them again. Everything seems perfectly fine.

"What is the tablet saying?" Jemma asks.

"The tablet still just says to make the right connections." Harrison shifts from one foot to the other. Over and over he bounces from foot to foot. "It hasn't changed a single bit."

Lucy frowns and steps back from the puzzle. "Trey, maybe you should double-check the cords?"

Trey checks the ports and cables just as carefully as Lucy did. He jiggles the inputs and tightens the outputs. But there is no clicking and no change on the tablet screen.

"Is it possible we're wrong about any of the facts?" Jemma asks.

"I don't know," Lucy says. Her throat feels tight and her eyes feel hot. "I'm sure they're right. I don't know why it isn't working."

"This is sort of ridiculous," Jemma says. "The tablet should say something, shouldn't it?"

"I think it's not working because of the electronic locks," Lucy says. "They're broken all over the park and now we're stuck just like Alex."

Her throat is feeling even tighter now. She tries to swallow, but her body won't cooperate. A panicky rush of heat bubbles up in her middle. And then the bubbles become fizz and her stomach swings back and starts to roll forward.

She can't be stuck in this enclosure. She can't let something bad happen to Tabora. Lucy's breath is coming too fast and she needs to slow down. She can feel the attack coming on. She takes a deep breath and then another. And then one more. Then she remembers the story technique and she begins to tell herself a story.

She is just a girl having a feeling in the middle of a wildlife sanctuary. The feeling is partly fear and partly stress and while it feels super overwhelming, it's only a feeling, and feelings don't last. This feeling will go away and she will be okay. The end.

It's a very nice story, but there's one teensy-tiny problem. Lucy doesn't believe it. Not even a little bit. Her stomach is doing somersaults and her face is hot. Her heart is pounding and pounding and it's not stopping.

Why won't it stop?

It should have stopped!

Suddenly, the hot, tight, somersault feelings explode in Lucy's body and every single part of her begins to shake.

"Something's wrong with me." The words blurt out super loud, and the tears are coming too. She can already feel them rolling down her cheeks. "I don't think I'm okay. I'm not okay!"

"What's wrong?" Jemma asks, and she sounds really worried. Which scares Lucy even more. She begins to pace back and forth and back and forth.

"I think I'm sick. I think something's wrong with me! I have to get out of here!"

"I think you're okay," Trey says in the same calm voice.

"She doesn't seem okay," Harrison says, and he looks worried too.

Jemma shakes her head. "She doesn't. What should we do?"

Lucy is still pacing and her heart is pounding and she's crying in great hiccupping sobs and it's all so loud. She was almost screaming and everyone heard! They're all hearing now and there's nowhere to go.

"I don't know what to do," Jemma whispers.

"We don't need to do anything, I don't think," Trey says.

"I'm not okay," Lucy says again around a sob.

"I think you are okay," Trey says again, and his voice is soft and gentle. And familiar.

His words are absolutely, positively familiar.

The realization breaks through the terrified fog surrounding Lucy. She stops pacing and turns to Trey. She hiccups on a sob, but her heart feels maybe 10 percent slower. Where has she heard those words before? He just blinks his dark eyes at her and says the words one more time.

"I think you are okay."

Alex. Alex says that to her when she's having a panic attack. Those words tend to give her a moment to regroup. When Alex thinks she's okay, she has to consider the possibility that she *will* be okay, because Alex is very smart and would never lie to Lucy. She trusts her sister.

But does she trust Trey? Lucy thinks about his steady presence beside her on the platform stairs, and his smile when they shared animal facts. Lucy thinks maybe she just might trust him.

Lucy's heartbeat keeps slowing. And a little bit after that, her tears stop. Everyone is still looking at her and her cheeks burn again, not with tears, but embarrassment. Why is this happening to her?

Trey is still calm as ever, but the others look very, very worried. Almost scared.

Harrison's shoulders are hunched right up to his ears. "Um . . . are you feeling better?"

"Yes. How do you feel?" Jemma asks, and she is not looking at Lucy like she's annoyed. It seems like she's genuinely concerned.

"I feel . . ." Lucy trails off, feeling heat flood her cheeks. She had a panic attack. A short one maybe, but she acted like a baby in front of these people and they all saw it. They all saw how weird she really is. Lucy's voice is very soft when she answers. "I feel embarrassed."

"Why?" Harrison asks.

She looks up at Jemma, Harrison, and Trey. She's never told anyone about her attacks. But she's never let anyone see them either. She usually goes to the nurse's station or hides in the bathroom, or like her earlier attack on the platform, curls into a ball to hide. But there's nowhere to hide out here, even now.

Harrison plops down on the ground with a sigh. "Did you know I once threw up in front of the whole class? And I wasn't even sick. I put an eraser in my mouth and I was spinning around in my chair and then the eraser got caught in my throat and I couldn't breathe so I ran to the teacher and she had to give me the Heimlich maneuver and I threw up the eraser and my lunch in front of the entire class."

"Oh my gosh, that's a total nightmare," Jemma says. "And kind of gross, no offense."

"It was pretty gross," Harrison says. And then he laughs a little. "It's funny now, but it sure was embarrassing."

Harrison sounds strangely calm and still, which is unusual for Harrison. Lucy turns around, daring a peek. Harrison is on the ground with his hair sticking up and his grin extra wide. He turns to Trey. "What about you, Trey? What's your most embarrassing moment?"

"I went to school on a Saturday."

"What?"

Trey shrugs. "I don't know why. I just got up like normal and put on my backpack and went to school, but it was a Saturday."

"Well, that's not too embarrassing. You probably just went home, right?" Jemma asks.

"Not at first," Trey says. "I wasn't paying attention and I'm always very early, so I didn't notice that there weren't any other kids. I went to the library, where you're supposed to wait if you're at school early, and I sat down and started reading."

"How?" Lucy asks, sniffling. "Wasn't the school locked?"[74]

"No," Trey says. "There was a special athletics meeting at the same time. So the entire football and lacrosse teams walked into the library and the coach asked if I was okay or if I needed help."

"Oh no," Jemma says, looking mortified. "And what did you say?"

"I told them I was just waiting for the bell to ring. Both teams started laughing and one of the coaches explained that it was Saturday."

"That sounds really awful," Lucy says.

Trey nods. And then Jemma clears her throat. "I cut my own bangs. And not like when I was in the third grade. I did it a few months ago. I saw this video and it seemed really easy,[75] but it was terrible. They were really crooked and Mom had to take me to get them cut again, but then they were super-duper short. I had to pin them back for two months."

Everyone chuckles, and then Lucy knows she's supposed to say something. That's how it works. Everyone else shared things and now she should too. But her stom-

---

74 The school is almost always locked after school hours are over, even though there are lots of doors. One time, Lucy missed a tryout (she doesn't even count that one) because she couldn't find the right unlocked door to get inside to actually do the trying out.

75 Videos have a way of making things that are a very bad idea look like a perfectly good idea. Lucy learned this when she tried to film a wasps' nest to learn about their activity but instead wound up getting stung four times and cracking her phone screen when she dropped it.

ach and throat are doing all the terrible things that got her here in the first place.

She doesn't know if she can do it. It feels impossible. But then she opens her mouth to explain about all the things she can't tell them, but the truth comes tumbling out instead.

"I have these things sometimes where my stomach feels bad and it's hard to breathe. It's like an attack."

"Like a panic attack?" Trey asks.

Lucy is surprised, but she nods and Trey goes on. "My sister had panic attacks. She doesn't now. She's on medicine."

"I'm on medicine too," Lucy says. And it feels weird. She's never admitted that out loud to anyone outside of her family. But to her shock, none of the kids looks at her like she's weird. They don't even look surprised.

"They don't know if we have the right medicine or amount," she says. "It's better, but I have to keep checking in with my doctor."

"That happens to me all the time," Harrison says, spinning around on the ground. "I've been on medicine since the second grade and we've had to switch it a few times. But we found one that works really good this year. I know you will too."

Lucy nods, feeling her face heat up. And this time it doesn't feel tomato-red hot; it just feels warm and cozy, the way she feels after finishing a great book or when she comes home from school to find her mom baking cookies.

"So you had a panic attack just now?" Jemma asks. Her

voice is very gentle, and Lucy decides she sort of likes this side of Jemma.

"Yes. I feel better now. I think it's hard being trapped in here. Especially since Alex is trapped somewhere else. And Tabora might be in trouble. I feel so helpless."

"I think I understand," Jemma says "I do hate that we can't do anything. But maybe we can. There's got to be a way to get out of here."

"We could wait for the electricity to turn back on," Trey says.

"We could climb out," Jemma says, and there's a wicked gleam in her eye.

"Maybe we should just body-slam into the gate or try to kick it open like one of the X-Men or something. Like hi-yah!" Harrison demonstrates with a pretend kick to the gate.

Except that he actually does accidentally kick the gate. And as soon as his foot connects with the metal, the gate clicks and clanks and then swings wide open.

CHAPTER 31

Harrison blinks and then scratches his head. "Dudes . . . do I have superpowers?"

"Don't be ridiculous," Jemma says. "Something must have happened."

"Or he has superpowers," Trey says.

Lucy doesn't really believe in superpowers, but she doesn't say that. Instead, she looks for an explanation. The gate is open, but the tablet still shows the solved puzzle with no happy chimes or bright lights.

Wait, is it possible that the Ambassadors finally solved a puzzle and somehow that unlocked the gate? But no. Lucy sees that the scorecard has not changed. Whatever is happening with the Ambassadors, they are either not solving puzzles or their tablet is not reporting when they solve them.

Lucy's eyes drift to the electronic lock above the gate latch. There is no red light. For that matter, there's no green light or any other kind of light. The lock looks like a plastic square and nothing more.

"The lock isn't functioning," Lucy says. She grabs the open gate and pulls it closed and then pushes it right back open. Sure enough, there is no electronic clicking or beeping. Because there is nothing electronic happening in this latch.

"If the locks are turned off, we don't have to solve the puzzles," Lucy says. "We can just run through the rest! We should be able to get there in no time."

"Maybe you're right," Jemma says "Come on, everybody!"

Trey pushes the gate open again and they peer into the next enclosure. The path before them is very different from the Canopy Walk. It's less like a safari or a zoo and more like stepping into someone's backyard. There is green grass with lots of bare dirt patches. Mostly dirt, really, and the keeper access fence on the left side of the path is much closer. There is also a small building with a red roof at the opposite end of the enclosure.

"This is a small area," Trey says. "What animal lives here?"

"I don't know yet," Harrison says. "I haven't found one. But since there's a house up there, maybe we're the animals and this is our exhibit."

Harrison starts cracking up, but Lucy is still trying to figure out what's going on. The signs in this area seem to be in the process of being installed. She sees short poles here and there, but the wooden signs are still blank. The plastic signs she's seen in other parts of the park haven't been attached. So she'll need to figure it out by clues. Like the bare patches of dirt and the plastic kiddie pool half full of water. There are two doors leading into the building. The one on the trail is human-sized, but the one attached directly to the yard is much shorter, but wider.

"There aren't any signs," Jemma says.

"Well, whatever lives in here runs around as much as I do," Harrison says. "All the grass is trampled."

"Or eaten," Lucy says. "But I don't see an animal. Maybe it's inside the building. There's an animal access door there."[76]

Lucy looks along the tall access fence, which rises up on the far left side of the enclosure. There are lots of big boulders near the fencing, so maybe this animal likes to climb? Lucy notices the little square electronic lock on the keeper access gate.

"That lock back there is just like the others we've seen, and I don't think it's working either," Lucy says.

Jemma nods. "You're right. There's no red light."

Lucy nods. Just like the lock on the gate entering this enclosure, the lock on this gate is not blinking or shining. It's just sitting there doing nothing to hold the gate closed. And then, as if the gate realizes nothing is actually holding it closed, it wiggles.

"Um, why is the gate moving?" Jemma asks.

The gate wiggles again, pushing open a few inches.

"Maybe it's a security guard," Trey says.

But Lucy can clearly see there isn't a person opening the gate. In fact, she doesn't see a person anywhere other than the four of them.

---

76 Many zoos and wildlife sanctuaries have doors like this that allow animals to choose the inside or outside areas of their habitats. They're like giant versions of the pet doors some people install at home!

"I don't see anyone," Lucy says.

"Maybe it's a ghost!" Harrison hops up and down three times. "That would be so amazing. What if this whole park is haunted and some sort of ranger ghost is running around letting animals out of cages and that's why the locks aren't working!"

"Ghosts aren't real," Jemma says, but then the gate opens another few inches and she frowns. "Are they?"

"No, definitely not," Lucy says. And then she sees something at the base of the gate, one of those big brown boulders. Only, the boulder is moving. Only it isn't a boulder. It's a giant tortoise!

"We're in Leonardo's enclosure," Lucy says. "He's a giant tortoise and he's Alex's favorite! She said they were moving him to a new, larger enclosure. This must be it!"

"They could have given him some nice grass if it's new," Jemma says.

"I'm sure they did. He probably ate it,"[77] Lucy says. "He's been here for several months; it's just the first time I'm seeing it."

"Well, several months or not, he must not like it here very much," Harrison says.

"Why's that?" Jemma asks.

"Because it looks like he's on his way out," Harrison says.

Sure enough, the gate pushes open farther, and Leonardo trundles forward. Lucy's heart squeezes with the

---

77 Giant tortoises can go up to a year without eating if necessary, but they love fresh grass and will happily graze on any they find until there's nothing left but dirt.

same fear she felt when she saw that truck driving toward Tabora. It's the fear that something bad is about to happen. But this time, she knows how to stop it.

"Come on, you guys." Lucy steps over the railing that keeps Leonardo off the footpath.

"Um, what are you doing?" Jemma asks.

"She's breaking the rules, I think," Trey says.

"That's true, but I don't think we have a choice. We have to save Leonardo." The tortoise in question is already halfway through the gate. If she doesn't stop him, he could wander into the elephant area or the Serengeti enclosure. There are so many animals that could step on him and hurt him.

"How on earth do we save a giant tortoise?"[78] Harrison asks.

"I'm still coming up with a plan, but we're going to figure it out," Lucy says, picking her way carefully across the small enclosure, trying to stay on the bare patches of dirt.

"Let's do this," Jemma says, and she climbs over the fence to join Lucy. "Giant tortoise rescue mission, here we come!"

Lucy stops when she's close enough to see that the giant tortoise is currently stuck in the fence. The right side of his shell is catching on the gate's frame, which might be the only reason he hasn't pushed the gate all the way open.

"We've got to get him back inside before he figures out

---

78 In most situations, giant tortoises don't need saving because they don't have natural predators, but they also don't normally live where elephants can squash them to pancakes.

how to get unstuck," Lucy says. "And we need to move really slowly. We don't want to scare him."

"But if we scare him, won't he run back inside?" Jemma asks.

"If he's scared, he might pull into his shell."

"Well, couldn't we just turn him around if he does that?" Harrison asks. "He'd be like a giant Frisbee."

Lucy turns to Harrison. "Leonardo weighs four hundred and eighty-two pounds."

"That's a really heavy Frisbee,"[79] Trey says.

"Uh, that's way too big to move," Jemma says.

"I know how to do it," Lucy says, because Alex has helped with Leonardo's care, and Lucy has heard a lot of stories,[80] including stories about how to move him.

"So, what do we do?" Jemma asks.

Lucy smiles a little bit of an ornery smile. "I think we need to tickle him."

---

79 The world's heaviest tortoises are the Galápagos tortoises, which can weigh more than 900 pounds. Even heavyweight Frisbees don't weigh much more than 200 grams, which is less than half a pound.

80 Leonardo, like many tortoises, is a creature of habit, and when his round plastic baby pool was replaced with a rectangular plastic baby pool, he investigated the pool briefly and then went inside and refused to leave the indoor portion of his enclosure for a week. Alex had to lure him out with a trail of grapes.

CHAPTER 32

Lucy knows you don't just randomly tickle a giant tortoise. You need to think it over first, to make sure your tickling pushes the tortoise in the right direction. And Lucy wants to be double, triple, quadruple sure before she does this. She walks to the left and she walks to the right. She tilts her head until she's seeing the problem (and the tortoise) almost upside down. There are lots of questions in her brain. Does Leonardo know he's stuck? Does he know how to get unstuck? And why does he want to get out of his enclosure in the first place?

Leonardo stretches his head forward. His long neck strains and his mouth opens and for a moment, Lucy wonders if he's about to cry out. She doesn't think tortoises make noise beyond hisses and clicks, but she could be wrong. But then Leonardo lowers his head and his mouth closes on a clump of green, green clover.

He pulls back and munches slowly and thoughtfully, his head turned to the side so he can watch Lucy, except that's when she remembers.

"Leonardo is blind," she says. "Remember? Alex mentioned this earlier. He might not be totally blind, but he's not really seeing us."

"Then why is he outside the gate?"

"I think he smelled the clover outside." Lucy gestures at the tortoise, who is reaching for another clump of clover. "Leonardo loves clover. Well, he loves papaya too, according to Alex, but that's not the point. I don't think there's any clover left inside his enclosure."

"So he's going to keep wiggling until he figures out a way to get out," Jemma says.

"Probably," Lucy says. "Which is why we need to stop him."

"Okay, what do we do?" Harrison asks. "How do we stop a four-hundred-eighty-two-pound turtle? If we had Wookiee, he might be able to play tug-of-war with him. But I don't know if turtles play tug-of-war."

"Tortoise," Lucy corrects. "And like I said, we're going to tickle him."

Jemma waves vaguely. "Turtle or tortoise.[81] Either way, that's a whole lot of animal to get turned around. What's the tickling going to do?"

"It will annoy him a little, so he'll try to move away from it." Lucy carefully and slowly steps closer to Leonardo, who is reaching again. "He's pretty spry for an eighty-year-old."

"Wait a minute." Harrison shakes his head. "Did you mean an eight-year-old?"

"No, giant tortoises live to be well over a hundred in captivity," Lucy says. "There was one named Harriet who lived to be a hundred and seventy-six years old."

---

81 Turtles and tortoises aren't the same thing. Turtles have flatter shells that are streamlined for swimming. Tortoises have more domed shells.

"Dude, is there some sort of tortoise immortality potion? Or wait . . . are turtles secretly vampires? That would be so cool," Harrison says.

Lucy laughs. "No, they just live a long time. But that's beside the point. If the keepers need him to move, they get him to move by gently tickling his hind legs. Which is what I'm going to try to do."

"Won't that just make him move forward?" Trey asks.

Lucy nods. "I thought about that. My plan is to tickle his left leg only. If he pulls away from that, his body should move to the right. Does that make sense?"

"Tickling a tortoise to get him to move out of a gate he's trapped in?" Harrison blinks. "Um, no, it doesn't make sense. But I'm willing to try. How can we help?"

"I need someone to climb to the outside of the gate without scaring him."

"Oh, me!" Harrison raises one hand and then the other and then leaps up and down. "I can totally do that. It's like parkour, and I've been practicing parkour forever."

"Okay, but you can't hurt him. Or scare him."

"Dude, I totally have this! I've been climbing and wiggling and sneaking around my whole life. I was born for this!"

And sure enough, it looks like he was. Harrison drops his backpack by Lucy and then climbs onto the fence. He pulls himself up over the tortoise's giant shell, pivoting around him to the other side of the fence. There is one wobbly moment where Lucy is sure Harrison will fall. Or maybe make a noise and scare poor Leonardo. But Harrison swings his whole body around the fence and steps quietly onto the grass just at Leonardo's left side. Fortunately, at that moment, Leonardo's head is bent far to the right to grab another small patch of clover.

"Okay, now try to get on the other side of the actual gate so you can push it gently closed when he starts to move," Lucy says.

"You want me to push him with the door?" Harrison's voice is squeaky with worry.

"No, no. Just make sure he can't go back out. Every time he moves backward, you're going to close the gate a little more."

"Should we try to entice him?" Jemma asks. "Does he like carrots, like Archibald does?"

"That's a good idea!" Lucy says. "But Alex left them back at camp, I think."

"I have some in my backpack in a plastic baggie," Harrison offers.

Lucy does not know why Harrison has carrots in his backpack, but to be fair, she doesn't know why he has a lot of the things that he has in his backpack. Trey unzips Harrison's bag, which is still on the ground, and for one second, Lucy thinks he might pass out. Which sort of makes sense. Trey had every single lunch plate perfectly arranged and now he's peering into Harrison's backpack, where it looks like a small tornado formed inside and left all the contents in a jumbled heap. To his credit, though, Trey just retrieves the baggie of baby carrots and offers them to Jemma. But she shakes her head. "No way. I don't know anything about turtles."

"Tortoises," Trey corrects.

Lucy takes the carrots and pulls one out of the bag. She moves slowly so Leonard can see, and then remembers that he can't see well or maybe at all. She waves the carrot gently in the air instead. For a minute, Leonardo doesn't do anything. Then he slowly stretches forward, searching for the carrot. Lucy takes a step back, but the tortoise is already moving in, his mouth open wide.

Lucy drops the carrot and Leonardo sniffs back and forth at the ground, finding the carrot very quickly. He snaps onto the carrot with surprising force, moving his massive body to the left as he does. The gate creaks as Harrison closes it a few inches.

"Good job," Lucy says softly, watching in fascination as Leonardo chomps the carrot, finishing it quickly. He lunges toward her, looking for more, and she stumbles back. She's falling! Lucy catches herself on her butt and elbows and gazes up at nearly five hundred pounds of tortoise, which is definitely not lodged in the gate anymore and is instead coming right at her![82]

"Leonardo!" Jemma says.

The tortoise startles at her voice, and Lucy hears the gate creak again. She tries to slowly rise to sit up.

"Keep going, Harrison," she says, though her voice is very shaky and Leonardo is still much too close.

Leonardo's leg is only inches from Lucy's knee, and she's never thought of tortoises as dangerous in the least,

---

82 Tortoises are slow, with a max speed just over one mile an hour, but three-toed sloths are actually the slowest land animal at most zoos. They only move one foot a minute, so sixty feet would take an hour! Still, anytime a 482-pound thing is moving in your direction, it's normal to be alarmed.

but one look at his long toenails has her thinking again. And then thinking a third time.

She pulls open the bag of carrots and spills out two more. Leonardo is almost completely out of the gate opening now. Just a couple more steps and he'll be safely back in his enclosure. If they can figure out how to actually lock the gate to keep him in the enclosure, that is.

The tortoise takes a step and bites the carrot. Lucy fishes another one out of the bag and scoots back another foot. "Is he clear of the gate yet, Harrison?"

"Almost," Harrison says. "Just a few more inches."

"We need to find something to lock the gate once he's in," Lucy says. "Is there a manual lock?"

"I think so, but it's the kind that needs a key," Harrison says.

Lucy notices Trey standing up a little straighter. "I can tie knots."

"Can't everyone tie knots?" Jemma asks.

"Possibly, but I can tie forty-two different kinds of knots. Maybe more, but I'd have to look them up."

"I didn't even know there were forty-two kinds of knots,"[83] Jemma says.

"It's not going to matter if we can't find string," Harrison says.

"It's not going to matter if we can't get Leonardo to go for another bite of carrot."

---

83 There are 196 basic knots, but thousands of variations when you consider all the different combinations and flourishes that can be added. This is normally not the kind of fact Lucy would be interested in knowing, but she studied knots hoping they'd be part of the Ambassador tryout.

At that moment, Leonardo lunges forward. His mouth gapes open, and Lucy is surprised by how pink his tongue looks, considering every other part of him is brown and gray. She pulls the carrot back a few inches and lays it in the grass. Leonardo finally moves another step forward.

Harrison quickly slips back inside the enclosure and closes the gate as Leonardo finds and chomps the carrot on the ground.

"Well, that's one thing solved," Harrison says. "Now we just need rope."

"What if we cut my headband?" Jemma asks. "Is that long enough to use for a knot?"

"It should be," Trey says. "As long as we don't think this tortoise is going to be able to pick a knot loose."

"I think he'll be preoccupied by carrots for a bit," Lucy says. She feeds him another and begins to leave a couple here and there. There are only nine left after she feeds the first few, so she has to make them stretch. She leaves them around the enclosure, being careful to keep them as far away from the gate as possible.

Leonardo begins to amble toward the first pair of carrots, and as he passes, Lucy allows herself a gentle touch of his shell. It is the most wonderful thing she can think of, somehow smooth and bumpy all at once. Best of all, the shell feels warm from the sun. Lucy closes her eyes and tries to memorize exactly the way it feels to touch a giant tortoise's shell.

Is it something she might get to do again if she gets to be an Ambassador? Speaking of the Ambassadors—she still can't help but wonder where they are and what's happening with them. She wishes she could leave something for the Ambassadors—some sort of flag or signal to tell them they're in trouble. But the Ambassadors are on the total opposite side of the park. It feels hopeless!

Harrison closes the gate, and the noise brings Lucy back from her thoughts.

"Dudes!" Harrison says. "We saved a giant tortoise!"

All four kids cheer and clap, and then the cheering is so loud. Shockingly loud. Like a blaring trumpet is right in the enclosure. Lucy takes a sharp breath and her heart does a double thump. They all fall silent and Lucy can't hear a thing except for the sad, rasping trumpet in the distance.

Except Lucy knows it is not a trumpet at all. It's Tabora, and Lucy's absolutely, positively sure the baby elephant is in trouble.

CHAPTER 33

"We have to hurry," Lucy says.

"I'm trying to rip the headband," Harrison says.

"Let me try," Jemma says, but as hard as she pulls, she can't tear it either.

"Maybe I don't need to tear it," Trey says. "It might work if I just stretch it and use a more basic knot."

Trey gestures for the headband and loops one end through the other. When Trey said a basic knot, Lucy expected something like tying a shoelace, but his long, dark fingers are quickly twisting and looping the headband until it's a large knot jutting out from the gate latch.

"Do you think it will hold?" Jemma asks with a frown. "I mean what if that tur—tortoise gives it a push?"

Trey shrugs. "I think a determined-enough person could get it open without much trouble. I'm not sure about a very determined tortoise."

"Well, let's hope he's more determined to find all the carrots," Lucy says, wiping her hands on her pants. She steps back to watch as Leonardo stretches out his long neck and then slowly moves toward the next pair of carrots.

Harrison balances on his right foot and then bobbles left to balance on the other. "You know, I thought tortoises were slow. Leonardo is pretty speedy."

Lucy nods. "Tortoises aren't as slow as people think.[84] I don't think Leonardo is fast enough to chase a cheetah, but we need to try to be that fast. We can't forget about Tabora and those trucks. I think we need to go through the building. Can you check our route, Jemma?"

Jemma pulls up the map. "We have to go through the building to leave the savanna and enter the forest. The forest is a smaller section, and I think it starts inside the building here. Which I think is for lots of reptiles, not just the tortoise."

The little elephant trumpets again in the distance, and this time, the sound feels almost hopeless. Has Tabora given up? Is she injured? Or is she just scared because she can't find her mom? And for that matter, where is Mwanza? She should have shown up by now, unless something bad happened. The idea of it makes Lucy's chest feel heavy with worry.

"Let's hurry," Lucy says. "I don't like the way she sounds. And I don't know how long it will take them to unstick that truck, but it won't be forever."

Lucy leads the others inside the building. Everything looks just the way Alex described it. There's a soft glow from behind the wall panels on the right and left. The giant tortoise does have a special indoor area with a warming lamp, lots of foliage, and a large indoor pool; but Lucy's eyes are drawn to the other glass-fronted enclosures lining the hallway ahead.

The building itself is distinctly warmer than the air

---

84 And they aren't as slow as sloths, as noted before.

outside,[85] which is only one of the ways Lucy can tell they have entered a new habitat. Each of the enclosures to her right has lots of leafy branches and floors that resemble a forest floor. Even the building itself is shady, with giant tree branches crisscrossing the ceiling. Dark green leaves of various shapes and sizes dangle down from the limbs, and Lucy has to move more slowly while her eyes adjust to the dim light.

"There's a door leading to outdoor forest exhibits," she says, pointing to a sign overhead.

Jemma shakes her head. "That's a dead end. It's just a short loop through an area with deer and sloths and a few other forest things, I think."

"Okay, let's keep going," Lucy says, leading them quickly down the main hall. She resists the urge to read the various signs beside the enclosures, because she loves reptiles and wishes she knew more about them. This would be an excellent place for learning—that is, if they weren't desperately trying to release Lucy's trapped sister, save a baby elephant, and ensure that all of Wildlands' animals are back in their correct enclosures.

Jemma comes to an abrupt halt in the middle of the building, her sneakers squeaking on the tile floor. Lucy turns at the sound, surprised by the way Jemma's hands have come up in front of her, like she's trying to stop a bull.[86]

---

85 As cold-blooded creatures, most reptiles do best with heat lamps in their cages and warmer temps altogether. It's almost always summer in reptile habitats.

86 For the record, holding your hands up will *not* stop a bull. Actually, the only way to stop a bull is to keep your distance and a sturdy fence between yourself and said bull so it doesn't get started in the first place.

"Um." Jemma's voice is small and shaky. "Are there snakes in these exhibits?"

Lucy nods. "All of Wildlands' reptiles are here, and I know they have several snakes. Definitely a black rat snake and a milk snake, because those are both Ohio natives. They could have . . ." Lucy trails off, realizing that Jemma isn't moving. "Are you okay?"

"She looks kind of freaked out," Harrison says, and he takes a few steps back toward Jemma too. "Dude, are you freaked out?"

"Yes I am freaked out!" Jemma whisper-screams. Her hands are clenched into fists and her eyes are very, very wide. "I don't like snakes. I don't."

That's right! Lucy remembers the tents at camp and Jemma's snake comments then. Now they're with real, live snakes, and poor Jemma looks like she's seen a ghost. Lucy looks around. There is an enclosure to the right where a black rat snake is curled up near his water dish, just as she suspected. And she sees another snake, some sort of python or boa, she thinks, in the enclosure to the right of the black rat snake.

"Well, I know they take in injured snakes, and all sorts of reptiles that have been rescued from the pet trade after being abandoned. Often people will buy things like pythons or iguanas, but then when those iguanas grow far larger than expected, the people no longer want them."

"But there's nothing poisonous in here, right?"

Lucy absolutely, positively doesn't want to tell Jemma about the red circle with the word *venomous* typed on the glass on two enclosures just left of the boa. Unfortunately, her face must give everything away, because Jemma's eyes widen to teacup saucers. And then to dinner plates. "Do you mean to tell me we're in here with a poisonous snake? And the locks are broken!"

Harrison, who has clearly also seen the *venomous* sign, takes a few steps toward the enclosure. "Whoa, there are poisonous snakes in here? That is so cool!"

Lucy tries to think of something reassuring to say, because Jemma is breathing in fast, shallow pants. "I don't like snakes," she says. "I don't like them. I do *not* like them."

"I don't *think* they make electronic locks for these kinds of enclosures," Lucy says.

"You don't *think*?" Jemma asks.

Lucy squirms. "Well, I can't be two hundred percent sure, but it doesn't seem likely."

Impossibly, Jemma's eyes get even bigger. Her voice is so squeaky now that she doesn't sound like herself at all. "So you aren't two hundred percent sure that there isn't a poisonous snake trying to escape his cage right this minute?"

"Well, this one isn't trying to escape right now," Harrison says, peering into the enclosure.

"See?" Lucy asks, gesturing at Harrison.

"How do you know?" Jemma asks.

Harrison shrugs. "Because he's not in there at all."

Lucy looks at Harrison and Harrison looks at Trey and Trey looks at Jemma. And then Jemma screams and starts running as fast as she can through the building.

Lucy takes off after her, with Harrison and Trey just

behind. They race past the venomous snake enclosures,[87] and several other reptile enclosures, including one for an iguana and one for a chameleon. Lucy spots the other end of the building and the exit door they're looking for just in time to see Jemma push it open and burst outside.

The tablet pings in Harrison's backpack, but he doesn't pull it out. Instead, they all glance at the puzzle on their way out. Lucy just makes out enough to know it has something to do with animal speeds and looks like it might involve math. If you ask Lucy (and the people who designed this whole thing might want to ask, because she's got some strong words about backup systems for them), math shouldn't be included in this sort of challenge.

Jemma stops abruptly ten yards into the next area. She bends over with her hands on her knees. Her face is bright red. "Please tell me there are no snakes out here."

"Well, I don't see any snakes," Lucy says. What she does not say is that there are snakes on every single continent except Antarctica,[88] so there probably are snakes somewhere nearby.

But now that she's looking, there aren't any animals nearby. Lucy scans the area they're in. A few benches and tables are nestled under tall trees and three pathways

---

87 Lucy notes that one is for the eastern copperhead and another is the timber rattlesnake, which are two of the three venomous snakes in Ohio. Neither is likely to be looking to bite anybody, but it still would be best not to sneak up on one accidentally.

88 There are twenty-six different species of snakes in Ohio, so chances are there was probably a snake near enough to have their feelings hurt by Jemma's comment.

leading off in different directions. Lucy spots a sign and checks it quickly. One path leads to the forest animals and the reptile building, and that's the path they just came from. The other two lead toward the parking lot and the aquarium, respectively. So which one would be a faster route to get help?

"Dudes, snakes are supercool," Harrison says. He's balancing on one foot with his arms out like airplane wings. "They don't even need arms and legs to do stuff. They're awesome."

"They can be awesome somewhere else," Jemma says with a shudder.

"Where does the map tell us to go next?" Lucy asks.

"The aquarium," Jemma says automatically.

"Would the parking lot lead to people or the guard area more quickly?" Trey asks.

Jemma pulls out the map and squints at the areas. "It's honestly hard to tell. The parking lot might be closer to the road, but the aquarium eventually leads us to the Lakeside Pavilion, which is where the two teams are supposed to meet."

And that reminds Lucy of something else, the fact that the Wildlands Ambassadors are totally out of contact and may have no idea what's going on. A terrible feeling swells in her chest. "Harrison, check the score on the tablet."

Harrison pulls out the tablet and quickly frowns. "It hasn't changed."

"I'm worried about that. The Ambassadors' score hasn't changed."

"Like I said earlier, maybe we're just good," Jemma

says. "Or maybe it's the bad signal we are having, like with the walkie-talkies."

"Maybe, but wouldn't they try to come over to check on us?" Lucy asks. "That's why they're here too. To help out with the testing, and if their score isn't updating, ours might not be either. So wouldn't they try to check in?"

"Maybe they're having trouble with locks in whatever area they're in. Maybe they're stuck, like Alex," Trey says with a frown.

"The Ambassadors were supposed to be on the other side of the park, weren't they?" Harrison asks. "Is that the side where the truck was?"

Lucy sees Jemma check the map and also sees her face crumple just before she nods. "It is the same side."

Lucy's chest feels extra, extra heavy. "You guys, those trucks are bad news. If they ran into the Ambassadors, I don't know what they'd do. We have to get help."

CHAPTER 34

"I know we've just been trying to make it through the puzzle, but what if we could signal someone now—like a mayday flag?" Jemma says. "Maybe we could alert the guards or find the Ambassadors?"

"What about this observation tower?" Harrison asks. "Maybe we could see some people from up there—people that could help."

"What observation tower?" Lucy asks, but as soon as the words are out, she sees it, tucked in behind a tree near the building. She doesn't know how she missed it, but it's there now—exactly the same kind of tower where everything went wrong for her before.

Lucy's mouth feels sour. The last thing on earth she wants is to climb up another observation tower, but if it gives her a chance of finding a security guard? Or maybe a keeper or someone who might be able to help them and get these bad guys away from baby Tabora . . . Well, that's worth facing all the scary stuff in the world.

"This is a great idea," Jemma says, and she's already rushing for the tower, bounding up the rickety stairs two at a time. Harrison and Trey quickly follow.

Lucy turns away, feeling her stomach clench. Then it

swings back and rolls forward at all the bad possibilities that could happen. An invisible hand seems to squeeze her throat, and her heart starts going faster. But then she remembers, she did the Canopy Walk. She got through that just fine, and that was high up.

Lucy takes a deep breath and then another. No matter how she feels, she has to keep going. She has to keep putting one foot in front of the other.

She climbs very, very slowly, and holds the rail very, very tightly, and feels very, very frightened with every step. But after a lot of steps, she reaches the top. She closes her eyes and her stomach rolls over with a flop. Everything around her feels windy and wobbly. It also feels 100 percent terrible, but if she's completely honest, it is maybe 3 percent less terrible than the last time she climbed something high. Three percent isn't much, but it is something. Maybe 3 percent will make it easier to look again too? Because she has to look. There's a chance that looking could save Tabora and maybe other animals too.

Lucy cracks one eye open and then the other. The park is all around her, green grass and rolling hills and blue skies. Her heart is pounding again, super fast, but she just holds the handrail tighter and keeps taking one slow breath after another. Just like the steps on the Canopy Walk. Just like the hike at Arches National Park. She spots some of the enclosures she's passed and then the area with the white truck that chased Tabora.

But Lucy remembers something from earlier. There

was a second truck. She looks at the railing where the other kids are peering out instead of clinging to the handrail at the top of the stairs like her. "There should be two trucks. Does anyone see a second white truck?"

"I see the truck that got stuck," Jemma says.

"Hey, there's some writing on the door, I think," Harrison says.

Lucy looks out and spots the truck. She squints extra, extra hard, because she sees the writing Harrison is talking about. And she can almost make out the green letters on the driver's-side door.

"Is that *BTP*?" Lucy asks. "Or is it *HTP*?"

"It's definitely an *H*," Harrison says. "I'd recognize the *H* anywhere because my name starts with an *H* so I write it a lot, you know."

"But I can't tell about the *P*," Jemma asks. "I think it's a *P*?"

"It's an *F*," Trey says, his soft voice strong and confident. "The letters are *HTF*."

Harrison shifts to balance on his left foot. "Yeah, like Hang Time Friday. Or Huge Turkey Feet. Or Hip Tadpole Fashion."

"Or Happy Time Farms," Lucy says, her heart dropping. "Alex talked about this farm, remember? Mr. Swendel did too. There was a man trying to access animal areas. He was from Happy Time Farms. That's why they installed all these electronic locks!"

Jemma frowns. "But now those locks aren't working."

"Maybe someone *made* them stop working," Lucy says.

"I think the men in that truck are from Happy Time Farms and I think they are up to something really bad."

"What do you think they're doing?" Trey asks.

"They wanted some of Wildlands' animals, and after everything we've seen today, I think . . ." Lucy trails off because what she's about to say feels so scary and terrible. But sometimes you have to face the terrible, scary thing. "I think they're here because the park is closed, so they knew there wouldn't be much staff so it would be a good time to steal Tabora."

"That's why they were chasing Tabora," Jemma says, looking shocked. "And that's why they have such a giant truck. What do we do? And where is Mwanza?"

Lucy shakes her head. She has no idea where Mwanza is and no idea what to do, either.

"I see a second truck!" Harrison shouts. "Well, wait, it's gone. I think it went down that hill way, way over there. It has to be moving slow."

Lucy follows the direction Harrison is pointing in. The road winds up and down hills all over. "Jemma, can you tell me where that road goes?"

Jemma squints at the map and then gasps. "I think it goes right by the field with Tabora."

"And then where?" Lucy asks.

"If they keep driving all the way to the end, I think there's a back gate. They can get to the main road."

And get away with stealing Tabora. Dread sinks through Lucy's middle. If they don't stop that truck, the most adorable baby elephant in the world might disappear forever!

Suddenly, they hear a faint elephant noise, not too far away,[89] and definitely in a different direction. Lucy whirls around, but she can't see an elephant anywhere. And much, much worse, there's something else she can't see. The white truck that was in the area with Tabora earlier? It's gone!

"Does anyone see an elephant?" Lucy asks. "And what about the truck in the field, because it isn't where it was earlier."

Lucy doesn't know everything there is to know about African elephants, but she knows this much: Elephants are far too large to be easily hidden. But a giant white delivery truck would be big enough for a baby, at least.

"Look for people too," Jemma says. "We should be able to see the Ambassadors or the guards or something. There has to be something here other than mysterious white trucks!"

"Well, I do still see the giraffes and zebras and those kangaroos in the Canopy Walk. I think they really like it there, by the way, so maybe they should let them visit sometimes when they get this all sorted out.[90] Anyway, I can see our truck way, way over by the camp too."

"But we don't need to see our camp. We need to find the security guards or the Ambassadors and their camp counselor. That's all over there."

---

89 Elephant noises come in a variety of volumes and pitches. Many elephant noises are too low for human ears to detect.

90 Kangaroos probably would like any savanna habitat, but forests wouldn't work at all. Since kangaroos move by jumping and have a difficult time walking, too many obstacles would be a real problem!

Lucy searches in the direction where Jemma's waving, which is the other side of the park. She realizes too that they've walked half a circle. If Wildlands is a wheel, they have walked the top half and the Ambassadors are on the bottom half. Meanwhile, the security guards are somewhere in the middle, which is a long, long walk away. Lucy checks the area a little closer than the guard station, where a collection of unfamiliar roofs and fenced-in areas sprout up here and there. Several barns and paddocks are among the other buildings, but they don't look like the brightly colored buildings for Wildlands guests. Are they behind-the-scenes buildings?

"What's over that way?" Lucy asks, pointing to the area. "Is that maybe an area where we could find a keeper? They're coming back too, right?"

Jemma looks at the map with her thinking frown. She turns it this way and she turns it that way. And then she steps closer to Trey. "I don't see any of that on here, do you?"

"No."

"Maybe that's more of the backstage area," Harrison says. "My aunt in Florida works at Disney World, right? And I don't know if you've been but it's really cool and there's this super-fun hill at the Pirates of the Caribbean ride. It's my favorite ride, but it smells funny like an old person's house but also fireworks? There aren't fireworks, though. You should know that going in, because I expected them. Anyway, my aunt says there are large parts of the park that guests can't see so that we can just enjoy the experience of being in a magical land."

Lucy gasps. "Harrison, that's brilliant! Alex talks about off-exhibit areas for animals that are recovering or need a temporary space for enclosure improvements. Plus, some of the larger animals, like elephants and rhinos, have their winter barns away from the visitor areas."

"I see it," Jemma says. "That big barn right there? The one beside the road? It's attached to the big area with the hill where we saw Tabora."

"I see something," Harrison and Trey both say at the exact same time. But when Lucy looks, they're staring out opposite sides of the tower.

"Wait, what do you both see?"

"There is an orange shirt stuck in a building, and it's got a weird black blob. No, two black blobs," Harrison says. "Maybe a circle and a square?"

Lucy and Jemma look at each other and frown.

"What are you talking about?" Lucy asks.

Harrison points at the opposite side of the park. "Look way, way, way over there. Use the spyglass thing."

He scoots over to reveal a spyglass viewer mounted on the observation tower railing. Lucy inches closer bit by bit, her hands and legs shaking at the height. But then she grabs the spyglass and leans down to see better. There, far across the park, is a regular-looking storage building— nothing special at all if you don't spot the orange fabric dangling from an air vent at the top. It looks like it's been pushed through the vent from the inside.

The fabric is orange, like Harrison said, with a large black dot and another shape that's lost in a fold of fabric. It's way too far to see clearly, but one thing seems pretty obvious to Lucy. "I think someone pushed that through on purpose."

"Why would anyone be in there to begin with?" Harrison asks. "Isn't that like a storage shed or something?"

It is. And Lucy has a feeling that orange flag means something.

"What did you see, Trey?" Jemma asks.

"The truck that was stuck in the field isn't gone. It's backed up to that big barn."

"That big barn is in the same enclosure with Tabora," Jemma says, sounding worried. She turns the map so Lucy can see. "Look? See how they are all connected? It gets a little narrower here, but that makes sense. If that big building is their barn, they have to be able to get to it if it's cold or rainy or whatever, right?"

Fear crawls up Lucy's back like cold fingers. "Can you show me the truck?"

Trey points and Lucy's whole body tenses when she sees the white truck with *HTF* on the door. It's backed up close to the barn, and the tailgate looks like it's open. Worse still, there are two men getting out of the truck, and just like the two men in the elephant enclosure, they are definitely not wearing the khaki uniforms the keepers wear.

Lucy can't see any of the men's features, so she has no idea if they're the men from earlier or new ones. But she can absolutely, positively see the ramp that stretches from the truck bed to the ground in front of the barn. The men are standing on that ramp, waving their arms like they're gesturing at someone inside the barn.

"What is that ramp for?" Jemma asks.

Lucy isn't sure, but those men are definitely trying to get someone to come toward them. It's the way Lucy might try to get a frightened child to come out of hiding.[91]

"You don't think Tabora ended up running into that barn, do you?" Jemma asks.

But Lucy *does* think. She thinks of the men chasing Tabora in the paddock. And Mwanza's angry, frightened cry much earlier. Mwanza has been missing since they heard that cry. Maybe the reason she's missing is that she somehow got trapped in the barn and separated from Tabora. If that happened, the baby elephant would be desperate to get back to her mom. She would probably search anywhere, including inside barns.

But where is Mwanza? Lucy's stomach has that twisty intuition feeling again. The feeling that tells her those men did something to get the baby elephant away from its mom. They might have trapped Mwanza in one barn, and now they might be cornering Tabora in this one!

Lucy knows she can't be sure of anything, but just at that moment, a small, frightened trumpeting sound drifts through the air. It is 100 percent the sound of a baby elephant. And it is 100 percent coming from inside that barn. It's Tabora. Lucy is absolutely, positively certain!

Lucy gasps. "Those men are trying to steal Tabora now!"

---

91 Though the more she thinks on it, the more Lucy thinks it's a terrible way to coax anyone or anything from a hiding spot. Usually, it just makes said person or creature feel cornered.

CHAPTER 35

Lucy does not have time to be afraid when she runs down the stairs from the platform. She feels winded at the bottom, but the others seem to be breathing hard too. Lucy points to a path that leads to the road, and the group quickly runs to a wide wooden gate carved with various birds. Lucy sees a sign that reads AVIARY above the double doors before she pushes them open and steps inside.

"Are we sure this is right?" Lucy asks.

"Positive," Jemma says. "The aviary is the shortest route to the road."

Lucy looks around at their new surroundings. They are in a wide tunnel, with netting carefully spread above them and on both sides of the path. Trees and shrubs flank the walkway and a small stream bubbles along, crossing under a low bridge in the habitat. As beautiful as it is, Lucy is disappointed by the total absence of birds. Alex warned her that the birds weren't going to be moved into the aviary until the safety zone was created with an additional gate at the entrance and exit. Lucy can see the beginnings of these frames, but the construction isn't even close to complete. So basically, they're the only animals in this exhibit.

"Over there!" Jemma says, pointing at the far side of the enclosure. "I see a puzzle."

Lucy spots the puzzle and picks up her pace with the others. When they get close, the tablet pings with a puzzle notification. Lucy ignores it and tugs on the gate latch, but it doesn't budge. Jemma tries and then Harrison and even Trey, but it's definitely locked. And that's when Lucy notices the red light shining from the lock on the gate.

"Guys, the electricity on this lock is working," she says.

"Seriously?" Jemma says. And then she sighs. "Okay, let's just solve it fast."

"This is . . ." Lucy looks at the puzzle and then frowns. There are four vertical channels with different words or groups at the top. *Songbirds. Waterfowl. Raptors. Wading Birds.* She did an Ohio Birds project in 4-H in the third grade, but she doesn't know how much she remembers.

"Those are different bird group types, but I don't quite get what they want," Lucy says.

"I think it might have something to do with these little coins." Harrison points at a small tray beneath the puzzle, which is full of small wooden discs.

READER NOTE!

TIME TO GET OUT YOUR
PENCIL AND PAPER!

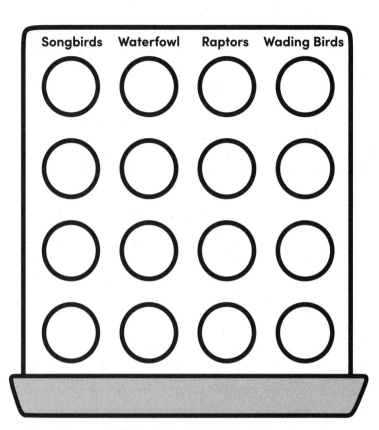

Songbirds Waterfowl Raptors Wading Birds

"Are those checkers or is there something on them?" Lucy asks.

"There are birds on them," Harrison says, and he picks one up and shows her.

"Ohhhh, I get it," Jemma says. "We have to figure out which category each bird disc belongs to and then slot them in. Like that old game with the checkers."

"Connect Four," Trey says. "It does look a little like that."

"Do the discs have bird names on them?" Lucy asks.

Harrison grabs one of the checkers and turns it over to look at both sides. "No."

"Well, then it's a good thing I know birds pretty well because we need to do this fast," Lucy says. "Tabora could be loaded onto that truck and driven out of here any minute!"

Jemma picks up one disc. "I actually know this one. It's a cardinal because of that crest. I know a cardinal is a songbird because we have them at our house a lot."

Lucy can think of other birds that also have the crest, like a blue jay or a cedar waxwing, but technically those are both songbirds too. "Okay, that's a good start. What's next?"

Harrison holds up another disc that has a bird with long talons on its feet and a curved, sharp-looking beak. "This one looks like a ninja bird. Look at those claws!"

Lucy nods. "I think that's some sort of a hawk. That's a raptor[92] for sure."

---

92 Other raptors include eagles, kestrels, and kites, and if you ask Lucy, which maybe someone should, they are by far the coolest bird group ever.

"Awesome!" Harrison slots the two birds into the corresponding slots and grabs the next one. A mallard, which is super obviously a waterfowl. Then there is a bald eagle, and a great blue heron. The list goes on and on, and Lucy doesn't miss a beat, but when she puts the last wooden coin, a bluebird, into the songbird slot, the tablet makes a low-pitched buzz. The screen turns red and large letters appear over the instructions: WRONG COMBINATION.

"What?" Lucy looks at the puzzle. "I'm pretty sure these are right."

"At least one of them isn't right," Trey says.

"Is it the last thing? You said it was a bluebird. Do bluebirds swim or anything?"

"No, bluebirds are definitely songbirds," Lucy says. "I don't know what we got wrong. I think they're all right."

"I think it's going to be one of the wading birds or waterfowl," Trey says. "You'd mostly find those in similar areas, right?"

"But they're completely different. All the waterfowl are really obvious. They have webbed feet and are generally made for swimming."

Lucy's voice is getting high and loud, the way it does when her anxiety is getting worse. She takes one deep breath and then another. And it does not make everything 100 percent better, but it is at least 10 percent better. And this time 10 percent is enough. Maybe she's getting better at this.

"I'm just not sure where I made the mistake," she says, much more softly.

Harrison balances on his left foot and then hops to his right. "Alex taught me that when you make a mistake, it's best to start the problem over. Let's take them all out and make piles."

Lucy quickly pulls the wooden discs out and separates them into piles that match the different categories. Lucy makes sure at least one other person agrees with her on the robin and the cardinal. There are a few others, like the great egret and the brown thrasher, that no one else knows, but when she's moving the thrasher, Harrison stops her.

"Are we sure about that one being a trasher?"

"A thrasher. I think so. Why?"

"I don't know. It seems like it has kind of a longer bill than the other songbirds. The raptors all have curved beaks that kind of come to a point. Like an upside-down hook. And all those waterfowl birds have beaks that are rounded like spoons. Which makes sense because eating bugs out of water is like eating soup, right?"

Lucy thinks about that, because Harrison has a point. But when she looks at the wooden coin she thought was a thrasher, she isn't sure where this bird belongs. "But this one doesn't have a rounded bill or a hooked bill."

"No, it's longer," Harrison says.

Trey nods. "True."

Lucy suddenly realizes exactly which birds this looks like. The wading birds. And then she notices something else that's different about the bird. The thrasher has a long tail that sort of sticks up behind it. This bird's tail is almost nonexistent.[93] Because it isn't a brown thrasher or any other kind of thrasher. It's a sandpiper!

"Harrison, you're right!" Lucy feels fizzy with excitement. "This isn't a thrasher; it's a sandpiper. And a sandpiper is a wading bird, just like you guessed."

Lucy moves the sandpiper from the songbird pile into the wading bird pile. Then each of them snags one group of the wooden coins and starts feeding them in. Lucy is the last one to drop a bird coin—the bald eagle—into a slot.

The tablet sings the happy chiming song and the screen flashes green, green, green. The kids cheer as they push the gate open and enter the next exhibit. This platform walkway is elevated maybe six feet off the ground, and a large plexiglass roof of sorts stretches across the entire enclosure two feet below the fence, where it is suspended by sturdy-looking bands. It's a little like being in one of those outdoor picnic shelters. If it rained, they wouldn't get drenched, but they sure wouldn't stay very warm.

Lucy looks around and notices that everything is quite different from the tortoise enclosure or the reptile building. "We're not in the forest habitat anymore."

"Nope, definitely not," Jemma agrees. "There were signs that pointed to the forest animals back by the viewing platform, but the map said we'd be heading here next."

---

93 The primary ways to identify a bird include color, size, habitat, and activity, but beak shape can be a very important indicator, which Lucy learned from her 4-H Ohio Birds judge, who was a very nice older man who smelled like a mix of old attic and dryer sheets.

Lucy turns back and forth, looking for some sort of information. "And where is here?"

Jemma starts to unfold the map again. "I'm not sure. It isn't marked on the map, but a lot of these areas are new, right?"

"We followed the path with the sign that directed us to the parking lot," Harrison says.

"Okay, so we just need to keep moving through here. Whatever here is," Jemma says.

If you ask Lucy, and they just might about this particular situation, *here* certainly looks like an animal enclosure. There's the fencing, for one. And there are large, sturdy boulders scattered around the enclosure. The rest of the ground is covered with sandy soil and scrubby-looking plants. It looks like the desert, except for the excessive number of holes.

"Why are there so many holes?" Harrison asks. "It looks like Swiss cheese around here."

"Didn't you say meerkats are burrowing animals?" Trey asks.

And at that exact moment, three things happen at once. Lucy sees a MEERKAT MANSION sign carved into the handrail. Jemma looks up from her map with a grin. And two tiny furry heads pop out of two different holes in the enclosure.

They've gotten to the meerkats!

"I have never seen a cuter animal in my life," Jemma whispers. And then, as if she is actually melting, she droops over the handrail until her chin rests on the wood.

Not that Lucy blames her. The first meerkat that poked

its head out is unbelievably cute, with its dark eyes and small ears.[94] The second meerkat had ducked back down, but now it's back too. It pulls itself completely out of the hole, and then two others emerge quickly from another nearby burrow entrance. Their long arms hang loose on either side of their furry bellies. And they stand up tall, dark whiskers twitching as they look this way and that.

"Omigosh, there are four of them, just like there are four of us," Jemma says.

"She's right!" Harrison says. The meerkat on the far left suddenly drops to all four feet, its thin tail rising like a flagpole behind it. It stands up and then drops back down. Up and back down, and then it rolls on one side to chew the tip of its tail. "Okay, that one that won't stop moving is definitely me."

"Then that tall one is me," Trey says.

"That leaves the middle ones for us, I guess," Jemma says. "What do you think, Lucy?"

What does she think? Well, she certainly doesn't think of herself as adorable, but one of the two meerkats in question is standing in the back and holding very, very still. That one has watched them all nonstop since it emerged.

"I think I might be that one that looks worried," Lucy says with a laugh.

"I don't know if that other one does anything that feels like me," Jemma says, and then, as if the meerkat wants to prove their connection, it suddenly sprints around the full

---

94 Meerkats, which are actually not related to any cat, are even cuter when they're close together, which is often, since meerkats are super-social animals.

loop of the enclosure. It's a blur of light brown fur rushing under the bridge and then down into a hole on the other side of the path.

All four kids giggle, and then the meerkat pops out of another hole and sprints back to the group, circling around them to try to get them moving. Now the kids' giggles are turning to full-on laughter.

"Okay, okay, the bossy fast one definitely feels like me."

"That's our team, then!" Harrison says. "We're the Meerkats!"

Everyone laughs, but even as the laughter fades, Lucy feels warmth spread through her chest. She mouths the team name silently to herself. Meerkats. So much has gone wrong with this escape challenge, and Lucy knows they aren't out of the woods yet. Alex is still trapped, that truck is still out there, and if those men manage to lure Tabora out of the barn, they really could kidnap her. But even with all of that being true, Lucy has to admit that being part of a team with a real name for the first time in her life feels pretty nice.

Lucy enjoys the feeling for one moment. Then she straightens and starts toward the other end of the enclosure. "Come on. We should go before they get Tabora into one of those trucks."

"Do you really think they can?" Jemma asks. "I mean, I know she's a baby, but she's a really big baby."

"You're definitely right," Lucy says. "Maybe she will be able to—"

Something slams in the distance, interrupting Lucy's sentence. She steps away from the meerkat rail, feeling a cold wave rushing up her insides. She hears a series of cheers from far away. The voices are low-pitched and grown-up and scary. Lucy's stomach turns to ice.

"Was that sound the tailgate of a truck slamming closed?" Jemma asks. Her worried face tells Lucy that she's already pretty sure about the answer.

"I think so," Lucy says, and she feels as close to crying as she's felt since she climbed the platform earlier.

"Does that mean they got Tabora?" Harrison asks.

"If they did, then we failed," Jemma says, her eyes welling with tears.

Suddenly, all the sad and frightened feelings in Lucy's chest harden into a tight, hard knot underneath her ribs. It feels a little like she ate too many hot dogs and a lot like she's really, really angry.

"No." Lucy balls her hands into fists. "If they haven't driven out of this park, then we still have a chance to stop them. We can still save Tabora!"

CHAPTER 36

They race for the enclosure gate with all four meerkats following behind, popping in and out of holes.[95] The meerkats keep their distance, but Lucy thinks they must be super-curious critters, because they are definitely watching the kids.

When they reach the gate, Trey stops to look out. "I can see the truck."

"What are they doing?" Lucy asks. "Are they driving?"

"No, they're looking at a map, I think," Trey says. "And talking on a walkie-talkie."

"They must be talking to the other guys. Their truck is outside," Harrison says. "Oh, maybe they need some sort of all clear! Mr. Swendel is up front, right? So maybe they're trying to figure out how to get the elephant-stealing truck out without passing the guard station."

"Maybe they don't know about the back gate?" Lucy asks.

"They'll figure it out soon enough," Harrison says.

"Okay, we have to get through here and then we can

---

95 Meerkats have very elaborate burrows with multiple entrances and exits for speedy getaways, or maybe just to create a supercool racetrack home.

dart out using this path," Jemma says, pointing at the map. Lucy sees the small trail that leads out of the animal exhibits to the main road.

"What if the truck drives through the fields again?" Lucy asks, remembering the horrible chase from earlier.

Trey shakes his head. "They can't. The truck will be too heavy with Tabora inside. They already got stuck once."

"Then they *have* to stick to the road, which means they'll avoid the guards if possible," Lucy says. "If they head the other way, we have a little bit of time. We might be able to cut them off."

Trey nods. "Then we need to find that puzzle, because this gate is working too."

"Yeah, good point," Harrison says. "Where is that puzzle? The tablet should ping."

"Maybe part of this puzzle is the fact that it's hidden," Lucy says. "Try to walk around."

"Dude, that's supersmart." Harrison slowly paces the length of the fence on either side of the gate, holding the tablet straight out in front of him. He walks one way and then the other, but there's no change. Then he walks straight back a few steps and—

Ping!

"Did you hear that?" Jemma asks.

Lucy rushes closer, looking all around Harrison for a puzzle. "Is there a message?"

Harrison pulls the tablet up and frowns. "The tablet says 'look down.'"

All four kids look down at the same time. At first,

Lucy only sees the boring wooden planks that make up the walkway. There doesn't seem to be anything different about them, until she sees a circular hole at the end of one of the planks.

"I think I see something," she says. Then she crouches down and carefully curls two fingers around the edge of the circle. It's dark under the walkway, and Lucy is worried. What if there's a spider? Or a bunch of biting ants? She'll have to take that chance.

Lucy pushes her fingers inside the hole and pulls. Three of the wooden planks come loose at once, swinging up like a tiny trapdoor!

"Whoa!" Harrison says. "It's like a secret compartment."

"Is there something in there?" Jemma asks.

"Tactical flashlight!" Trey says, rummaging in his pockets to produce one.

"I knew those would come in handy!" Harrison says.

Lucy turns the flashlight on and directs the narrow beam of light into the dark compartment. A sturdy wooden frame is resting inside. She tugs it out, and it's heavier than she expected. When she turns the frame over, she spots an old-timey phone keypad attached to the center. Each row has three buttons, and the first three have numbers like a cell phone keypad.

Trey moves in closer. "I think this is from an old pay phone."

"The tablet says to dial the numbers in the right order," Harrison says. "Press the pound sign between each dial."

"Which one is pound?" Jemma asks.

"I think it's the hashtag," Lucy says.

"Look at the clues that just came up," Harrison says. He turns the tablet so that Lucy can see five sentences below the keyboard. Each one of them has a blank to be filled in. And every last one is about meerkats.

READER NOTE!

TIME TO GET OUT YOUR PENCIL AND PAPER!

The meerkat's closest relative is the _____ (8).

A group of meerkats is called a _____ (3).

The meerkat that keeps a watch out for the group is called the _____ (6).

A meerkat's_____ (4) is nearly as long as its body.

As eaters, meerkats are primarily_____ (10).

"Okay, we have to do them in order," Harrison says.

Lucy nods. "A group of meerkats is called a *mob*, so I'll fill that in. And they have a *tail* as long as their body. Or almost as long, at least."

Jemma claps her hands. "Okay, let's just do what we did in that earlier enclosure. We'll run back to read the information signs and you fill them in as fast as possible."

"Oh, and if you have time, write down the numbers," Harrison says. "That way as soon as we have them all we can punch everything into the keypad and get out of here fast."

Lucy stays with the keypad and her trusty pen while the others rush back and find the other answers throughout the exhibit. The meerkat that keeps watch is a *sentry*, and though they do occasionally choose a fruit or other plant, meerkats are *carnivores*, and mostly eat insects and larvae. The closest relative is a problem, because no one can seem to find it.

"It's not on anything," Jemma says. "We all looked."

"Okay, well, it would have to be something like a weasel or a ferret or . . ." Lucy trails off, because none of those words are eight letters long, and she's pretty sure it needs to be.

"What's that animal that can kill cobras?" Harrison asks. "I once saw a video about that and they're way smaller than the snakes, but they're basically superhero mutants because they're immune to the venom."

"Mongoose!"[96] Lucy says. "There are lots of different

---

96 While mongooses are resistant to snake venom, they are not entirely immune and do not always win, though if Lucy were a snake, she'd steer clear of any mongoose, especially one that seemed to be having a bad day.

types, but it's probably the gray mongoose you're thinking of!"

Trey's face brightens. "*Mongoose* has eight letters, right?"

Lucy grins. "It definitely does!"

She turns to quickly punch in each of the answers in the order they are listed in. She goes slowly and double-checks that the right numbers correlate with the right letters. And as soon as she enters the final animal, the gate buzzes and clicks open.

CHAPTER 37

"**M**aybe the lights have nothing to do with the gates?" Harrison guesses as he tugs the gate open wide.

Lucy shakes her head in frustration. "I don't know what's happening with these locks and I don't really care. I just want to help Tabora."

Lucy steps out of Meerkat Mansion with the other kids right behind her. They are on a narrow pathway with tall fencing on either side, and the large square shape of the aquarium rising up on the left. Lucy turns, looking for signs, and then, there it is. She absolutely, positively cannot think of four more beautiful letters in the whole world.

"Dudes!" Harrison shouts. "It's the exit!"

A burst of energy rushes through Lucy's whole body. They can do this! They can still save Tabora! Jemma pushes open the exit door and they all tumble through. Lucy looks around the new area, which has four round picnic tables, restrooms, and an attached storage shed labeled LANDSCAPING. Four paths lead away from the picnic tables, including the one they just came from. One path has a sign pointing to the Canopy Walk, another sits next to a BACK TO CAMP sign, and a third points to the main entrance.

"This is the Picnic Pavilion," Jemma says. "I bet we're supposed to meet the Ambassadors here."

But it's crystal clear the Ambassadors aren't here. Lucy decides they don't have time to worry about that yet. First, they have to get to Tabora.

Lucy points at the third sign. "Let's get to the road!"

Jemma nods. "But how are we supposed to stop a truck with a baby elephant inside? I don't even know many adults that could do that."

"We could try to find some tire spikes to lay across the road!" Harrison says, hopping from one foot to the other. There's a wicked gleam in his eye when he goes on. "Ooh, or we could slash the truck tires like they do in action movies! We just need really sharp, pointy knives. Or swords. Swords would totally work."

"I don't think we have road spikes on hand," Trey says.

"Or a sharp knife to go stabbing tires with," Jemma says, looking concerned.

"Bummer, dudes. It would have been totally cool. We are dealing with bad guys, right?"

"They are definitely bad guys. Remember how Mr. Swendel and Alex were talking at the gate? They were glad he was gone, but he's back with friends, and they're trying to steal a baby elephant."

"Why would anyone do that?" Jemma asks.

"Because elephants are super popular. Maybe they want to sell her. A private zoo far away would pay a lot of money for Tabora, or trade another valuable animal."

"I just don't know how to stop them," Jemma says. "They're grown-ups."

Harrison nods. "Four grown-ups, and they're really big, but there are four of us. Hey, it might be a stretch, but do any of you guys know karate or tae kwon do? Or maybe jujitsu?"

Everyone shakes their head, but Lucy jumps in before Harrison can get going again. "I don't think *we* have to stop them. Now that we're at the road, we just need to get to the security guards at the gate. After we tell them what's going on, they'll take over and save Tabora."

Jemma pulls out the map. "Well, the front entrance isn't even half a mile from here, so it should be pretty easy. We just need to follow the road—"

A distant slam interrupts Jemma midsentence. She looks up from the map, and her eyes are very big and wide again.

"That sounded like a car door," she says.

Trey frowns. "Or a truck door."

Lucy tenses. "If it's a truck door, that means they're going to go!"

CHAPTER 38

"We don't have time to get security," Lucy says. Her stomach twists and twists with worry. "We have to do something fast."

"You're right," Jemma says. "So what can we do?"

"What about the weight thing?" Harrison asks. "Is there a way to force the truck off the road and into some swampy area? But not like a big swamp, because we don't want the truck to sink, just get stuck—"

"Wait," Lucy says, and she turns to the landscaping shed, raising her hand like she's ready to speak, because an idea has come into her brain and it's a super-extra-good one. "I know how we can stop the truck, but we've got to get into that shed. And we need an outdoor faucet."

"Outdoor faucet?" Jemma asks.

Trey steps forward looking 100 percent excited. And if there's one thing Lucy has learned about Trey, it's that he doesn't get excited easily.

"You want to use the hose to flood the road, don't you?" he asks. "If you can get it wet enough, it will turn muddy and soft."

"And if it's muddy and soft, then the heavy truck might get stuck just like the truck got stuck near that hill earlier," Jemma says.

Harrison turns to her, looking very, very surprised. "Are you trying to say that you need us to go and make a bunch of mud?"

When Lucy nods, Trey breaks out into an extra-huge grin. Jemma claps her hands like she does when she's ready to take charge.

"Okay, you heard her, everybody! Let's get to work."

Lucy crosses her fingers when they walk to the shed door, but she's happy to find the same unlit electronic lock they've seen on some of the animal enclosures. The doorknob twists easily and the door swings open without a noise.

The light in the shed doesn't work, but when Lucy pushes the door wide, she sees that it's less like a regular shed and more like a garage. There is a golf cart with storage in the center, and shelves line the walls with stacks of bagged mulch piled underneath. Lucy scans baskets of gloves and rows of hooks with shovels of various sizes. And there on the floor beside a stack of mulch bags is a thick coil of garden hose. Bingo!

"This is it!" Lucy says. "Did Harrison find water?"

"A faucet thingy?" Harrison asks from outside. "Yes, I did. And I turned the knob—and, dudes, the water is just shooting out all over the place!"

"Turn it off!" Jemma cries, and she rushes out of the shed to find Harrison. "We have to attach the hose, and we can't do that when the water is on."

Lucy and Trey pull the hose out of the shed. It's much heavier than it looked coiled up innocently on the floor like a sleepy anaconda. Fortunately, they manage to carry it out of the shed and around the side of the building to where Harrison is standing in a large, muddy puddle. There is mud spattered on his shirt and face, even in his hair!

"What happened?" Lucy asks. "We were only in there for two minutes."

"Oh, well, I turned on the water. And then this happened. On a bright note, I definitely made things muddy pretty quickly."

"Let's hurry and uncoil it," Jemma says. "Lucy, you can run closer to the road and drag the sprayer with you."

Lucy starts off the second they hand her the hose. But as soon as she reaches the clearing for the road, she stops. The road is a narrow two-lane route, which is small enough to handle. But the surface of the road isn't dirt, it's a long stretch of fresh white gravel.

Lucy's heart sinks and her shoulders droop. "This won't work. The road is gravel."

"Gravel?" Jemma asks. Lucy feels the hose go slack, probably from Jemma dropping it. "We can't make mud out of gravel."

Lucy squints at the narrow lane. There has to be something they can do. This isn't even a big road! Suddenly, there is a soft clomping, followed by a familiar grunt. Something tall and brown steps out of the bushes and up onto the road.

"Archibald," Lucy whispers.

The camel is still chewing[97] as he walks to the center

---

97 Lucy is a little astonished at the endless chewing, even though she remembers the documentary that clearly stated that camels actively graze, eat, or chew for fourteen to sixteen hours a day.

of the road and stops dead in his tracks. He watches her with a lovely, dark eye and lips that chew and chew and chew. Suddenly an idea sparks in Lucy's brain. She whirls to face Jemma, who is frowning at the edge of the path to the road.

"We can block the road," she says.

"With what? Our hopes and dreams?" Jemma asks.

"We have that golf cart!" Harrison shouts. "The key is in it, and we could load it full of bags of mulch and stuff from the shed. Like the way people put sandbags up before hurricanes."

"That's a good idea," Trey says.

"Um, except we are twelve years old!" Jemma says. "We can't drive anything."

"Well, honestly, how difficult can it be?" Harrison asks.

"It's not difficult," Lucy says, but her heart is already pounding and her throat is already so tight. "I know how to drive a golf cart."

She's pretty sure she'll never forget driving a golf cart, because the first time she did it was also the first time she had a panic attack. Does that mean she'll have one again?

"Wait," Harrison says. "You've driven a golf cart? Like on a golf course?"

"Um, no. I haven't driven on a golf course. My grandparents live pretty far out in the country on a farm, and they have a really long driveway. Pops taught me to drive it last year."

Out of the corner of her eye, Lucy notices Trey walking back to the shed.

"Still," she says. "I'm not so sure I can do it."

"Not sure?" Jemma asks. "You said you can drive! Let's do it!"

"Driving a golf cart caused my first panic attack, I think," Lucy admits, and her eyes are already filling with tears.

"How did a golf cart cause them?" Harrison asks. "Did you run someone over?"

"No, I was in a field," Lucy says. "But we did hit a hole and my pops hurt his shoulder. I'm just not sure I can do it again."

"Ohhh," Harrison says, and then he shakes his head. "Well, that might not be exactly how it happened. I got a detention right before I got diagnosed with ADHD."

"A detention?" Jemma looks scandalized, and Lucy totally understands this. Even hearing the word *detention* makes her feel squirmy and nervous. Squervous!

"Oh yeah, I was in the second grade, and I heard this noise in the playground and asked the teacher if I could go check it out and she said no, but the noise kept happening so I ran out of the room and found an emergency exit in the lunchroom so I could sneak into the playground. Anyway, it tripped the fire alarm and the fire department came and it was a whole thing. So I got a detention and my mom took me to my doctor and then they started these questionnaire things and found out I had ADHD."

"Oh, that sounds . . ." Lucy isn't actually sure how that sounds, or what point he might be trying to make. Fortunately, Harrison waves his hands like he's not quite finished.

"The thing is, me sneaking out that day wasn't when I got ADHD. That was just the time it became super noticeable to everyone around me. Maybe that's what the golf cart was for you."

"Yeah," Jemma says. "And you've done better all day with heights. I think you can do it!"

Jemma has a point. Lucy has done better. Still, maybe it would be safer to carry the bags of mulch, even if it does take a bit longer. Lucy has started toward the shed with the others following when suddenly Trey appears, pushing the shed door wide open.

"What are you doing?" she asks.

"Well, as soon as I heard you could drive the golf cart, I decided to load it up. There are six bags in the back and it's ready to go."

Lucy's face feels hot and her knees feel rubbery, but Jemma and Trey and Harrison are looking at her like they are 150 percent positive that she can do this. Maybe they're right.

Plus, there's only one way she can think of to help Tabora get out of that truck, and that way involves driving the golf cart. Which means there's really only one thing left to do.

"Well, I guess we better do this thing, then," Lucy says.

She jogs back to the shed and climbs onto the golf cart. It's different than the one she has at home, a little bit wider and higher. And being up in the seat reminds her that she doesn't have permission to drive this golf cart.

Lucy isn't sure this won't get her into trouble. She also isn't totally sure it's legal. She also isn't totally sure there isn't a hole somewhere on the path that will tip the golf cart like the cart on her grandparents' farm, but it's a chance she has to take to keep Tabora safe!

"I think we'll need three bags end to end to cross the road," Jemma says. "It's a guess, but it's a sort of mathy guess."

"We can carry a couple more bags, since the golf cart's full," Harrison says. "Go on, Lucy! We're right behind you."

Lucy takes a deep breath and reminds herself of all the things her friends said. The golf cart didn't cause her attacks to start happening. It's just a golf cart. Her hands shake when she turns the key to the *on* position. And then a low, rumbling noise starts up in the distance.

Trey looks at Jemma, Jemma looks at Harrison, Harrison looks at Lucy, and Lucy looks at the open door of the landscaping shed. That noise is the sound of an engine starting up. And there's only one engine Lucy can think of nearby. The one inside the truck that's trying to elephant-nap baby Tabora!

There is no more time to think about anything. Lucy grips the steering wheel and hits the gas.

CHAPTER 39

Here are the things Lucy hopes she does not get arrested for:

1. Stealing bags of mulch (because she's not stealing, only borrowing).

2. Stealing the golf cart (again, not stealing, only borrowing!).

3. Driving the golf cart without a license. (Lucy is 79 percent sure this is a real crime because she's not on her grandpa's farm in the middle of a field, but she's hoping that if a police officer finds out, they will understand that this was an elephant emergency. An eleph-ergency!)

She drives the golf cart slowly, slowly, slowly out of the shed and then more quickly to the end of the gravel path and down the path to the edge of the road. She stops and turns off the golf cart. In the middle of the road, Archie stops chewing. He stares at her with one dark camel eye. And then he moseys off the road and into the tall grass on the other side.

Lucy jumps into action, stepping out of the golf cart to get the bags of mulch. She starts unloading the first bag before Harrison even gets there. He's out of breath from running, but as soon as he drops his mulch on the road, he rushes back to help Lucy.

Harrison grabs the other end of the bag, and together they start toward the road. Lucy decides in that moment that if there's one thing more awkward than unloading a bag of mulch, it's definitely, positively carrying one while walking backward.[98] When they lay out two bags of mulch end to end, they realize that the second bag of mulch doesn't quite stretch to the middle of the road.

"Okay, let's scoot them down," Harrison says, dragging the middle bag to the middle of the road.

Lucy drags the first bag about a foot away from the edge of the road.

"Do you think this will work?" she asks, and she hopes so, because the engine noise seems to be getting a little bit closer.

"As long as the space around the middle bag is narrow enough, the truck won't be able to straddle them with the tires."

"Good thinking," Jemma says. She is also breathing hard and pink-cheeked when she and Trey walk past, dropping the third bag on the far side of the road. They work in teams of two, hauling the bags out of the golf cart and to the makeshift blockade as quickly as they can.

---

98 Fortunately, Lucy is a human being and not a kangaroo or an emu, neither of which can walk backward.

When the second row is complete, Trey stands up, and his eyes go very wide.

"The truck is only two hills away," he says.

"Hurry!" Jemma says. "We don't have much time!"

As big as the hills at Wildlands are, it won't take more than a couple of minutes for a big truck to get there, even one moving extra, extra slowly. Lucy tries to hurry, but her noodle arms are sore and wobbly, and even Harrison, who usually moves faster than an average person, is starting to slow down.

They put third bags on the first and second pile at the same time. Then they sprint back to add the final row on the far side of the lane. Lucy and Harrison are wrestling one of the remaining bags across the road when Lucy stumbles on a rock. The bag splits, the plastic ripping open right in the middle. Mulch spills down Lucy's front and across the gravel. Just like that, one of their precious bags is gone.

Lucy feels like she might cry, looking at the mostly empty, torn bag, but Jemma and Trey are already on their way with the next one.

"It's okay," Jemma says. "We're getting another. Just get the last one."

But Lucy suddenly knows it is definitely, positively not okay. They only have two bags of mulch left. And another scary fact has jumped to the top of Lucy's mind. They were able to get these bags here pretty fast. It will stop the truck for a few minutes, but she knows that two or maybe even four full-sized men will be able to move those bags of mulch out of the way pretty quickly.

There will be nothing any of them can do about it, and Happy Time Farms (which is 1,000,000 percent not a happy time) will get away with stealing a baby elephant.

"This isn't going to work for very long," Lucy says. "Someone needs to run for the guard station and fast."

"But the guard station is over a mile away," Trey says.

"I can run a mile," Jemma says. "I can run a mile in less than ten minutes. I'm pretty fast." [99]

"Is that fast enough to get there before the truck comes and moves these bags?" Lucy asks.

"I'll make it fast enough," Jemma says, and then she grins the biggest grin Lucy has ever seen. "I have to, right? My team needs me."

Her team? Jemma takes off, and Lucy's chest feels funny as she watches her go. Does Jemma really feel like they're part of her team now?

Less than a minute after Jemma runs, the engine noise becomes much louder. Harrison and Trey drop the last bag and turn toward the noise of the engine. But Lucy, who is still at the edge of the road, sees it first, and the sight of the giant white truck makes her stomach tumble into an instant somersault.

"Guys, we should probably not stay here," Lucy says.

The black metal bumper and round headlights of the truck bounce as it jostles over the gravel. After one particularly bad bump, Lucy hears another noise over the en-

---

99 The fastest human runner in history is Usain Bolt, whom Lucy learned about in PE class. He reached a top speed over 27 miles per hour! That's fast for a human, but lots of animals are faster. Even warthogs and house cats can run 30 miles per hour, which is probably why you can never catch a cat after it steals your hair tie.

gine, a frightened, small trumpety cry. Her heart squeezes painfully in her chest.

Tabora! Tabora is in that truck, and she is scared, maybe even hurt.

The truck is coming closer, and some small part of Lucy wants to run up, pull the tailgate open, and somehow set Tabora free. But she is too small and the truck is moving too fast. Lucy's shoulders sag in defeat, but then Trey grabs Lucy's arm.

"It's our turn to run."

"The driver sees us," Harrison says. "He's pointing, you guys, and he looks really big and mean."

Lucy looks up at the truck long enough to see the small, hard eyes and puffy cheeks of the man behind the wheel. The driver's window rolls down and the truck begins to slow. And then the same man, with his small eyes and big cheeks, leans a balding head out of the window. Lucy has one tiny second to realize that Tabora isn't the only one in danger. And then Trey tugs her arm and they all run.

CHAPTER 40

"**F**ind out who those kids are with!" The man's voice is behind them, but Lucy doesn't dare look back. She doesn't get the golf cart or stop to tie her shoe that has come undone. She runs faster than she's ever run in her life. The way Jemma would run.

"They're chasing us," Trey says.

And sure enough, Lucy can hear the clomp of heavy feet on the road. They have barely any time at all!

"You three! Stop!"

It's a man's voice that Lucy hears behind her as she runs. And this is not the friendly, happy voice of her uncle Wayne, or her mom's friend Matt. This is a mean, gruff voice. The man's footsteps sound like they're slowing, but Lucy's legs already feel weak and wobbly. She knows she won't be able to run too much faster or for too much longer. And she doesn't even know where they're going! Everything they know in Wildlands is behind them.

"Up here," Harrison whispers, waving them to the right as the path curves. There is a giant building here with enormous double doors and the smell of hay in the air. This must be one of the barns.

The double doors are closed, but Lucy finds a normal door on the right that has been cracked open. She slips inside and waves for Harrison and Trey to follow. Enormous stalls rise up on the right, with thick bars and huge troughs for food.

The first two stalls are empty, and the building seems quiet and dark.

"Is this a barn?" Trey asks.

"Yes, this is one of the off-display areas for rehabilitation," Lucy says.

"What do they keep in here?" Harrison asks.

"I'm not sure," Lucy says, but what she is sure about is that whatever animals are housed here, they are probably pretty large. The ceiling towers overhead, and everything she can see looks giant-sized.

Lucy turns left and finds herself staring down the length of the barn. This area is even more spacious, with sections of equipment and more stalls. Lucy peeks to the left, where a single room is lit, the door thrown open wide. Inside, she sees cabinets with various brushes, files, and large jars of tablets and powders. There are also extra-large needles that send the hairs on the backs of Lucy's arms up.

"Is that the pharmacy?" Trey asks.

Lucy blinks and then startles. "You might be right! Or at least I think it's some sort of animal care area. Those files and big clippers are for some sort of hoof or foot care."[100]

"And what about those vials and that needle?" Harrison

---

100 Hoof and foot care (including trimming, filing, and careful inspection) is an important part of animal care in zoos and wildlife parks and is critical to keeping animals healthy. Who knew pedicures could save lives?

says. "Because they're just sitting there on that table and something about that feels super not safe."

Lucy examines the needle and vials again and chills race up and down her arms. He's absolutely right. She doesn't know anything about animal medicine at Wildlands, but she's watched dozens and dozens of wildlife veterinarian shows, and they are always meticulous about where things are stored and how they're organized. But there are two vials lying on their sides on a worktable with two giant syringes. Plus, there's an open cabinet overhead. None of it looks safe at all!

"You're right," Lucy says. "I think someone has been in here messing with this stuff. I just don't know why."

The sound of a door flinging open cuts off their conversation. Lucy's knees knock as footsteps *thump-thump-thump* into the building. There is a bad guy inside the barn with them. And he's walking this way!

Lucy looks at Harrison and Harrison looks at Trey and then Trey looks at Lucy again. Lucy knows they are as afraid as she is, and this time it is not just an attack; it is a real fear. This man is up to no good!

Thump-thump-thump.

A staticky crackle. *"Kev, come in!"*

Lucy squeezes her hands into fists as they listen to the man wrestle what must be a walkie-talkie off his belt or pocket or whatever place he had it.

"I haven't found 'em yet."

"Just leave the kids. We need to get out of here."

"We don't know what they saw."

"I don't care what they saw. They're just stupid kids! We need to get this thing out of here before that security guard gets loose and before the keepers get here for evening rounds!"

"What if the big one wakes up?"

"All the more reason for you to get out of there! Now hurry or I'll leave you here to take the fall for their precious missing elephant!"

"I'm on my way."

The footsteps start up again, but this time they're heading away from Lucy and the others. Lucy holds her breath tightly until the bang of the shutting door echoes through the barn. Harrison exhales long and loud, like a balloon losing all of its air in a rush.

"Dudes, that guy was creepy. What did he mean by *What if the big one wakes up?*"

If you ask Lucy, and she supposes Harrison just did, it can't mean anything good. "I'm not sure, but I have a bad feeling it has something to do with those big syringes."

"The ones that look like they've been used?"

Lucy feels cold all over. "Let's keep going."

They take a few steps forward and then Lucy hears a loud, slow huffing. And another huff. And then there is a huge rustling ahead of them like something very, very large is moving around in the barn. Lucy takes a few tentative steps forward and peers into the darkness. At first . . . nothing. And then finally, finally her eyes adjust. She sees a gigantic shape in the dim overhead lights. Suddenly the enormous doors and needles and clippers make all the sense in the world. They are in an elephant barn.

And Lucy's sure of it because the giant thing snuffling and moving in the dim light is an elephant.

"Is that . . ." Trey doesn't even finish his sentence, but Lucy is already nodding.

"That's Mwanza," Lucy says. "We found Tabora's mom."

CHAPTER 41

Lucy looks at the four enormous and empty stalls on the right. Then she looks at the one super-enormous and not-empty space to the left. There is a metal railing between the walkway they're on and the bare ground where the elephant is still sleepily nudging the door, but is that railing tall enough to keep an elephant away?

Lucy isn't so sure.

"I feel like we are way too close to that elephant," Harrison whispers. "Couldn't it jump over that tiny little fence and squash us?"

Lucy shakes her head and whispers, "Elephants can't jump."[101]

"True," Trey says, but he still sounds worried.

Lucy nods and watches Mwanza closely. The giant elephant shakes her head once. Twice. And then a third time. This third time seems to shake off any confusion she had left. There is a distant rumble outside the barn. Then Mwanza swings her mighty head around to look not at the door but at the kids.

---

101 This is true. Elephants (like hippos, tortoises, porcupines, and several other animals) can't jump. But they can definitely climb over objects, so Harrison is smart to be nervous!

Lucy freezes, realizing three things in a single instant:

1. The rumble Lucy heard was the truck's engine starting again.

2. Which means the men have moved all of the bags out of the way.

3. And that means they will be driving out of the park with Tabora right now.

There is the barest, tiniest hint of a baby elephant noise beyond the truck's engine, but the noise is enough to send Mwanza into a frenzy. She trumpets loudly and desperately, pushing at the hinge in the double doors, testing the seam with the tip of her trunk.

"What's happening?" Harrison asks. "Why is she so upset?"

"I think she heard her baby," Lucy says. "She's trying to get to Tabora."

"Well, maybe we should let her," Trey says.

Lucy looks up then and realizes that Trey is right! The only chance at all of helping Tabora is by letting Mwanza out of this barn right now. As if she's agreeing with Lucy's thoughts, Mwanza lets out a mighty trumpet and pushes her whole body against the seam between the big double doors. They shift but do not open.

"How do we open them for her?" Lucy asks. She points at a box beside the doors. "Is that a control panel?"

"I think so," Harrison says. "But, dude, you can't go in there. You'd be on the other side of the railing and that elephant is super worked up. She could squash you flatter than a pancake!"

"She won't squash me," Lucy says, though in truth, she isn't sure that won't happen. The only thing she's sure about is that she has to try.

She rushes around the railing until she's as close to the control panel as she can possibly be while still being inside. Lucy can see it's no use—no matter how far she leans or stretches, she cannot reach that panel. Mwanza is trumpeting again and the truck engine is coming closer to the barn. They are closer to the road than she realized! Which is even more reason why Lucy should try to get Mwanza out there!

"Okay, how far do you think it is between me and the control panel?" Lucy asks.

"Maybe ten feet," Trey says.

"We'll be right here and we can pull you over the rail. You just need to run over, hit the button, and run back," Harrison says.

Lucy hesitates for one second and then for another. And then Mwanza turns her mighty head away and Lucy knows this is her only chance. She leaps over the railing and sprints to the control panel the way she imagines Jemma would sprint. She stretches up onto the tips of her toes, and then a loud, blaring trumpet shakes her to her bones.

Out of the corner of her eye, she sees Mwanza turning toward her. The big elephant's ears spread out wide, like two satellite dishes. She shakes her head once with a mighty snuffling sound.[102]

"Hurry, Lucy!" Harrison says. "She looks upset!"

Lucy's hands are shaking when she presses on the control panel. The screen lights up. There are two green buttons and both are arrows, but which one will open the doors?

Mwanza trumpets again, and Lucy jumps. She presses the first green button and it's like it was a button telling Mwanza to charge, because the elephant suddenly starts barreling toward her. Lucy jerks away from the panel.

"Lucy, get out of there!" Harrison cries. "Hurry!"

"I am hurrying!" Lucy says. But the first button didn't work. Lucy leaps forward, darting her hand in to smash the other green button. She can feel Mwanza's footsteps now and can see the shadow of her trunk moving along the floor. It's too late! Lucy will never make it out before she's crushed!

"Lucy, run!" Trey and Harrison say together, and then there is the loudest clunk of all the clunks Lucy has ever heard.

The clunk is right behind her.

Lucy freezes. Harrison and Trey freeze too. And the giant elephant behind her? She freezes just like everyone else. There is only one thing in here that is still moving, and it's the doors. The enormous doors are grinding open!

"You did it, Lucy," Trey says softly.

---

102 This is one of the many ways elephants display apprehension, and work to scare off potential threats by showing how large they are. Given that the elephant is maybe four times taller than Lucy, someone could tell Mwanza that the ears bit isn't necessary to drive that fact home.

Lucy can't believe it. She's 90 percent sure she must be imagining it, but then Mwanza rushes through the open barn doors, a loud, angry trumpet trilling behind her. Lucy turns to the open doors, and it's one of those times when everything feels like slow motion. Lucy can see Mwanza's tail raised as she thunders toward the road. The truck trundles slowly forward on the gravel road, and one of the men inside begins pointing frantically outside the window. Pointing at the giant elephant that is dangerously close to charging the truck.

"Is Mwanza going to hit the truck?" Harrison asks.

Lucy has no idea. But if she does, it could be terrible! It could knock over the truck, hurting the men inside and poor baby Tabora, who is trapped in the back!

Harrison and Trey both leap the railing, and Lucy waves them closer. "She's going to knock over the truck!"

"She's not," Trey says. "She's going in front."

And then, just as Trey suspected, Mwanza rushes in front of the truck. She plants her front feet hard on the ground and flaps her ears as wide as they will go. Her trumpet is like a scream, and Lucy is sure that the truck will hit her, or go around her or some other terrible thing.

But the truck stops right in the middle of the road.

"Now what happens?" Lucy asks.

A low, rumbling engine sound rises in the air, and Lucy squeezes her hands into fists. "Oh no, they're going to go around her."

But the truck doesn't move. Lucy double-, triple-, quadruple-checks, but the engine noise keeps growing louder and the truck keeps not moving.

Harrison gasps beside her. "Lucy, look! It's a Wildlands truck!"

And sure enough, as soon as the words leave Harrison's mouth, a tan pickup truck with the Wildlands logo on the side zips down the road into view. It's heading right toward the elephant too!

CHAPTER 42

The delivery truck has stopped about thirty feet away from the elephant, and for one second nothing happens. No one moves. Mwanza flaps her ears and gives a low trumpet. The tiniest, most distant trumpet answers. It's baby Tabora.[103]

Mwanza rushes toward the back of the delivery truck, and the men inside get out. Lucy sees the faintest trace of blue light flickering across the road once. Twice. And then a third time.

"Oh no, what if those men try to run someone over?" Harrison cries.

But Lucy is already grinning. "Oh, I don't think those men are going anywhere!"

Suddenly, one police car pulls up behind the first truck and another comes down from the other entrance. And then the tan pickup truck doors open and Lucy sees the best thing she can imagine seeing in the whole wide world. Jemma Louise Sparks is standing on the road with her hands on her hips and the Wildlands cavalry behind her.

"Jemma, you did it!" Lucy shouts.

---

103 Sadly, Tabora would not be the first baby elephant kidnapped. Baby elephants can be illegally sold for a lot of money, so plenty of bad people have stolen them in the wild for this exact evil reason!

"Well, of course I did. I told you I hate losing!"

Lucy feels a laugh bubbling out of her so fast. And before she knows it, they're all laughing with one another. And if there's one thing that's better than laughing after a really scary thing works out okay, it's doing that laughing with three of your best friends.

Jemma pops her hands on her hips again, and Lucy grins.

"She looks just like a captain in a pirate movie," Harrison says.

And suddenly, Lucy remembers something else. The orange fabric with black shapes. She's seen that before, and now she knows where.

Lucy rushes past the other kids and right up to the security guard, Mr. Swendel.

"Mr. Swendel!" Lucy says. "I have to talk to you."

"Oh, you kids are so brave! Jemma unlocked the guard shed and got me out! Now, don't worry. A couple of the keepers arrived right after Jemma, so they're already going to get Alex out of that ostrich enclosure."

"It's not Alex I'm worried about right now, it's the Ambassadors."

Mr. Swendel's eyebrows scrunch together in worry. "The Ambassadors! They aren't with you?"

"No, but I have a question about sailing."

"Sailing?" Now Mr. Swendel looks truly perplexed.

"Yes. Is there an orange flag in sailing? One with black shapes? Like a circle and—"

"And a square?" The old guard's confusion is starting to turn into concern. "If it's an orange flag with a circle and a square, then you've got a true distress flag. It's an SOS emergency signal."

Lucy looks left where Jemma and Harrison and Trey have circled around. Jemma gasps.

"Olivia goes to sailing camp every summer! She would know that flag!"

"Mr. Swendel, would Wildlands have any orange fabric in storage sheds that someone could use to make that flag?" Lucy asks.

Mr. Swendel rubs his chin. "Well, come to think of it, we do use a lot of orange tablecloths for special events."

Lucy nods at Jemma and then looks back at Mr. Swendel. "I think the Ambassadors got locked up just like you, Mr. Swendel. And I think they made that flag to signal for help."

"We better get one of the officers over here to start a search," Mr. Swendel says.

"You don't need a search," Lucy says. "Our team can show you exactly where to go."

CHAPTER 43

It takes ten minutes to load back onto one of the safari trucks, but this time, Mr. Swendel is behind the wheel. For a guy who makes Lucy think of her grandpa, Mr. Swendel drives pretty fast! Or maybe it feels fast, because he takes them on the authorized-personnel-only loop, which Lucy learns is an extra-bumpy dirt road that leads around the backs of the enclosures (like the place Leonardo tried to escape) and between the equipment buildings and off-exhibit barns.

"It's going to get bumpy," Mr. Swendel says.

"It already feels pretty bumpy," Jemma says.

"True."

This time, Lucy is especially grateful for the cushy seats, because Mr. Swendel meant it when he said *bumpy*. The road feels rougher than crocodile scales and armadillo skin! Lucy also doesn't really recognize this area of the park, because it's not where they were solving puzzles. They're in the Ambassadors' side of the park, or the behind-the-scenes part of that side, at least.

"Okay, we are between the largest pasture and the south viewing platform. Can you tell me where you saw this flag, using the map?" Mr. Swendel asks.

Lucy freezes, gripping her extra-cushy armrests. She doesn't really know where either of those things is. And she doesn't know if she could point it out. She's not sure she can help!

But then she hears the map rustle behind her, and Jemma clears her throat. "I can, Mr. Swendel. There should be a turnoff path coming up on the left. I think we all need to look for the flag down there because that's directly across from the platform where we saw it."

"Wow, Jemma, that's kind of amazing. You're a map-magician!" Harrison says.

"You really are," Lucy says with a grin.

Mr. Swendel turns the safari truck left and they go bump, bump, bumping down the new road. And then Lucy spots something out the window of a plain, rectangular building. "There it is! I see the flag!"

It all happens extra, extra fast from there. It's only a few seconds before Mr. Swendel is skidding to a halt. It's less than a second after that that the engine is off and all five of them throw open the doors and jump down, using those supercool stepping bars.

Jemma, who really would make an awesome gazelle or cheetah or ostrich, flies ahead of them, calling her friends' names.

"Olivia? Isaac? Adam?"

"Here! We're in here!" The voices come from inside the windowless shed.

"My friends are in there!" Jemma cries, but then she tugs at a padlock on the latch. "How do we get them out of here?"

"Some horrible guys locked us in here!" a small voice calls.

"We're going to get you out, Olivia!" Jemma says.

"We might have to get some bolt cutters from the truck," Mr. Swendel says.

"Mr. Swendel? It's me, Leah. We're okay in here, but you have to call the police. That awful guy from Happy Time Farms is back. We've been trying to use our walkie-talkies, but the signal isn't working at all."

"You're right, he is back," Lucy says. "And he wasn't alone."

"They sabotaged our signal booster and our electrical circuits," Mr. Swendel says. "And locked me up too!"

"But we stopped him," Harrison says. "All of us together!"

"Hang on just a second. I have an idea," Mr. Swendel says. He heads back to the safari truck and opens a compartment in the back. Then he pulls out a small toolbox, and more importantly, a large screwdriver.

"There's always a solution if you think hard enough," Mr. Swendel says. And then he proceeds to unscrew all of the screws that hold the latch itself to the door.

Within seconds, the padlock, latch, and hinge all drop to the ground and the door swings open. Jemma swoops in to hug her friends before they even get outside. And suddenly everyone is talking at once.

"That was so scary!"

"Those guys waited until we were inside putting all our camp stuff away."

"They were like ninjas!"

"It was awful. The door just slammed shut!"

"We didn't even know anyone was out there."

"Until we saw from the vent, but by then it was too late."

"But a few seconds later, we spotted a giant white truck."

"That's when I knew it was the Happy Times Farm guy," Leah says. She is tall like Alex, with long black hair and very kind eyes. "How did you catch him?"

"Them," Mr. Swendel says. "There were four of them. And these awesome kids caught them on the road."

"Alex must be so proud of you guys," Leah says, with a smile that's just as friendly as her eyes. But then she frowns. "Wait, where is Alex?"

Suddenly, two short horn blasts toot through the air.

"Well, that's where," Mr. Swendel says.

"That's where what?" Lucy asks, feeling a little wiggle of worry.

"The two short horn blasts are a code we use in emergencies. They tell us that everything is A-OK with the other safari truck. That means they've found your sister!"

"Wait, does anyone know *we* are okay?" Trey asks.

Mr. Swendel's blue eyes twinkle. "I don't think they do. Does someone want to do the honors?"

For some reason, everyone looks at Lucy, and Lucy feels a little rush of excitement as she follows Mr. Swendel back to the safari truck. She climbs up into the driver's seat and takes a deep breath as she looks at the big shiny steering wheel and the horn button right in the middle.

"Two short blasts, right?" she asks.

"You've got it," Mr. Swendel says.

Lucy takes a deep breath and taps the horn two times to tell the whole world that they are absolutely, positively okay.

CHAPTER 44

Two hours later, Lucy scoots in beside Alex at the campfire and carefully rotates her marshmallow. If you ask Lucy—and actually, everyone did ask Lucy about this—the key to a perfect s'more marshmallow is patience, patience, patience.

"See?" she says. "If you're careful to keep the marshmallow near hot coals and away from the actual flames and you turn and turn and turn . . ."

Lucy holds up her marshmallow for demonstration; it is a perfect golden brown on all sides. A couple of the aquarium keepers clap, and Phoebe, who is in charge of Mwanza and Tabora, claps too. She has only been able to stop by for a few minutes. She'll be very busy with the vets making sure Tabora is okay after the awful ordeal in the moving truck. And while Mwanza didn't get jostled around, she did get heavily sedated by someone who relied on Google for tranquilizer information. Those giant syringes Lucy saw were just as bad as she feared.

Lots of the Wildlands staff have come over to round up animals and to join the impromptu campfire feast. First, Alex made fish tacos, with the fish grilled in baskets over the fire. Trey worked with one of the aquarium keepers to collect some early greens from the Wildlands garden for a salad, and Harrison helped with assembling all the supplies for s'mores. But the s'mores? It was the Wildlands Ambassadors themselves who brought those supplies. After their own ordeal of being locked up, most of the Ambassadors opted to go home, but Isaac and Emma, the team captains, insisted on staying behind. Right now, they're sitting with Jemma, and even though she's feeling a million times better about everything else, Lucy is a little sad to see Jemma so quickly back with her old team.

But then again, maybe it isn't her old team. Maybe the Ambassadors are still her real team, and a good friend would support that, wouldn't they? Lucy feels a pang of sadness wondering who will get the Ambassadors spot. No matter who gets it, Lucy will be sad for someone. Every one of her new friends seems to deserve that spot, and deep down she feels like she might deserve it too.

Alex offers Lucy a prepared graham cracker with three chocolate squares on top. "I'm super proud of you. You totally did it. And wow, it must have been scary."

"It was."

"But you didn't melt down like this marshmallow."

Lucy squishes the marshmallow between the graham crackers and chocolate and takes one crumbly, gooey bite. After chewing it a bit, she nods. "I definitely melted down. You can ask Jemma."

Lucy sees something move out of the corner of her eye. It's Jemma. And she's standing right beside her! Lucy cringes, worried about what Jemma might say, but to her surprise, Jemma shakes her head. "You know, I don't think it was a meltdown. And besides, it barely lasted a minute. I hardly remember it."

Jemma smiles an extra-big smile, and even though it's a little bit untrue and Lucy isn't too sure about lying to a grown-up, even a brand-new grown-up like Alex, she thinks maybe this isn't quite the same as most lies. Maybe this is Jemma trying to be kind.

A scuffle of footsteps announces Mr. Swendel's arrival. "Well, everybody, I think it's all squared up now. Our IT pro fixed the broken signal booster, and the locks are all functioning properly."

"Plus we've reinstalled good old-fashioned padlocks as a backup measure," Phoebe says.

Mr. Swendel nods. "Best of all, I can confirm that every last animal is tucked back in the right enclosure."

"I still say those kangaroos should get a visiting pass to the Canopy Walk area," Harrison says. "They loved hanging out with the zebras and giraffes."

Phoebe laughs. "We'll keep that in mind. I'm going to head back and check on my girls. Before you leave today, why don't the four of you stop by the elephant barn? You've all earned the special experience of your choice, and I'll help you square those away. But I think you should all get a peek at the elephants you saved."

Harrison flops back like a starfish, with the biggest imaginable grin on his face. "It's happening! I'm finally going behind the scenes with the kangaroos."

"You all deserve it," Alex says. And then she turns to Josie, an aquarium keeper who's also a manager at

Wildlands. "But I think there's something else Josie would like to say."

"Is it about the police?" Harrison asks. "Because I really hope they didn't leave without letting me sit in the police car. They promised I could."

Josie—who has lots of long black braids twisted into a single, thick braid—laughs and shakes her head. "No, they had two big trucks to tow and four men to take down to jail for processing. They'll be here for a while yet."

"Jail!" Lucy stands up, surprised. "They're really going to jail?"

"For now they certainly are," Josie says. "Their plan breaks a lot of laws. In addition to stealing an endangered animal, they also intentionally sabotaged our animal security system. That could have created major safety problems in the town."

"Even a single wildebeest could have caused plenty of issues," Alex says.

Fortunately, none of the larger animals were out of their enclosures. And Lucy later learned those that had wandered loose were more than happy to return to their proper areas once their keepers arrived with their favorite treats in tow.

"I still don't understand how they could get away with stealing an elephant," Trey says.

Lucy's been thinking about that same thing. "He's right. You guys already knew to look out for Happy Time Farms. Wouldn't you just have had the police check there right away?"

"We wouldn't have known they were even in the park without you four," Josie says. "They snuck in a side gate because we were closed and had lower security. Once they disabled some of the electricity and that signal booster, they were able to get around pretty easily because Wildlands is so huge."

"And their plan wasn't to keep Tabora for Happy Time Farms. They were going to sell her for other animals," Mr. Swendel says.

"That's so terrible," Lucy says.

"But it does explain things," Harrison says. He's back up from his starfish sprawl and is balancing on one foot again. "That's why our walkie-talkie wasn't working and why some of the locks were broken. And it's also why they chased us. Until we bumped into them on the road, they'd been witness-free. They'd managed to trap everyone else without being seen."

"Pretty devious stuff," Josie says. "They even knew to cut the phone lines so Mr. Swendel couldn't call out once they trapped him in the guard shack."

"How did you not see anyone?" Lucy asks.

"They were smart enough to call me on the short-range radio," Mr. Swendel says. "When I turned to hear the radio better, my back was to the door. Someone must have been hiding and waiting for just that thing, because before I knew it the door was locked and there was no one in sight. Of course, we now know they weren't in sight because they were already working on getting into the elephant enclosure."

Lucy's chest squeezes. "That's when they tranquilized Mwanza in the barn, isn't it?"

"That's right." Mr. Swendel nods. "They thought it would be easy from there, running little Tabora out of the barn and into the truck, but elephants are smart animals and she took them on quite a chase."

"But they still almost got her," Harrison says. "The men got her in the truck! She could have been gone forever!"

"Except she isn't," Alex says, and when she looks at Lucy, Lucy's whole heart feels big and warm. "They didn't get her because you guys had the best escape challenge ever."

"And that's why it's time for someone to become the next Wildlands Ambassador," Josie says.

Now Lucy feels like her heart will beat its way right out of her chest! She still wants the chance to be an Ambassador so much. But does she want it more than anything? Does she want it so much that she's willing to take it from Harrison, who sees the good in everyone, or from Trey, who has been so kind to her? Or what about Jemma? Could Lucy really feel good about keeping Jemma away from the team she's been with all along?

Josie gives them all a very big, warm smile and then nods at Isaac and Emma.

"Isaac and Emma know all about the adventures you had today. You all deserve to be Ambassadors, but right now our funding only allows for one addition to the primary team. So we decided that instead of simple points, the Blue Team should vote on who deserves the spot."

Lucy's feels a little shaky, and Jemma is looking at her

feet. Josie pulls five index cards out of her backpack, along with five pencils. She begins to hand them out, but Lucy can barely pay attention. All she's seeing is the way Jemma is looking at the ground, her hands in fists at her sides. She looks so, so sad.

"Now, this will be a secret vote," Josie says, but Lucy leaps to her feet.

"We don't need to vote."

Lucy startles at the words. She'd meant to stop the vote. It had been her idea—the whole reason she stood up. But it wasn't Lucy who said those five words. It was Jemma.

Jemma stands up slowly, sharing a small smile with Isaac and Emma, who nod supportively.

"Go ahead, Jem," Emma says.

Jemma turns to Lucy, giving her the best and warmest smile she has. "Lucy should be the next Wildlands Ambassador. I thought I wanted the position, but the truth is, I don't love animals the way Lucy does. And I know she'll be the best Ambassador Wildlands has ever seen."

Harrison and Trey both stand up.

"Jemma's right," Harrison says. "I mean, Jemma's always right because she's supersmart and awesome. But when it comes to animals, Lucy is the best of us. Being an Ambassador sounds so cool, and I know Lucy will be amazing at it!"

"True," Trey says.

Lucy doesn't say anything. She just turns to Alex with tears blurring her vision. Even through her happy tears, she can see her sister smile. "You've always had my vote,

Lucy. Though technically, I didn't get to vote on this at all!"

"So what do you say, Lucy?" Josie asks. "Do you want to join the best team in the world?"

"I say . . ." Lucy wipes her eyes and walks closer to Jemma. "I say that I've learned a lot about being part of a team through this adventure. And while I am super excited about being an Ambassador, I have to admit, I've already been on the best team in the world."

Jemma rushes in, wrapping Lucy in an extra-squeezy hug. Harrison and Trey join in and even though Lucy is 150 percent surprised, she's 200 percent happy to hug them all back.

* * *

An hour later, they're enjoying a private tour of the elephant barn. Phoebe even invited them to watch Mwanza and Tabora have a special veggie treat in a small training enclosure. They're all seated at a safe distance, but it's still amazing to watch the elephants play.

Jemma lifts her chin. "I signed up for the Adventure Camp for my experience. I get to rappel and go whitewater rafting and everything."

"That sounds awesome," Harrison says. "I think we all know what I picked."

"The giraffe feeding?" Trey asks, and when Harrison blinks in surprise, he laughs. "Just kidding. We know you'll be hanging with the kangaroos."

"What about you, Trey?"

"There's a horticulture camp. That's the whole reason I came," Trey says. "I was never too sure about the Ambassador thing, but I definitely wanted to win."

"Those camps sound really cool," Lucy says, and they do. As for her, she has no idea what she'll pick. Becoming part of the Ambassadors is already her dream come true.

Lucy watches Tabora and Mwanza walking together in the little side yard just outside the barn. Phoebe leaves them and heads toward the kids, wearing big galoshes and carrying four blue shirts over her arm.

"Hi, Phoebe," Lucy says.

"Are the galoshes to keep your feet safe from poop?" Harrison asks. "Because I've heard elephants do a whole lot of pooping."

"They are indeed," Phoebe says. "And elephant poop is no laughing matter around here. Moving poop is a huge part of my job."

Jemma frowns. "Are you sure you want to work with animals, Lucy?"

Lucy nods. "Two hundred percent sure."

"Well, I'm glad to hear that, since you'll be an Ambassador soon," Phoebe says. "But before that, I think you've all earned a little something for your incredible teamwork today."

Alex steps out from the side, where Lucy didn't realize she'd been standing. "Phoebe and I decided *Blue Team* wasn't quite good enough. So if it's okay with you, we've decided you guys are the Elephant Rescue Team."

"The Elephant Rescue Team?" Trey asks.

Phoebe hands each of them one of the blue shirts.

There is a Wildlands logo on the front and an elephant on the back, and best of all? Each jersey has a team member's name printed above the elephant.

"Sorry it took a few minutes to get these together," Phoebe says. "We had several keepers working on it while you had s'mores. We knew we wanted to test the escape challenge, and you certainly did a great job of that. But you also kept Mwanza and Tabora safe, and that's more important than any challenge we could ever create."

"This is really, really cool," Jemma says.

"Yeah, dude, I love it!" Harrison adds.

"Thank you," Trey adds.

But Lucy doesn't say anything. She can't seem to make her voice work. Maybe because she's too busy running her fingers across the letters of her name at the top of the blue shirt. From the *L* in *Lucy* to the last *a* in *Spagnola*, this shirt is the best thing she's ever received. If there's one thing Lucy has wanted more than saving an elephant or a chance to touch a tortoise's shell or proving that she can climb up one of those overlooks without freaking out, it's being part of a real team.

"So what do you think?" Phoebe asks. "If you're interested, we'd love to have you back to help groups tackling the escape challenge. Once we get the challenge fixed, that is."

"That sounds completely awesome," Jemma says. "I'm totally in!"

"Me too," Trey says.

"Double yes!" Harrison says. "All the double yeses!"

"Wait," Jemma says, and she smiles one of her real

smiles. "I would love to come back sometimes, but only if Lucy's in too. Can she be with us and still be part of the Ambassadors?"

"I don't think we'd have it any other way," Phoebe says with a smile. "So what do you say, Lucy? Want to be on two teams?"

There is clearly only one thing to do. Lucy pinches the blue shirt carefully between her thumb and forefinger. And then she pulls the shirt on over her head.

"Absolutely, positively!"

ACKNOWLEDGMENTS

Writing Lucy and her friends has been an amazing adventure, and there are many people who helped me shape this book into the one you're holding today. Thank you to my fantastic editor, Kelsey, who helped me navigate the swampy uncertainty of a first draft and made every step of the editing process a true joy. I also can't express enough gratitude for my amazing agenting team at New Leaf, Suzie and Olivia. Your support, wisdom, and creativity are gifts I treasure! I'd also like to thank my publicist, Leann, who has been a transformative force for good in my writing life. You are an absolute star!

Special thanks go out to Edith Pattou, Margaret Petersen Haddix, and Lisa Klein for sage advice, moral support, and many laughs. And no book of mine would see the light of day without the guidance and support of Jody Casella, who never remembers names or titles but always knows exactly how to find the heart of my story. Thank you.

I've had a lot of other tremendous folks supporting me through this adventure. Thank you to Ben, who talks me off the ledge, is always down for brunch, and provided lots of helpful model train facts. Thanks also to Rick, who makes most of the furniture in my house, including a small sign that encouraged me to begin. And a huge thank-you to all my animal-lover readers who inspired me to write this to begin with!

And always, always, always, thanks to my kids, who really aren't kids anymore. To Ian, for our road trips and playlists and thirty-thousand-step days. To Adri, for her endless compassion, fierce will, and willingness to spend endless hours in search of warblers with me. And to my Itty-Bitty Lyddie, who fills every room and every corner of our family with love and light and a little bit of ridiculousness. I love you three so much.

READ ON FOR ANOTHER SURVIVAL STORY BY NATALIE D. RICHARDS, ABOUT A GROUP OF FOUR CLASSMATES FORCED TO NAVIGATE THE WILDERNESS FOR AN EXTRA-CREDIT PROJECT WITH NOTHING BUT THE PAGES OF A SURVIVAL HANDBOOK—AND EACH OTHER—TO SAVE THEM.

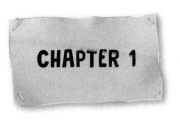

CHAPTER 1

DECEMBER 16, 3:25 P.M.—MONTANA

Our car grinds to a halt at the head of a narrow gravel drive. I look up from the back seat, seeing nothing but trees and mountains in every direction. I slouch lower and feel my throat go tight.

Is this really a fitting punishment? I mean, I already lost my spot on our school's e-sports team thanks to my active school discipline status. And it was just a few text messages.

Okay, fine, a few text messages and a Know and Grow team disqualification. For the record, they shouldn't have disqualified us, because we weren't cheating. We were just sharing our feelings with one another. And by feelings, I mean our dislike for one another. And by dislike, I mean loathing, but I already tried explaining that back when it all happened. That's when a funny little line showed up between Dad's eyebrows and Mom put her hand on her chest like she was trying not to cry and I decided that it was probably not a good idea to bring up the fact that it's kind of Mom's fault. She's the one who was all, "You four will make a great team for this class, Baxter."

Usually our elective courses at Lincoln are kind of awesome. Last year I took a class with three of my friends in a team to build and compete with derby robots. I figured a team trivia competition couldn't be that bad, even with Emerson, Turner, and Abigail. Didn't quite have that one right, did I?

Anyway, the day after Mom and Dad met with our teacher, they informed me that I would not be going on the tropical holiday cruise with them over winter break as planned. Instead the other Team Starbright members and I would be going for a weekend of responsibility and teamwork in the remote mountains of Montana with Mom's uncle Hornsby. And somehow, while doing all that, we're supposed to think of a group project we can do for replacement credit.

Dad steers around yet another curve. We've been weaving through mountains and forests for eight bazillion hours. How are we still in the middle of nowhere? Where are all the cities? Heck, for that matter, where are all the houses? Or farms? I think I'd get excited if I spotted a random barn on the side of the road at this point.

"Doobledee. Cookie." My baby sister, Vivi, offers this conversation starter from her car seat beside me.

"It sure is beautiful," Dad says with a low whistle. "I almost wish I could stay with you."

I doubt it. Dad and the other parents are going to Aruba while we're here, which is so unfair. But I make a strangled noise that might sound like agreement.

"You may thank me for this, Baxter," Mom says, her pink nails *tap-tap-tap*ping at her throat while she beams at the snowy pine trees. "It's an amazing opportunity."

I squirm in my seat, because this does not feel like an opportunity. A missing-child-in-the-mountains news report, maybe. I know Uncle Hornsby managed summer camps, but is this *really* the right environment for a school project?

"*Coo*-kie." This time Vivi enunciates each syllable clearly, tapping her chubby toddler knee with her pointer finger, just in case Mom wasn't sure where said cookie should be deposited.

"Just a minute, Peanut," Mom tells her, grabbing for the diaper bag.

Dad whistles his little up-down tune and shakes his curly hair. "Beautiful!" he says again.

I slouch even lower, until I can barely see over the side of the door and out the window. Not like there's much to see anyway. Like someone coded an infinite loop of trees, snow, and mountains.

Mom fishes a couple of animal crackers out of a plastic container and hands them to Vivi. Crumbs stick to her pink nails, and she looks at me, her matching pink lips smiling.

"Oh, Pumpkin, I just want the four of you to remember how much history you share. Remember in the third grade when you all went to the state fair? You were *precious*."

I give a weak laugh, because I definitely do remember it, but I'm sure Mom has the whole thing remembered in Mom Mode. That's the weird moms-only version of memory where everything past tense turns into a soft-focus video with a fairy-tale ending. If you ask my mom about the fair, she'll talk about sticks of cotton candy and all four of us giggling on the Hula Bula in one car. But her version of this event magically omits Abigail losing her headband (and her mind, briefly, as a result) and Emerson throwing up on me and Turner.

Mom has especially Mom Mode memories about everything involving the Getalong Gang. That's what she calls us. She loves to point out that she was the one who came up with this moniker first, and everyone had *better* remember it. As if any of us would try to take credit? Anyway, I think that's why she was so upset about the Know and Grow disqualification incident. I think that until she read the transcript, she completely believed we liked each other. The truth is, we are the Don't Getalong Gang.

When you're really little, you don't choose your friends. Heck, you don't even choose your clothes or what you eat for lunch. You wear stupid shirts with frogs on them, eat weird, mushy organic vegetables, and hang out with your parents' friends' kids.

For me those kids were always Abigail, and Emerson and Turner. Mom and Dad started a business with Dr. Walters years before Abigail or I came along. And Mr. and Mrs. Casella joined in right after they had the twins. They bought houses in the same neighborhood. We all four went to the same daycare and then preschool, and our parents were sure we would be the best friends ever, just like them. None of us were consulted on the matter. And since I never felt like I had much choice about Mom's suggestion, we weren't really consulted on entering the Know and Grow elective class as a team, either.

Dad pulls to a stop at a four-way intersection and looks back and forth. And back and forth.

"Uh, Dad," I start. "Are we lost?"

Dad shakes his head at his phone and gives a sad, low whistle. "This phone is maybe not working at a hundred percent right now."

"Reception is probably terrible out here, pumpkin," Mom says. "Oh! I have directions."

She digs out a neatly folded letter with scary black printed directions. That's the note Uncle Hornsby sent, and it's all we've got to go on, because apparently we're beyond the reach of GPS or any other modern device. My palms feel sweaty at the idea.

"So where exactly is this cabin?" I ask. It looks like we're driving deeper into the armpit-of-the-middle-of-nowhere.

"Deep in the Montana mountains!" Dad says. "If we were any farther north, we'd be in Canada. Just look at this snow." He whistles appreciatively and maybe I should press my hand to my chest like Mom, because I feel a little bit like crying too.

"We'll be there in fifteen minutes," Mom corrects. "Uncle Hornsby said it's fifteen minutes down the gravel road. Baxter, maybe you should time it. Get started on some of those responsibility skills."

"Well, if Uncle Hornsby says so," I say, reaching for my pocket. And then I remember: No phone to use for a stop-watch. No phone or tablet or gaming device of any sort whatsoever. Mom hands me a watch from the Dark Ages, and I have no idea what to do with it, so I just start counting in my head and hoping I won't lose track.

"Uncle Hornsby knows so much about these mountains," Mom says. "He led the camp here for almost twenty years, and he taught lots of kids how to work together and how to be responsible. This is a great opportunity for you, Baxter."

Ms. Westwood thought it was a great opportunity for the four of us to tackle teamwork again too, but I don't get it. What does wandering around the wilderness have to do with a team trivia class? Maybe Uncle Hornsby has a Fountain of Opportunity out here somewhere.

Great-uncle, actually. I've never even met him, but Mom went to his camp every summer, starting when she was very small. Sometime when she was in college, the camp shut down. Mom blames cell phones and video games, but she likes to blame cell phones and video games for lots of things. I think the kids just got smart. Who would want to spend two whole weeks of summer break getting bug bites and blisters from hiking boots while walking a zillion miles a day in the mountains? But whatever it was, after it closed, Uncle Hornsby moved on to some half-finished cabin off the grid. Like, way, way, way off the grid.

"How much time is left, buddy?" Dad asks.

Oh, crap. I stare at the watch, hoping it will whisper the answer to me. "Um . . ."

We rumble over an old bridge that rattles my teeth. I see a river burbling underneath us.

"More cookie," Vivi says.

A sign in her room back home says VIVI IS MADE OF SUGAR AND SPICE AND EVERYTHING NICE. I guess they don't make signs that say MADE OF CRUMBS AND DROOL AND BABY DOO-DOO.

"Oh, it's lovely," Mom says, tapping her pink nails together again.

"All that snow!" Dad says with a happy three-note whistle. "It's going to be the perfect weather for wilderness training."

"Don't people die in the cold and snow?" I ask, because I feel like Dad should consider it. Also, I'm pretty sure no one ever died from sending or receiving unfriendly messages on a group chat.

"Oh, no one will die, Pumpkin."

"Cookie!" Vivi's finger stabs into the air again. "Doobledee dee dee!"

Mom hands her another cookie while more trees and snow and yuck fly past my window. I sigh and Mom pats my hand.

"It might be better than you think, you know," she says.

Three days with three of my least favorite people while my real friends back home will all be celebrating their initiation into the Game Brigade by raiding the GrobGoblin Fortress in *Forever Life*. Four thousand experience points *each* and a full set of Invisibility Armor for the team to split. I was supposed to get the gloves, which is all I need for a complete set. Now I'll be gloveless forever. And in real life I might get buried under a snowdrift or eaten by a yeti.

If it's the yeti, Abigail, Emerson, and Turner will probably offer him a napkin when he's done polishing me off.

Our tires *bump, bump, bump* over the crunchy ruts and dips in the snow-covered road, and then we zip down a hill. My stomach tumbles end over end.

"More!" Vivi says. "More *whee!*" She shakes her tiny fist. Some days I really worry about that kid. I think she has dreams of ruling a small country.

Six million years and a couple of scary, creaky bridges later, Dad turns left and puts our Subaru into a low gear to descend the ridiculously steep and long driveway curving down to the left. We slide three times, but finally he finishes the corner and I see the edge of a squarish pile of logs and sticks.

Wait. Is that pile of logs and sticks Uncle Hornsby's cabin? I stare until my eyes hurt, but it doesn't change anything. This is definitely his cabin. I have seen some rustic places, but this is a whole new level. Some of the logs making the walls still have bark and twigs attached. There are windows, sure, but they're all a little crooked—like whoever built the place didn't have a level and instead just eyeballed everything.

Leaning against the door is a long axe, which tells me firewood is going to be a thing this weekend. Chopping it. Hauling it. Burning fires that don't heat the cabin enough but make us all reek like a campout. Dad had a thing for rustic cabin weekends for a while, so I know about firewood.

Mom opens the door, and three things happen all at once: Dad gives an alarmed whistle. Mom gasps. And a gigantic moose appears through the windshield.

ABOUT THE AUTHOR

Natalie D. Richards is the *New York Times* bestselling author of *49 Miles Alone, Four Found Dead, Seven Dirty Secrets, Five Total Strangers, Six Months Later,* and *One Was Lost,* among other young adult thrillers. *15 Secrets to Survival* was her middle-grade debut, and her latest middle-grade adventure story is *Survive This Safari*. Natalie lives in Ohio with her three children and a ridiculously furry dog named Wookiee.

nataliedrichards.com